Works by Frank A. Ruffolo

Jack Stenhouse Mysteries
Shadow of Death & Saturnalian Affect

Gabriel's Chalice

The Trihedral of Chaos Trilogy
The Crescent Star
The Falcon's Canticle
Yellowcake

"Loved Loved Loved this book - kept me in suspense - easy read can't wait for the third in the series."
~ Lorraine

Tres Archangelis

Frank A. Ruffolo

Printed in the United States of America
Edited by: Kathy Ree
Cover Design: Linkville Graphics

Linkville Press
linkvillepress.com
linkvillepress@gmail.com

ISBN-13: 978-1-947794-14-6
ISBN-10: 1-947794-14-0

A portion of all proceeds goes to Villalobos Rescue Center.
vrcpitbull.com

To Alicia, Michael, and Anthony

PROLOGUE

The Day of Judgment ended quickly. With everyone given the opportunity to choose, some chose well, and went on to live in peace and prosperity. But one-third of the world's population chose poorly, and was lost.

While the years following the Great Judgment saw Christians and Hebrews unite together in faith, the generation that followed slowly began to lose that faith, allowing small pockets of non-believers to grow and spread across the planet. But despite this growing unbelief, the majority of the population is still being drawn to visit the newest holy sites around the world and on the Moon. Pilgrims are basking in God's beauty and grace at the miraculous altars at Yellowstone National Park and Russia's Kuril Lake, and also at the basilicas built in Rome to showcase Gabriel's Chalice and the Ark of the Covenant. Together with these earthly sites, the Garden of Eden on the Moon is also drawing thousands.

Soon after the Day of Judgment, archeologists were overjoyed to discover the resting places of several religious treasures that had been lost to history for thousands of years. The Ark of the Covenant was found in an area under Jerusalem's Temple Mount and is now presented in all its glory in a basilica that was built in the large garden behind Saint Peter's Basilica in Rome. And the Holy Grail, the chalice that was used by Jesus during the Last Supper, was found hidden in a support beam in a church in Scotland that was built by the Knights Templar. This priceless holy relic is now displayed reverently on the main altar of Saint Peter's Basilica itself.

The altar sites, the basilicas, and the Garden of Eden at Moon Base

Challenger came into being when God manifested His glory by sending His messenger, the Archangel Gabriel, to mankind. The archangel came to the Moon with a symbol—a crystal chalice—to foretell the day of the coming of God's Son, and to display God's saving power.

However, even though the Son of God appears and walks among His children on Earth, man still leans toward the delights of Earthly living, and Jesus and His Father grow weary of man's weakness for greed and power.

In this, the twentieth year of the one thousand years of peace that was foretold to follow the Great Judgment, many of those involved in bringing Gabriel's Chalice from the Moon to the Earth are now living out their lives in relative anonymity.

Pulmonary specialist Doctor Stanley Simons is operating a family practice business in San Francisco with his wife, Josie, who quit her job as head of the Emergency Department at Bayside Medical Center to assist her husband with his business.

Former astronaut and engineer John Stevens retired from his job at Challenger Base and moved to a retirement community in South Florida with his wife, Clara.

Colonel Jonns, the former Air Force commander of Challenger Moon Base, retired from the military and moved to his ranch in Montana. He recently passed away after being thrown from his horse.

Raphael "Matt" Matteo, who was chosen to bring Gabriel's Chalice to the world, is also retired. He hopes to continue to live out the rest of his life in peace with his wife, Jennifer. Their son, Peter, who turned down a chance to go to West Point after graduating from Stanford University, is an archeologist for the Smithsonian Institution in Washington, D.C. Peter is currently working at a new dig at the Temple Mount in Jerusalem.

The only ones of the original team from the Moon who continue to be involved with the Moon base are Joe Toteda, and the husband and wife team of James and Christine Reynolds. The trio lives in the biosphere on the Moon where they work as groundskeepers and tour guides. The work is fulfilling for each of them, but the Reynoldses miss their son, James Junior, who has moved back to Earth to work for Johns Hopkins University as a software engineer.

All is well in the world.

Or is it?

CHAPTER ONE

Doctor Senjali has Raphael's test results in his hands as he walks into his office.

"Matt, there's no easy way to say this, so I'll just give it to you straight. You have amyotrophic lateral sclerosis, commonly known as ALS, or Lou Gehrig's disease."

For Raphael and Jennifer Matteo, who were nervously waiting to learn the reason for Matt's muscle spasms and difficulty breathing, hearing the actual diagnosis is difficult to bear. Jennifer breaks down in tears and Matt is stunned into silence, as if all the life has been taken out of him. As he processes the information, he sits quietly for a few moments and then erupts in disbelief.

"No way, Doc! It can't be! Not after what I went through. Something's wrong!"

"I'm sorry, Matt. We ran the tests twice. The disease is the reason you have breathing problems and muscle spasms. We have drugs that will slow the disease's progression and help with the symptoms, but as of now there is no cure. You need to know that you will get progressively worse."

"What? How long do you think I have left?"

"It's not as bad as it sounds, Matt. I believe you can live another ten to twelve years with this disease, and with more treatments on the horizon, my outlook for you is optimistic."

Matt turns to his sobbing wife and gives her a hug. When she composes herself, she asks, "What therapies are available now? What can I do to help Matt?"

"Mrs. Matteo, please remain positive. I will start Matt's treatment right now with a drug called Laptatrin, which will need to be injected twice a month. My nurse will give him his first dose, and then she will show you how to administer it to Matt. Listen, we've made great strides in treating this disease and its slow degenerative process. With physical therapy and a continued drug regimen, Matt should do fine. I'll go and prepare the first dose now."

When the doctor leaves the room, the Matteos reflect on the diagnosis.

"Matt, what are we going to tell Peter, our friends, and my Mom?"

"We'll tell them the truth, Jen. It is what it is. I'll be fine."

After a few minutes, the doctor's nurse walks into the room and prepares to inject a dose of Laptatrin into Matt's posterior. Matt squeezes Jennifer's hand and whispers, "I love you."

The nurse administers the shot and then explains the procedure to Jennifer, who listens attentively and asks numerous questions.

CHAPTER TWO

Deep in the asteroid belt, mining is continuing on one of the largest asteroids in the Solar System. At 1,000 miles wide, the Prometheus asteroid is so large that some astronomers actually call it a mini planet. That is why, about ten years ago, NASA sent a probe to the space rock to gather information about it and its components for possible industrial and commercial use.

When the data from that probe was analyzed, scientists were elated to find that their theories about the minerals on the asteroid, and its gravitational pull on objects around it, were accurate. The success of the probe was instrumental in attracting intense interest from the international industrial and scientific communities. The data it returned encouraged them to invest in a project to extract the high concentrations of iron, gold, titanium, and lithium that were found on the asteroid. And about five years ago, NASA and two large international corporations collaborated to establish a robot mining colony on that floating rock in space.

The initial establishment of the robotic mining colony on Prometheus caused an intense period of adjustment but eventually a routine procedure was established for harvesting its valuable minerals. Now, two shuttles continually commute between Moon Base Challenger and Prometheus with the bounty collected by the robot colony.

The invention of hyperdrive engines allows the shuttles that leave the Moon to reach the asteroid in three weeks, but only when Prometheus' orbit is close enough to the Moon's orbit around the Earth. That orbit brings the asteroid within achievable traveling distance from the Moon only four months in every eighteen-month period.

Currently journeying within that four month period, the mining shuttle Atlantis is en route to Prometheus and scheduled to land on the asteroid's surface in one week. The second mining shuttle, the Voyager, is making the reverse trip from the asteroid back to the Moon.

The De Beers Moon mining venture is going strong. Demand for moon diamonds is increasing, which keeps the De Beers workers busy, and the company's owners happy.

A separate group of laborers at the Moon base is also busy. They are breaking down the water found on the planet into its various components to produce the fuel needed for further space exploration.

The humans who are conducting these projects on the Moon live and work inside a biosphere, an area surrounded by a field of energy. The energy field acts like a curtain and holds the breathable atmosphere inside the biosphere while keeping the vacuum of space out.

The lunar mining and fuel projects require regular flights for workers to go to and from the Moon, but those jobs are not the only reason people are traveling there. The Moon's miraculous areas—the Garden of Eden and Saint Michael's Cave—have ignited people's imaginations. As a result, several tour companies have sprung up to whisk pilgrims out into space to visit those wondrous sites.

When the tours first started several years ago, married couple James and Christine Reynolds accepted jobs with an interplanetary travel company and moved to the Moon's biosphere. They now work there as guides for the many pilgrims who make the long trip from Earth.

On the Moon, the Reynoldses' work day is almost over. With the last tour of the day completed, Christine is currently assisting pilgrims in the souvenir shop. After the group leaves the store, the Reynoldses will make their way through a covered portal to return to the Moon's hotel, where they reside while they're working. The hotel is also where they catch the shuttle whenever they need to return to Earth.

Meanwhile, Joe Toteda has just finished his routine gardening tasks inside the biosphere. Before he heads home, he takes a quick trip around the lake that sprang forth from Gabriel's Cave, the place where the Archangel Gabriel presented his crystal chalice to mankind and where he sent the message of the Good News to the world—the news that the Son would soon return to Earth. The water from the cave created the lake and a complete ecosystem on the Moon that eventually became the site of the little Garden of Eden.

Ever observant, Joe stops his utility cart when he notices a new and strange-looking plant on the west side of the lake. He pulls over to examine the plant and then calls James on the radio.

"Hey, James? Can you come out here?"

"What's up, Joe?"

"There's a new plant growing on the west side of the lake. I'd like you to see it."

"A new plant? What kind?"

"I don't know. That's why I want you out here."

"No prob. I just finished today's tour, so I'll be there as soon as I see a guy about a horse."

Robotic drillers and jackhammers, or what the shuttle crew members call F.R.E.D.s—f---ing, ridiculous, electronic, devices—are gathering the precious metals that Prometheus is holding close to its heart. In the silence of the vacuum of deep space, these tireless mechanical workers continue their duties, unaware of the deep crack that has developed on the surface of the asteroid. The more they drill, the more they mine, and the deeper and longer the crack creeps across the surface.

The monitors located around the asteroid have not picked up this anomaly—yet.

Matt and Jennifer have returned home from the doctor's office and are waiting for a Skype connection with Peter. Peter knew about the testing his dad was going through and is anxious to hear the results. Matt is not eager to tell him the diagnosis, but as he said, it is what it is. Finally, the connection to Peter is established.

"Hi, Son. How's the dig going?"

"Dad, never mind the dig. How did the tests go? Sorry I couldn't be there."

Matt sighs. "Son, it's not good news. I have ALS."

CHAPTER THREE

J ames joins Joe near the utility cart on the west side of the lake.

"So, where is this plant you want me to see?"

"Right there, Jim."

The men turn toward the lake's edge and stare at the plant, which is about six inches high and looks like a perfectly-formed bonsai tree.

"You know, it looks like a mini oak tree."

"Yeah, but the leaves aren't green."

As the men approach the tree, its leaves begin to shimmer and twinkle in a rainbow of colors. They seem to reflect the light like tiny little prisms. The display has a calming effect on the men and they delight in its beauty.

Back on Earth, it is a beautiful fall day in the Gulf of Mexico, where the deep-water oil rig Genesis is routinely pumping black gold out of the bowels of the Earth. The operation has been running smoothly until alarms bells wail and the rig's pumps automatically shut down.

The pipe bringing up the thick crude has ruptured, spewing crude oil 2,000 feet below the surface of the water. The well is old, so the release of the oil is slow, but it is still a disastrous ecological and financial failure. As the oil company's emergency plans go into effect, a frantic call is placed for assistance by one of the rig's workers.

"We have a breach! This is Rogers on Genesis. We need a deep-water crew here NOW! Emergency protocols are in effect. There are no injuries, and there is no threat of fire. However, we're losing product into the Gulf at a rate of one hundred barrels an hour! Monitors are showing a ruptured pipe just above the sea floor. This is going to be bad!"

The project manager at Argon Oil's regional office in New Orleans reacts at once.

"Stage one will go into effect immediately, Rogers. It will take forty-eight hours to get our team out there with a pump head and valve to shut that thing off. But at the depth you're at, it's gonna take weeks to get it done. I'll contact Corporate, and they'll release a statement. The press is going to have a field day with this one. Do you have any idea what happened?"

"We're reviewing the tapes now. So far, it looks like a catastrophic failure of the pipe. She just…blew."

The last oil spill in the Gulf of Mexico occurred almost fifty years before, and at that time, the public was never told that it took nearly fifteen years for the area to fully recover. Sea life was severely affected by the spill, and the shrimping industry almost disappeared due to the oil pollution that genetically altered succeeding generations of shrimp.

The dire results of that oil spill were never fully revealed to the public. In its infinite wisdom, the government felt that it was better to keep the populace blind, dumb, and stupid.

CHAPTER FOUR

Peter Matteo ponders mixed feelings about leaving the dig in Jerusalem as he packs his belongings for a trip back home. On the one hand, he is grateful that the Smithsonian granted him a leave of absence so he can be with his parents. On the other hand, the ancient scrolls that he recently discovered are an incredibly significant find. As much as he wants to file a petition with the Smithsonian to allow him to begin to hunt for the relic described in the scrolls, he knows that his father comes first. He resolves to start the request process soon, right after he visits his father.

The scrolls that Peter found assert that a relic was left to mankind in the Middle Ages by the Archangel Raphael during one of the battles over the city of Jerusalem. They state that the archangel presented a commanding officer of the Crusades with an object—a large walking stick, or a staff—that protected the troops when they rode into battle. The documents describe a great power that was produced by the staff that vanquished all invaders from the city. The final entries in the scrolls indicate that the object was taken to Ireland after the fighting ceased.

Flying over the surface of Prometheus, Commander Jonathan Drake of the interplanetary shuttle *Enterprise* is routinely monitoring the robot workers—the F.R.E.D.s—from a holographic display in the shuttle's command center. His daily routine, which is usually pretty boring, becomes a lot more interesting when he notices a deep crack in the asteroid's surface.

"Hey, Sally! Come over here and take a look at this!" he shouts to Sally Fellows, his First Engineer.

Unstrapping herself, the first engineer floats over to the command center's display. "What's up, Boss?"

"Look at that," he says, pointing firmly at the display. "There appears to be a crack on the surface. It wasn't there on the last flyby."

When the alarms placed on the surface of Prometheus suddenly sound off in the command center, they look at each other in fear. Returning their attention to the display, they see that the crack is increasing in length and that it seems to be on a slow creep across the surface. After some quick calculations, they surmise that if it's not stopped, the crack may eventually encircle the entire asteroid.

Since the beginning of time, the Comet Hades has traveled through our Solar System, making a complete round trip around our Sun every one thousand six hundred fifty-three years. It has always entered our Solar System through the asteroid belt, and as far as we know, has never struck another object.

But in the vastness of space, nothing is set in stone.

"This is Fox News with a news alert. Yesterday in the Gulf of Mexico, the deep-water oil rig Genesis *experienced a catastrophic failure that is causing crude oil to leak into the waters of the Gulf at a rate of one hundred barrels per hour. There have been no reports of death or injuries in this incident, and repair crews are on their way to the oil platform. The U.S. Coast Guard has also quarantined the area surrounding the rig. Argon Oil, which owns* Genesis, *released a statement indicating that all emergency shutdown protocols have been successfully deployed, and that the company is working closely with the EPA and the U.S. Coast Guard to ensure minimal damage. However, by their best estimate, it will take at least two weeks to stop the spillage. Oil recovery ships and containment units have been sent to the area. No oil has made it to the surface yet, which experts have found to be very disturbing. Return to this station at eleven for a full report. This is Sam Williams, Fox News."*

Jennifer turns off the TV and helps Matt with his coat. The couple is on their way to Denver International Airport to pick up their son, Peter, for a short visit home.

Regular Laptatrin injections have eased Matt's breathing and reduced his spasms to the point that they've all but disappeared. He's still a little weak, but he's looking forward to starting a rehab routine in the morning.

As they walk toward the car, Matt looks up at the moon and sighs as he remembers the tiny Garden of Eden on its surface.

On the International Space Station, Admiral Simpson is closely monitoring the situation on Prometheus. Placing an urgent satellite call to NASA's Mission Control Center at the Kennedy Space Center in Florida, he asks, "Are you aware of the incident on Prometheus?"

"Yes, Admiral, we've been receiving all shuttle transmissions. If that crack continues, there could be a catastrophic event on the asteroid. At its current rate, we estimate that it would take approximately two weeks for the fissure to make a complete circle across the surface. If that occurs, we don't know what will happen next. Commander Drake and his crew will report back after they investigate the area first-hand."

"Burt, I don't agree that the crew should investigate. I feel that direct exploration may put them at severe risk, as they won't have enough fuel if they need to abort the mission and return to the Moon. Remember, they refuel at Prometheus. If conditions on the asteroid force them to abort before they can replenish their supplies, they won't be able to return to base. "

"We understand, Admiral, but we believe it's critical that we get boots on the ground for a personal observation of the situation."

"I formally object to this mission, and I want that duly noted on the record."

"As you wish, Admiral."

Admiral Simpson ends the transmission and walks away from the radio room in disgust. At their current position in space, Commander Drake and his crew will arrive on Prometheus in two days, well within the two-week window of the lengthening crack.

But the Admiral's concern is that the two-week estimate may not be correct.

Peter was able to get a lot of work done on the flight from Jerusalem to Denver, even though the hypersonic trip took only a couple of hours.

As he descends the escalator near the baggage area, unwelcome tears well up in his eyes when he spies his parents waiting near the conveyor belt. His thoughts are centered on his father and his incurable disease.

When the last step of the escalator disappears, he runs to his dad. With a warm embrace, he allows his tears to flow like a river.

13

CHAPTER FIVE

I t's a bright morning in Colorado Springs and with Pike's Peak dominating the landscape, the view from the rehabilitation room is spectacular. Matt tries to enjoy the view, even though the physical therapist is pushing him to increase his workout on the elliptical machine to keep his muscles toned and to improve his arm and leg coordination.

While Matt works out, Peter sits in the waiting room with his laptop, skimming through photocopies of the scrolls he discovered at the Temple Mount in Jerusalem. The manuscripts are written in Aramaic, the lost language of the region, and Peter and his colleagues believe they were written by the Apostle Thomas a few years after the Resurrection.

As he scans the documents, he quickly notices that a particular phrase, "*Tres Archangelis,*" is repeated throughout the text. The words stand out because they are Latin words in an Aramaic document. In English, the words mean, "Three Archangels."

Just as he has finished highlighting each position of that phrase in the text, the therapist walks in with his father, who is sitting in a wheelchair. He reluctantly closes his laptop and fleetingly wishes that he had more time to work on translating the ancient-language text but as soon as that thought crosses his mind, he feels guilty about his selfishness and dismisses the thought outright.

"Mr. Matteo, your father did very well today. The strength in his arms and legs is exceptional. We are very impressed."

Turning to Matt, the therapist continues. "Raphael—oh, sorry, *Matt*—remember that you need to rest for two days. Your next appointment is Friday.

We'll transition to a daily workout schedule after we build up your endurance. I suggest that you get an elliptical machine at home so you can continue your exercises there. You will soon be able to make appointments through your physician as he sees fit. You did great, Matt."

The therapist shakes Matt's hand and turns to leave. "See you Friday," he says.

Matt is tired. His morning workout would have stressed a healthy body. On shaky legs, he forces himself to stand and gives his son a big smile. "How about some pancakes for breakfast? I'm starving!"

Repair crews have finally reached the Genesis oil rig in the Gulf. Since no oil is visible on the water's surface, everything seems normal. But deep below, the thick crude continues to leak steadily from the ruptured pipe.

The crew has wasted no time in loading a well head onto their company's deep-sea submersible vehicle. The swift and precise placement of the well head is the best chance Argon Oil has of halting the leak. However, the task will not be easy. Due to the depth, temperature, and density of the water, the crude oil is remaining 200 feet below the water's surface. It now covers the size of three football fields and has oozed into the path of the Gulf Stream, the powerful current that circulates the warm waters of the Gulf of Mexico around the tip of Florida, up the coast of the United States, and across the Atlantic Ocean toward Europe. If the crude oil gets caught up in that current, the company knows that the oil could potentially pollute the entire Atlantic Ocean, from Florida all the way to England.

The Hades Comet is continuing its trek into the Solar System's asteroid belt. It is projected to pass within 1,000 miles of the Prometheus asteroid in about three weeks, a near miss in the immensity of space. The two enormous bodies are approaching each other at a rate of 833 miles a minute. Since even a slight deviation in their speeds or trajectories could cause a collision, the Sagan Observatory in California is monitoring their courses with extreme caution.

Peter has taken up his dad's offer of breakfast. With each of them having hearty appetites, their orders are similarly large—stacks of pancakes that rise over their plates like monoliths on a flat desert plain.

But before he picks up his fork, Peter eyes his dad and begins their mealtime conversation with a question. "Dad, please tell me the truth. How are you *really* feeling?"

"I feel fine now, Son. All of this started with some labored breathing, which I ignored. But when it progressed to a problem swallowing food, we went to the doctor. The medicine your mom is administering to me on a bi-weekly basis seems to be helping to manage my symptoms. My breathing has stabilized, and I can swallow food more easily now. I just need to eat smaller portions and chew my food completely. My arms and legs are still a little wobbly, but the therapist says they should improve, or at least not get any worse. I need to continue exercising to keep my muscles toned and my nerve pathways active. But you know, this treatment is not a cure, it's only a postponement. I could stay this way for a while, or get a little better. The doctor says that as I grow older the disease will progress at a faster pace. There's no way to predict how long I'll last with the disease, but I've been told that I should be around for at least another fifteen years. There are always new breakthroughs coming, so keep your fingers crossed. That's about all I know." Eager for a change of subject, he sits back in his chair and says, "But that's enough about me. Tell me about your find!"

"Oh, Dad. I'm so sorry you're not well. I'll do anything I can to help you."

"I know, Peter. But right now, I'm counting on you to keep my spirits up. So, tell me! What did you find?"

"Okay, well, we found two scrolls. One of them seems to have been written by Thomas, one of the Apostles. From what I can tell so far, it's about a vision or a message that he received from the Archangel Raphael. I haven't deciphered it completely yet, but I did find a recurring phrase in the document that is in Latin, not the Aramaic of the rest of the text. The phrase is, *Tres Archangelis.*"

"Wow! That means, Three Archangels!"

"Yeah! You know Latin?"

"No, not really. That one was pretty easy to figure out."

Smiling, Peter continues. "The other scroll seems to be much newer. It's about a rod or a staff that the Archangel Rafael apparently presented to the leader of one of the Crusader armies to help them in battle. The text indicates that the staff assisted in vanquishing the Moors from the Holy Land and that it was taken back to Europe after the Crusades. The text mentions that it was taken to Ireland, but it doesn't get more specific than that. However, I've heard rumors of a church in Ireland that has links to a staff like this."

Peter points at his dad. "But let's get back to you. How is Mom handling your health problems? And do you need me to stay here? I feel that I need to do something."

"Pete, the best thing you can do is to continue your work. Thanks for your offer, but don't worry about me. I have a good doctor, and your mother is making sure that I follow his orders. Now, has any person or any group tried to look for this staff of Raphael?"

"No, not that I know of, but it would be a great adventure, wouldn't it? I'd like to request some time off from my current assignment to look for it. Who knows, maybe I'll even find it!"

Atlantic Princess, a day-cruise ship that travels between the Bahamas and the Port of Miami, is on its way back to Miami with a ship full of happy passengers.

André Le Sueur, the ship's captain and a twenty-year veteran of the cruise ship industry, has just retaken the helm after a break. Looking out over the vast ocean, he checks the instrument panel and turns to his navigator with a puzzled expression.

"Larson, are you sure we're on course? We should have crossed over the Gulf Stream by now, but the sea is still quite calm."

Surprised by the question, the navigator re-checks his instruments and then looks over at the skipper with concern. "Captain, we should be passing over the Stream right now. It usually shows up in our imaging SONAR as an intense discoloration in the ocean. But sir, there is no Gulf Stream! It's not there!"

At that moment, alarms go off at the headquarters of NOAA, the National Oceanic and Atmospheric Administration, in Boulder, Colorado.

CHAPTER SIX

When Commander Drake and the rest of the crew de-plane from the shuttle onto the surface of Prometheus, the Commander gives a few orders and then leaves the crew members to their jobs. While they work at loading the latest yield of precious metals onto the shuttle, he takes a short walk across the rocky surface to personally observe the large crack before they leave the asteroid, possibly for the last time.

The crevice heads off into the distance as far as he can perceive through his helmet. It is about one foot wide and appears to have no discernible bottom. Drake takes a glow stick from the utility box attached to his space suit, activates it, and drops it into the crack. Almost immediately, he feels a slight shudder under his feet that is similar to an earthquake. The trembling lasts only a few seconds, but after it's over, the fissure is wider by at least five inches. Drake jumps back from the jagged crack and places a call to the shuttle.

"Sally, contact Moon Base Challenger. We have a situation here. The crack is getting larger and wider so we need to leave this rock sooner than expected. How long before we can lift off?"

"It'll take another two hours to refuel completely. Was that a quake I just felt?"

"10-4, but I don't know if we have two hours. I think the asteroid is going to split apart. Get the crew back on board as soon as possible. We may have to leave now."

With time a precious commodity, the crew dashes about as quickly as they can to replace the spent fuel cells with the charged ones that are stored on the asteroid for their frequent trips to and from Moon Base Challenger. At the same time, others store the spent cells in the shuttle's cargo bay so they can be recharged back at the base.

On Earth, archeological crews from the Smithsonian Institution and representatives from the European Union are preparing to investigate the Tunguska region of Siberia. The majority of the scientific community believes that a comet exploded over this area in 1908 and flattened millions of trees over 2,150 square kilometers, or 830 square miles. However, a local legend suggests a different explanation for the unusual event.

The nomadic people living nearby believe that the explosion was either the result of an unknown entity destroying something in the sky, or of an equally mysterious entity defending the Earth against some form of attack. They say that at the time of the event, three domes rose from the tundra, and those domes sent what looked like a beam of light up into the sky. The natives of the area believe that the domes were built by beings that came down from the sky, and they refer to them as "creatures of light."

Over the years, several investigations were conducted of the area, but their findings only increased the mystery. In the explosion zone, there are circular regions of the tundra that never freeze over. Two of those sections of ground are set in a straight line with each other, while a third is located a short distance away from the others in a pattern that is similar to the arrangement of stars in Orion's Belt, located within the constellation of Orion. During one study, metallic structures were found under the pools of water that eventually formed over the circles, and in another investigation, several investigators fell mysteriously sick and had to leave before completing their research. Still other researchers found a sizable concentration of radiation and a strong EMF (electromagnetic field) within the circles.

Because of those high radiation readings, the teams of scientists that have tried to investigate the anomaly could never remain in the blast zone long enough to examine it thoroughly. But now, technology has improved enough to allow humans to enter the bizarre area with specialized gear. That is why the combined team of Smithsonian and European Union scientists is there now. A crew of twenty archeologists and construction engineers equipped with land-moving equipment is in the region to attempt to raise any structures they may find there.

The question on everyone's mind is, *Was this really an explosion that resulted from a comet colliding with the Earth, or was it an encounter with aliens?*

Joe Toteda is once again making his way around the lake on his daily inspection of the Garden of Eden near Gabriel's Cave. When he stops near the glowing tree at the east side of the lake, he notices that it's now six feet high. The leaves are still golden in color, and prisms of light continue to circle and dance around the tree.

While he gazes at the tree, he senses that the spectacle is producing a profound calming effect upon him. He suspects that if he remains there much longer he may become mesmerized by the tree's beauty and enter a state of peaceful contemplation that could last for hours. With no time to dawdle, he sighs and turns away to continue his morning rounds.

Unaware of the new discovery on the Moon, President Geraldine Bush, granddaughter of former President George W. Bush, is in the Oval Office waiting for an update on the Gulf of Mexico oil spill. At the sound of a door opening, she watches with interest as Chief of Staff Levar Daniels rushes into the room.

"Madam President! We just received a call from NOAA headquarters in Boulder. Doctor Emil Gurov is on line one. You need to hear what he has to say."

"You seem overly serious today, Levar."

"Madam President, this *is* serious."

"I don't like the sound of that," responds President Bush as she presses the first button on her phone. "This is the President. What do you need to tell me, Doctor?"

"Hello, ma'am. I'm afraid I have some bad news for you. Our instruments in the Gulf of Mexico have detected that the Gulf Stream's current has stopped flowing. We believe that it has been interrupted by the oil spill."

"That sounds impossible. Are you sure?"

"Yes, I'm afraid so."

"Well, then, what are the effects of this situation, and how can we get the current flowing again?"

"Ma'am, the Gulf Stream brings warm water from the Gulf of Mexico up the Atlantic coast and then across the ocean to Europe. The stream of warm water is what regulates the temperature of the oceans. Without that steady flow, the Atlantic Ocean, as well as our entire planet, will eventually cool down. Oceanographers and geologists have theorized that the cause of the last Ice Age, when glaciers covered the Earth as far south as Florida, was due to the interruption of the Gulf Stream. Madam President, it is now late fall, the time of year when the Atlantic Ocean normally cools down. What is different this year is that the ocean's temperature is falling more rapidly than usual and the formation of ice in the Arctic Ocean and the Northern Atlantic Ocean is increasing dramatically. I'm afraid we may be entering a winter that may not end."

"What are you saying? We obviously need to get the Gulf Stream flowing normally again. What can we do to make that happen? Can we jump-start it somehow?"

"Madam President…we don't know if that's possible."

"Well, damn it, find out!"

CHAPTER SEVEN

Commander Drake is at the controls of the shuttle *Enterprise,* going through his checklist in preparation for lift off from Prometheus. Sitting next to him is First Engineer Sally Fellows.

"We're all set, Commander. It's time to get off this ticking time bomb."

Following protocol, Drake continues his pre-flight routine, but a large shudder suddenly sweeps through the asteroid and bounces them both around in their seats. This time, the shaking doesn't subside and continues to increase in intensity.

Looking over at Fellows, Drake drops his checklist. "Screw this!" he shouts, and clicks the button to speak to the crew.

"Brace yourselves for takeoff! We're getting out of here, *now*!"

In the nick of time, the engines ignite and the shuttle jolts off the surface. Prometheus is beginning to break apart.

As the space plane steadily increases its distance from Prometheus, the crew members crowd around the display from the aft cameras to watch what's happening behind them. They are horrified when the asteroid splits into two separate pieces that wobble around each other in space and ultimately collide with each other. One of the pieces, about four hundred miles wide, heads into the outer reaches of space while the other piece moves into a different orbit within the asteroid field.

Astonished by the asteroid's destruction, the Commander turns to his First Engineer and shouts, "I hope that rock doesn't hit anything!" Then he instructs her to call Challenger Base to let them know that Prometheus is no more. As an afterthought, he adds with a wry smile, "You know, we probably just lost our jobs, eh?"

At that moment, an alarm goes off at the Sagan Observatory in California.

The next morning, Matt works out on his elliptical machine while Pete shares breakfast with his mom.

"Mom, it's good to see that Dad is holding his own now. I hate to leave you two, but I really have to get back to the Smithsonian. I've deciphered more of the scrolls, and I need to pursue some information that I found in them."

Peter tastes his first forkful of pancakes and declares, "Wow, these are better than I remember! I sure do miss your cooking, Mom."

Smiling, Mrs. Matteo gives her son a kiss. "Peter, you know you can come home anytime you like." Taking a seat across from him, she asks, "But what information did you find?"

Before answering, Peter swallows a mouthful of food while maple syrup runs down his chin. After a quick wipe of his mouth, he replies, "Well, according to the scrolls, there were divine interventions in human events in the distant past. The text says the Archangel Raphael left a relic with a military officer during the Crusades, and from what I've been able to decipher, that relic was taken to Ireland. For years, I've heard rumors about a special relic, a large walking stick or a staff, that was in a church in southern Ireland. But I haven't heard anything else about it until now. Anyway, that's what I've been able to figure out so far, and that's just from one set of scrolls. There's another set that I'm having trouble translating. The only thing I've been able to decipher about those writings is that they concern three archangels and something they either did, will do, or left behind, here on Earth. I need to get back to the museum so I can get more experts to work on them. I also want to go to Ireland to try to find that staff."

"Oh, my goodness! All of that sounds wonderful, and it means that you're going to be very busy! Now, don't you worry about Dad. He understands the importance of your work, and he supports you one hundred percent. Actually, he was wondering how he could tell you that it's time that you went back home."

Jennifer reaches out and pats her son's hand. "We'll be fine, Pete. Your dad has stabilized quite nicely, and the strength in his legs has increased. Go on your quest. You know we're only a video link away."

Grateful for his Mom's reassuring words, Peter rises from the table and gives his mom a hug.

"Hey, where's my hug?" asks Matt mischievously as he walks into the kitchen. "Better yet, where's my coffee?"

Doctor Stefan Bell, chief astronomer at the Sagan Observatory, has been camping out at his office since he learned about the catastrophic events on Prometheus. Until the potential for disaster has subsided, the urgent situation in space is preventing him from leaving the observatory.

Currently asleep on a cot, the doctor is suddenly awakened by the sound of an incessantly ringing alarm bell. Half-asleep, he bolts out of bed and stubs his toe on the leg of his desk. Shouting out a verb and a pronoun, he limps his way to the control room, and makes a beeline for his computer to turn off the annoying bell.

When peace is restored, he looks at his monitor to find the cause of the alarm and stares in shock at the warning on the screen. The piece of the once-majestic Prometheus asteroid that broke out of its former orbit is now hurtling toward the Comet Hades, and a collision between those two celestial bodies is projected to occur within seventy-two hours.

Ignoring the pain in his toe, Doctor Bell places an urgent call to NASA headquarters in Houston. Around the world, similar alarms are alerting the doctor's fellow scientists to this critical new development.

The demise of Prometheus and the billions of dollars in lost revenue and equipment is sure to bring difficult financial troubles to the deep-space mining operation involving NASA, De Beers, and the two large internet companies. Their goal of reaping the benefits from Prometheus has now ended.

But their loss of income and machinery will be the least of the organization's problems. The remnant of Prometheus, a rock larger than Manhattan Island, is now on a catastrophic rendezvous with the Comet Hades.

"This is BBC News London. A freak fall storm has gripped this city in plummeting temperatures and blizzards of epic proportions. London could soon see an accumulation of snow in excess of one meter, with temperatures well below freezing…"

CHAPTER EIGHT

After finishing his rounds on the Moon, Joe walks into the visitor's center and interrupts James and his wife, Christine, during breakfast.

"Good morning, you two! It's about time you guys got up. Hey, Jim, our mysterious tree is now over six feet tall! I've been sending updates to the space station, but I think we'd better get a botanist up here to start investigating this thing."

Jim is about to respond, but is interrupted by the unmistakable sound of singing which seems to be coming from across the lake. Puzzled, the friends look out of the observation window and see a bright light in the garden area that seems to be pulsating in time with the singing. The voices sound as if they are coming from the area of the golden tree, which they can clearly see is now close to twenty feet tall. The sight of the tree and the sounds of the singing cause them to enter into an altered state of consciousness in which they are at peace with themselves, and with each other.

The Board of Directors of Spacegen, the conglomerate that ran the mining operation on Prometheus, has convened an emergency meeting at their headquarters in Johannesburg, South Africa. Chairman of the Board Karl Jarsberg of De Beers is about to speak to the entire board, which is anxiously assembled before him.

"Gentlemen, as all of you know by now, our mining operation on Prometheus has ended unexpectedly, and disastrously. The asteroid has split apart, and early indications suggest that it was caused by our deep drilling rigs. Now, even though we've reaped close to one billion dollars in profits from this venture over the past few years, our loss of equipment alone will exceed our profits, and that will essentially bankrupt this investment. Thankfully, no lives have been lost, but the disaster has already negatively affected our stock. Fortunately, our facility on the Moon is still in full operation, and that enterprise will stabilize Spacegen's bottom line. But the public is demanding to know why we didn't foresee this disaster as a potential result of drilling on a foreign object in space. And I want to know who is responsible for this lack of foresight! We should have had a plan in place for this! Gentlemen, there will be no further space ventures conducted by Spacegen. We cannot control what we cannot predict."

When the meeting adjourns, Karl Jarsberg stands alone in the boardroom. He is staring at financial information on his tablet and considering the company's next steps. Suddenly, a voice penetrates the silence.

"Fools, all. You have abandoned Me."

Upset that someone would have the audacity to call *him* a fool, Karl is about to chastise the speaker until he looks up and focuses on who is speaking to him. With a gasp and eyes as wide as saucers, he drops to his knees and stammers, "My *Lord*!" in a trembling and barely-audible voice.

Jesus shakes His head in sadness.

"My little child, you have forgotten My command. Your greed has caused you to tamper with My Father's creation. Revive your faith, and pray that all is not lost."

The Son of God departs as abruptly as He arrived, leaving Karl Jarsberg in a state of extreme shock.

With packed bags at the ready, Peter waits at his parent's home for the airport shuttle van that will take him to Denver Airport. He is headed back to his office in Washington, D.C., where he will immediately prepare for a meeting with his boss. He intends to request a trip to Ireland to search for the staff of the Archangel Raphael and to hand the scrolls that he has not been able to decipher to a team of experts in ancient languages. He hopes that the experts will be able to discover the meaning of the remaining *Tres Archangelis* writings.

"This is ABC News Washington, with incredible scientific news. Doctor Stefan Bell of the Sagan Observatory in California has reported that the asteroid where Spacegen has been mining for years has broken apart! Incredibly, there was no loss of life in the astounding incident that occurred moments after a shuttle crew left the asteroid's surface. The space plane,

piloted by Commander Jonathan Drake, had barely lifted off before the asteroid split in two. According to Doctor Bell, a remnant of Prometheus about four hundred miles across is now heading toward the Comet Hades and is expected to pass close enough to the comet to potentially collide with it in about seventy-two hours. If a collision occurs, Doctor Bell predicts that the resulting explosion will be large enough to be visible to the naked eye. Please stay tuned to this station for updates.

"In other news, extreme winter conditions are continuing to develop across the Northern Hemisphere. Unconfirmed reports have suggested that the Gulf Stream, which brings warm ocean water and warm temperatures to the northern areas of our planet, has stopped flowing. NOAA, the National Oceanic and Atmospheric Administration, has no comment at this time.

"This is Beverly Collins, ABC News Washington."

When James Reynolds finally snaps back to reality, thirty minutes have mystically come and gone. He shakes his wife, Christine, and his friend, Joe Toteda, to bring them back to reality as well.

"Chris! Joe! Come on back now!"

Rubbing her eyes to shake off her stupor, Christine sighs, "Oh, my, that was beautiful! The colors, the singing! I almost hate to come back!"

"Wake up, man!" James says as he shakes Joe. "You okay?"

"Yeah," answers Joe. "I'm okay. Thanks for bringing me back. If I stayed there any longer, I probably wouldn't want to come back at all."

"What the heck kind of a tree is that?" questions James.

With a shrug of his shoulders, Joe says, "Damn it, Jim, I'm a mechanic, not a botanist!" Smiling at his little joke, he adds, "I always wanted to say that."

"Okay, 'Bones,' " answers James, in a reference to the old television program, *Star Trek*. "Listen, we need to call NASA, pronto. They're going to have to send a botanist up here on the next flight, or at the very least, we need to get a video link set up with them so we can show them what's going on. Because of our past experiences in this holy place, it looks like we're about to get another message. Something's up."

President Bush is about to address an emergency meeting with her cabinet, her chief of staff, and the Chairman of the Joint Chiefs of Staff in the White House Situation Room.

"Good morning, everyone. Even though we've entered one thousand years of peace, it seems that now, things are about to hit the fan in other ways.

I've recently received two disturbing phone calls. The first was from Doctor Emil Gurov of NOAA. He informed me that the Gulf Stream is no longer flowing on its natural course, and he believes that the Argon oil spill has something to do with it. He advises me that if we don't get the Gulf Stream flowing again soon, we're looking at another ice age. As you probably know, London and parts of Europe are already covered by over three feet of snow, and additional snow is about to blanket the rest of Europe. Temperatures from the Arctic Circle to the panhandle of Florida are far below normal. The falling temperatures are destabilizing the stock markets, which are reacting by spiraling dangerously downward.

"But that is not all. The second call was from NASA Administrator Joseph Spolten. The Prometheus asteroid, where Spacegen has been conducting their deep-space mining, has broken apart! Amazingly, there was no loss of life in that disaster. The crew that was on the asteroid at the time of the failure managed to escape to safety. But a large chunk of the asteroid is now heading on a collision course with the Comet Hades. The two outer space objects are being closely monitored by NASA and the Sagan Observatory, as well as by other observatories worldwide. NOAA's Cray supercomputer and IBM's Hal 2020 have been programmed to run scenarios of a possible collision. I'm sorry to say that both supercomputers have predicted with a sixty percent possibility that a chunk of the asteroid will survive the collision and head toward the Earth."

President Bush waits as gasps and expressions of fear circle the table like a crowd doing the wave at a football game. After a moment, she clears her voice to get their attention.

"Now, it appears to me that our meddling in the natural order of creation is resulting in dire consequences. Even though we are currently under the grace of God, it seems that the actions that mankind has taken against nature and the universe have finally caught up with us. Our past actions may have caused an adverse effect on our present, and the result could ultimately be our demise."

After the president's closing words, the Situation Room suddenly becomes very dark. Concerned by what they assume to be a lack of power in a critical area of the White House, several staff members head for the door to get help, but they are surprised to find that they cannot open it. Turning back into the room, their gazes are drawn to a small and radiant ball that is floating slowly down through the ceiling. The glowing orb settles near President Bush's chair, and takes on the form of a human being.

"You naïve fools. The power you treasure is no power at all. You have

tampered with My Father's creations. You have changed the natural order of the universe. You must now fix what you have broken, for My Father has lost patience. But even so, We will not punish you, for your actions have resulted in your own chastisement. Return to faith in God and heed My words: You yourselves have caused this calamity; therefore, you must end it. You have the tools to do so; use them wisely."

The Son of God disappears in an instant, and the room's lighting returns to normal.

In the silence that follows, faces around the room stare at each other in disbelief and shock. When a semblance of composure returns, all eyes focus on the president to gauge her reaction to the incredible events. In response, Geraldine Bush raises her eyes upward and makes the sign of the cross.

"It's our arrogance that has caused this. Please join me in praying that we can find a way to save ourselves, and our world."

CHAPTER NINE

For the past few days, Peter Matteo has been camping out in his small, windowless office at the Smithsonian Institution. He has been working nonstop, eager to widen his research into the location of Saint Raphael's staff. His 10x20 office, which normally holds only a bookcase and a metal, industrial-type desk overflowing with books and paperwork, now also contains a sleeping bag, and many empty cartons of Chinese takeout.

Amid the clutter, Peter has been spending all his time poring over dusty church archives, barely taking time out for necessities like food or sleep. But his persistence has finally paid off. He has pieced together the most likely path of Raphael's staff—from a war-torn plain outside of Jerusalem, to a small church in the village of Cratloe, Ireland. Ancient records indicate that although the original church in Cratloe was destroyed in the late 1300's, the village re-dedicated it some 400 years later in a barn that was repurposed for its use. That church still exists today as the Church of St. John the Baptist.

Peter's zealous investigation also revealed that a very old statue of the Archangel Raphael is still believed to be located within that church, and his examination of long-forgotten letters from the office of the bishop of Ireland reaffirms local tales that the staff held by the Cratloe statue belonged to Saint Raphael himself. Those letters have provided Peter with the precise information he was searching for.

Excited by this new information, Peter prepares a detailed request for approval of a museum-sponsored trip to Ireland to search for the staff. Armed with the documents he discovered, he knocks on Curator Jameson's door.

At the same time, several floors below, the museum's historical archeologists are hard at work trying to decipher the scrolls that Peter discovered.

Unfortunately, *Tres Archangelis* is still refusing to release its secrets.

James Reynolds is busy setting up an intra-planetary connection so he can make a video call to NASA headquarters in Houston. He wants to speak to Major Ralston, commanding officer of Moon Base Challenger, who is currently at NASA on assignment from the Air Force.

"Morning, James! How are you today?" asks Major Ralston when James' face pops up on his video screen. "And how is your 'special' tree doing?"

"That's why I'm calling. I'm looking at the tree now, and it's almost twenty feet high! It doubled in size overnight, and as you can probably hear in the background, it's 'singing'...quite loudly! Major, it's absolutely mesmerizing! The singing and the dancing lights are utterly captivating, and it's taking all of our concentration to avoid being drawn into the tree's energy and beauty. This morning, all of us were wrapped up in a state of euphoria for over thirty minutes! I think we need to close the visitor's center until we can determine what's going on, sir. And I suggest that you send a botanist and a theologian up here ASAP to do an onsite evaluation of this phenomenon."

Before Major Ralston responds, James adds, "Major, can you hear that? Now, there's loud chanting coming from the tree!"

"Yes, I can hear it, Jim! What's going on up there?"

As abruptly as the singing started, it stops, and is followed by a profound silence that envelops the entire area. Several minutes of nothingness ensue. There are no sounds, no movement, no nothing. Then, a deep and powerful voice is heard throughout the garden.

"I AM WHAT I AM. I command the transporter of My angel's chalice to come forth, for I have a task that he must complete."

At the moment the voice stops speaking, the tree goes dark.

"Oh, my goodness! Major that was *God the Father*! This is *God's* tree, and His tree is no longer glittering! And...hey! The singing has stopped! Doctor Raphael Matteo is the one who brought the chalice to Earth before the Great Judgment. What kind of task would God want him to complete now? Is there anything going on down there that we need to know about?"

"Actually...there are a few things that I need to tell you about, and they're not good."

"What is it, Major?"

The commanding officer of Moon Base Challenger pauses slightly before he replies to James' question. "Well, for one thing," he begins, "we've been experiencing very strange weather patterns that are causing a lot of serious problems. And there was a major oil spill in the Gulf that may be leading us into a very cold winter, maybe even into an ice age."

"An ice age?"

"Yeah, but as bad as that sounds, it's not…that's not the worst of it. James, there's been an incident on Prometheus, and a large piece of the asteroid has broken off of it. The thing is…the piece that broke off is now on a collision course with the Comet Hades."

"What?!"

"I know; all of this could be very bad for us down here. I've heard talk of several possible outcomes of an asteroid-comet collision, but there's nothing definitive yet. Look, let me contact Doctor Matteo, and then I'll call you back. I'll get to work on sending you a botanist and a theologian, and I'll also try to get more information on the asteroid."

Unknown to anyone on Earth, the moment the tree on the Moon went dark, the Archangel Gabriel's Chalice began to glow in Rome.

Peter Matteo's boss, Stanley Jameson, is curator of the Smithsonian Institution. He is a political appointee who bought his job with campaign contributions. At the beginning of his relationship with Peter, he was more interested in himself and his position than anything that had to do with Peter's research. However, as today's meeting progresses and Peter presents more and more of the translated texts from Jerusalem, Stanley finally begins to act more like a curator, and less like an asshole.

But even with his increased interest in Peter's discoveries, Jameson still feels the need to lord it over his staff. He has been deliberately dragging out this meeting by making a project out of slowly and meticulously cleaning his eyeglasses. He is enjoying the sight of an employee squirming in the chair in front of his great oak desk, waiting for him to speak.

When he is finally satisfied that he has made Peter wait long enough, he announces dramatically, "Peter. You're here to tell me what you've found and to convince me to approve your request to go to Ireland. I will listen to your petition, however, before we discuss that, tell me about your father."

"Dad's doing fine, Mr. Jameson. The medication and therapy seem to have stopped his nerve degeneration, for now. But we don't know how long that will last."

"I see. Well, they're always coming up with new treatments. I'm sure they'll find a cure soon. Now, let's talk about the issues at hand. Convince me, Peter. Convince me."

CHAPTER TEN

F ive o'clock in the morning is Doctor Matteo's usual wakeup time. When the grandfather clock in the hall rings five bells, he rolls out of bed slowly so he won't wake his sleeping wife.

Fumbling through the dark house, he makes his way to the kitchen to pour himself a glass of cranberry juice. But just as he is about to flip on the light, a glow from the adjoining breakfast area stops him in his tracks. Curious, he inches his way toward the brightness in the next room and is startled when he encounters a human-like form bathed in a blue aura.

"I am Gabriel, and I bring you Good News. Once again, you have been chosen. Do not be afraid, for He is with you."

The figure disappears in a flash, leaving Matt alone in the dark. In the hallway, the grandfather clock chimes the quarter hour, but Matt ignores the familiar sound and strains to make out the other tones that sound astonishingly like angels singing.

In the bedroom, Jennifer is stirring. When she rolls over and notices that Matt is no longer there, she rises and walks toward the kitchen. Puzzled that the light has not been turned on, she flips the switch and walks through to the breakfast area, where she finds Matt standing in the middle of the room.

"What's going on?" she asks. "Who were you talking to?"

Staring straight ahead, Matt doesn't respond until Jennifer touches his shoulder and awakens him from what seems to have been a trance. "Jenn," he whispers, "the Archangel Gabriel just spoke to me. He told me that I've been chosen again."

At that moment, the phone rings and startles them both. Jennifer looks questioningly at Matt and then turns to answer it. But Matt hasn't moved. He remains motionless, staring at the place where Gabriel stood just a few minutes before.

"Matt?" calls Jennifer. "It's Major Ralston from NASA. He wants to speak with you."

Roused from private thoughts, Matt takes the phone from his wife. "Hello? This is Doctor Matteo."

"Good morning, Doctor. I'm sorry to call so early, but what I have to say is important. And since there's no better way to tell you than to be straight and direct, here it is. God has planted a tree in the Garden of Eden on the Moon, and he has summoned you back up there!"

"Yes, I know, Major. I just had a visit from the Archangel Gabriel!"

Silenced by that revelation, the Major says nothing for a moment. Then, he says, "Well. I guess there are no coincidences where God is involved."

"No, I guess not," replies Matt. "But I don't know how I'm going to do all that traveling. I'm not a well man anymore."

"Before I called you this morning, our people contacted your physician. He told us that the weightlessness of space and the reduced gravity of the Moon would actually help you to move around better because there will be less strain on your body up there. You can talk to him yourself, if you like. In fact, he's waiting for your call. But considering *who* has beckoned you, do you really think there will be a problem?"

Matt smiles, "No, probably not."

"Look, you need to find out what God wants, so we're going to get you to the Moon as soon as possible. We'll send a driver to pick you up tomorrow morning. You'll have to take a commercial flight from Denver to Houston, but you know the drill from that point forward. From Houston, you travel to the space station, then on to the Moon. You should be up there in less than three days."

Matt ends the call and looks at Jenn. "Looks like I'm going to the Moon again! In fact, I'm leaving tomorrow!"

Peter is excited! He has successfully secured the backing of the Smithsonian Institution and is eagerly preparing for his trip to Ireland. In the back of his mind he knows that if his research pans out, he will be the second Matteo to possess an artifact from a messenger of God. At this time, he is unaware that his father has been given another divine summons.

As he packs for his trip, the recurring sections of the scrolls that refer to three archangels refuse to leave his thoughts. He wonders whether it's a coincidence that he's now being drawn toward archangels just like his father was so many years before.

President Bush is about to receive her regular updates on the oil spill in the Gulf of Mexico, and the looming collision between the Hades Comet and the Prometheus asteroid.

"If it's possible, gentlemen, I'd like some good news today."

"Actually, Madam President," begins Chief of Staff Levar Daniels, "we do have some good news, but there is also some bad news. The pipe that has been leaking oil in the Gulf has finally been capped, and there is no oil on the surface of the water or on any of the beaches in the area. That's it for the good news, however."

"Okay, Levar. Give me the bad news."

"There are several areas of bad news, ma'am."

Sighing, the president gestures for Levar to continue.

"First, deep water sonar scans have plotted a fifteen-square mile area of oil 200 feet below the surface. This is the mass of oil that has halted the Gulf Stream. Second, snow is now falling as far south as Monaco and NOAA predicts that the freezing temperatures will create conditions in the United States where snow will eventually remain on the ground as far south as Miami."

Levar looks up from his papers to eye the president for her reaction to his report so far, but seeing no reason to stop, plunges onward.

"Third, the Coast Guard Icebreaker Sam Houston is stuck in Artic ice off the coast of Greenland. They were sent there to try to keep the shipping lanes open. We dispatched helicopters to rescue the crew, but the ice up there is building up so fast that it will eventually crush the ship's hull. We'll save the crew, but lose the ship.

"Fourth…"

"Fourth, Levar? How much more bad news is there?"

"This is the end of my report, ma'am. The wayward fragment of Prometheus is predicted to make contact with Hades within the next forty-eight hours and the collision will be visible in the night sky. Computer simulations put the Earth at great risk for debris fallout from the impact."

"How long before the debris arrives in our atmosphere?"

"We've been told that it may arrive within six weeks of the collision. But there are several impact scenarios. Others say the fallout could miss the Earth entirely."

"Okay, let's deal with the collision first. I want contingency plans in place for all possible outcomes." Looking around the table at the meeting's participants, she adds, "Get back to me tomorrow with what you've come up with."

Mrs. Bush pauses to give her people some time to scribble notes, and then continues the briefing.

"And now, about the oil spill. How do we jump-start the Gulf Stream?"

"Madam President," responds General Parkins, Chairman of the Joint Chiefs of Staff, "our problem is the depth at which the oil is located. Complete removal from a depth of 200 feet may be impossible, but we can try to disperse it. We can use depth charges to spread it out, but we don't know if that will have any effect on restarting the flow. I have ordered two naval destroyers from our Southern Command to the area to work on the dispersal, and they are on the way as we speak. But if breaking it up doesn't work, there is one other course of action we can take. We can try to push-start the flow."

"Push-start the Gulf Stream? How do you plan to do that?"

"We believe that if a large enough device is detonated in the area, the resulting concussion would do the trick."

This piques the president's interest. "What size device are you talking about, General?"

"Twenty kilotons of TNT."

Shocked, President Bush jumps up from her seat.

"You want to detonate a nuclear device the size of the Hiroshima bomb in the Gulf of Mexico?! The resulting tidal wave will wreak havoc on our coastlines, not to mention the contamination from nuclear fallout! Are you *crazy*?!"

"Madam President, a global ice age will wreak more havoc."

Livid at the suggestion of using a nuclear bomb, President Bush decrees, "That strategy will *not* occur, General! Not on my watch! Come up with a better plan by tomorrow's meeting. That's an order!"

"Madam President, we already have an alternate plan," offers General Parkins. "Instead of dispersing the oil, we can *try* to remove it from the water, even though the depth of the spill is still a problem. What we can do is use the filtration system that Argon Oil has been working on with NASA scientists. It hasn't been fully tested yet, but it should work. The system separates the oil from the water and pumps it into empty tankers. But because the oil field is so deep we can't get to it. It's trapped between temperature inversions in the Gulf, which are sections of water that are either warmer or colder than other areas. However, if we can disperse the oil with depth charges, it should rise closer to the surface since oil is lighter than water. Then we can capture it with what can best be described as a giant vacuum cleaner, and haul it away in the tankers."

Slightly calmer now, the president sits back down in her chair. "General, that plan sounds *much* more feasible than the first one you presented and you should have given it precedence. You have my permission to go ahead with it. Let's hope this strategy works, because your earlier option will *not* happen. Is that clear?"

"Yes, Madam President."

CHAPTER ELEVEN

While waiting for a cab to take him to BWI, Baltimore-Washington International Airport, Peter places a call to his dad.

"Hi, Dad. Sorry I couldn't call earlier. I'm on my way to Ireland! The Smithsonian agreed to allow me to look for the staff of the Archangel Raphael!"

"That's awesome, Pete! I really hope you find it. But I got you one better! I'm leaving for the Moon tomorrow! Apparently, because I was the one who brought Gabriel's Chalice to the world, I've been chosen to do something else. *God* has summoned me to the Moon!"

"Holy cow! I didn't know you were that 'connected.' What an honor, Dad! Are you sure you can go, though? I mean…you know."

"Yeah, I checked with my neurologist, and he said it was okay. I should be up there in forty-eight hours or so. But let's get back to you. Where are you going in Ireland?"

"I'm going to Cratloe. It's a little village in the midwestern part of the country. There's a statue of the Archangel Raphael in a church there, and the local folk believe the staff the statue is holding is the one that Raphael gave to a senior officer of the Knights Templar Crusaders. They say the staff helped the Crusaders to protect the pilgrims who were journeying to the Holy Land. I should know in a few days whether the staff is actually there or not."

"Well, Son, I guess the both of us have been chosen to do something awesome. It's a great feeling, isn't it?"

"Yeah, Dad. I hope I'm able to do accomplish whatever it is I'm supposed to."

"Me, too. Me, too."

Matt takes a moment to reflect on their individual responsibilities and then changes the subject. "So, anyway, how's the weather in D.C.? It's colder than a well digger's knee here. I know we should be used to it in Colorado, but cold is cold. We expect a major snow storm at the end of the week."

"There's snow on the ground here, and the storm that you're going to get is supposed to head east and hit us, too. It's gonna be a long winter. I've heard rumblings about the Gulf Stream and the oil spill, but so far, it's only rumors. The president is supposed to have a news conference tomorrow afternoon. Something is going on. D.C. is all abuzz."

"Yeah, I think this call to the Moon is related in some way to what's going on in D.C. I'll keep you posted. Godspeed, Son. I love you."

"I love you, too, Dad. Have a wonderful trip."

Doctor Isadore Kirk, lead archeologist for the Smithsonian, is directing the archeological excavation in Siberia. It's cold there, damn cold. Temperatures are well below freezing in the general area, but the ground at each of the three pools is not affected by the temperature. Amazingly, the ground in those particular areas is not frozen at all. In fact, the deeper the excavating equipment digs into the soil, the warmer it becomes. There is also a constant hum in the immediate vicinity, along with mild vibrations of the earth.

The workers at the dig are grateful that they have been issued high-tech protective suits to shield them from the harmful radiation and electromagnetic fields. Except for an outbreak of nosebleeds, there seem to be no other injurious side effects to working at the scene.

So far, the archeological team has managed to uncover three metallic-looking domes, each about nine feet in diameter. The actual composition of the structures is unknown, however. Their extremely hard exteriors have defied all attempts at identifying what they're made of. None of the researchers' equipment has even scratched the domes' surfaces. On the contrary, most of the equipment has been damaged in the process.

At California's Sagan Observatory, Doctor Stefan Bell is closely monitoring the remnant of Prometheus as it approaches the Hades Comet. The collision between the two cosmic entities is predicted to occur within forty-eight hours, and the event promises to be spectacular. Doctor Bell was hoping that there would be a direct hit between the two objects to assure the mutual destruction of both the asteroid and the comet, but it now appears that the impact will be more of a glancing blow.

That is not good. That is not good at all.

Matt has already finished packing for his trip back to the Moon, so he decides to retire early. Early the next morning, a limousine will arrive to take him to Denver Airport where he is booked on a private jet bound for Houston. Once he arrives in Houston, he will take a Virgin Galactic flight to the Empyrian Hotel, which is circling overhead in Earth's orbit.

That will be the first leg of his adventure.

CHAPTER TWELVE

It is cold today, much colder than usual.

Matt and Jenn are sitting together in their living room, waiting for Matt's limo. When the grandfather clock in the hallway chimes five times, the couple hears the doorbell ring.

"I guess that's my ride," says Matt as he rises from the sofa.

Rising with him, Jenn squeezes her husband tightly and gives him a kiss. "I love you, you know. Please come home to me safely."

Returning his wife's embrace, Matt says quietly, "Jenn, I'm going to be all right. I feel that I'm going to be well-protected on this trip." To lighten the mood, he adds, "I just hope I don't freeze like an icicle before I get there, though. It's colder than a witch's…heart out there!"

Chuckling, Jenn heads for the door when the bell rings again. As it opens, she is surprised to see an Air Force officer on her doorstep.

"Good morning, Mrs. Matteo," he says politely. "Is your husband ready?"

Joining Jenn at the door, Matt responds, "I'm as ready as I'll ever be," while he buttons up his overcoat and pulls on his gloves.

"It's very cold out here today, sir. I hope you're dressed warmly."

Peter's plane has just arrived at the International Airport in Dublin. It's very quiet in the terminal; not many people are flying today. With hypersonic speeds cutting travel time everywhere on the planet to just a few hours, he should have arrived in Ireland earlier, but his flight out of Washington was delayed because of severe ice and snow.

Peter passes easily through Customs and then boards the electric-powered shuttle bus that was sent to take him to a local hotel. It's early afternoon, but Pete will stay at the hotel overnight and rent a car in the morning for the two-hour drive to Cratloe. He assumes that his quest for the staff of Saint Raphael will end quickly in Cratloe, but everyone knows what happens when we 'assume.'

The snow that fell overnight in D.C. has blanketed the ground and is contributing to keeping capital's air temperature in the low twenties.

It is on days like this that President Bush is grateful to be living above her work area. She has just fished her breakfast and is now heading down to the Situation Room to conduct a meeting with the Cabinet and the Joint Chiefs of Staff. The only items on today's agenda are the crisis in the Gulf of Mexico and the runaway piece of Prometheus.

Arriving early, she seats herself at the head of the large oak table and reviews the latest reports while the other attendees enter and take their seats. After everyone has arrived and the door has been closed, the president begins the briefing.

"Gentlemen and ladies, good morning. Please make no comments until I have finished my remarks. I need to share a lot of information with you today, and we need to get through each item as quickly as possible." Pausing, she takes a deep breath before launching into the grim details.

"I have reviewed the latest reports prepared by Doctor Emil Gurov from NOAA and Doctor Stefan Bell from the Sagan Observatory. There is no way to sugarcoat their findings, so I'll just lay it out for you. As you already know, the warm Gulf Stream current has ceased to flow because of the oil spill. But what you don't know is that the destroyers I dispatched to the area to try to disperse the spill with depth charges have failed in their mission. The oil is too deep, and the spill encompasses an area too large for that approach to have any effect.

"Now, along with that ongoing disaster, and possibly related to it, are the extreme climate changes in the Northern Hemisphere where temperatures have recently plummeted by more than twenty degrees. We, along with the Russians, have lost the use of two Icebreakers because they are locked in place by thickening ice. There is currently snow on the ground in northern and central Europe, and it is creeping eastward toward Russia and China. Snow has even reached as far south as Naples, Italy, and climatologists claim that it will completely cover the southern half of Italy when the sea-effect snow begins to blow off the Mediterranean. In North America, there is now snow on the ground in each of the fifty states. It currently stretches as far south as the areas around Dallas, Texas, and Boca Raton, Florida but NOAA estimates that within a week, the snow will reach even farther south than that.

"As you can imagine, this type of weather pattern does not bode well for the future. If the current situation does not correct itself soon, we could enter a mini ice age. Doctor Gurov has submitted a scenario in which the snow cover does not melt at all during the coming summer. If that scenario occurs this year, then when winter hits again the following year…well, you can fill in the blanks.

"The one bright spot in this disturbing change in our climate is that at least for this year, the Southern Hemisphere will not be critically affected, even though it will experience lower temperatures. But if the conditions I've outlined persist, the future of the entire planet is questionable."

Mrs. Bush stops her report to take a sip of water.

"Now, about Prometheus. The piece of that asteroid is set to strike the Comet Hades within twenty-four hours. Our best and brightest scientists are checking and re-checking the rock's path every few hours, and the trend of their computer simulations is that after the collision with the comet, a fragment of the rock will remain intact and ricochet toward the Earth. At this time, we don't have any means of stopping it from heading our way, and it's too early to project a potential trajectory and impact site."

Murmurs and gasps flow around the room, but Mrs. Bush ignores them.

"Now, I have also been given an update on the events at the Garden on the Moon. It appears that Doctor Raphael Matteo has been summoned by God to make a return trip there but he was not told the purpose of that trip. Let's take a moment now to pray for divine intervention in our hours of need here on Earth."

After a few minutes of silence, the president resumes. "Alright, let's continue."

With a hard glance at General Parkins, she says, "I have received a recommendation that we detonate a nuclear bomb over the Gulf to jump-start the Gulf Stream. But as all of you are aware, the world dismantled all of its nuclear arsenals after Judgment Day. Therefore, no nation on Earth has the resources necessary to shoot down or stop an asteroid or re-start the Gulf Stream. But if our best minds conclude that a nuclear device is the best option to resolve our current problem, I will need to hold immediate discussions with world leaders. They will need to agree to the plan before we could even begin to think of building a radioactive device to explode over the Earth or detonate in our Gulf."

Staring once again at General Parkins, she pauses to emphasize her next words. "That is a moot point, however, because I've decided that detonating a nuclear bomb is not something that will ever happen on my watch. I need you all to provide me with other options."

Doctor Raphael "Matt" Matteo is now on the second leg of his trip to the Moon. His Virgin Galactic flight is on its way to the Earth-orbiting Empyrian Hotel for a short layover, after which he will board the next scheduled shuttle flight to the Moon. At an average speed of 50,000 miles per hour, the shuttle will arrive on the Moon approximately five hours after liftoff.

Matt is anxious to reach his destination to find out what God has in store for him. He was a much younger man the last time he was on the Moon—much younger, but far less wise.

CHAPTER THIRTEEN

P eter is also anxious to reach his destination—Saint John's Church in the small village of Cratloe. He is hoping that he will find the staff of Saint Raphael quickly.

Driving west along the M7 motorway to Cratloe, he is grateful for the heated interior inside the rented Mercedes, but disappointed that he is not able to see the famous soft green Irish countryside. Outside the car's windows, all he can see is a continuous canvas of white snow. Curious about the outside temperature, he glances at the car's gauge only to realize that it's in Celsius. Calculating quickly, he converts the minus ten degrees Celsius to a cold fourteen degrees Fahrenheit. "No wonder I was freezing out there!" he mumbles to himself.

On the drive, he keeps the radio tuned to BBC news, hoping to hear any updates on the confrontation between Prometheus and Hades. The world knows about the impending collision, but not about the potentially deadly outcome of the event for the Earth's inhabitants.

Doctor Matt Matteo is blissfully asleep his Empyrian Hotel room, floating effortlessly inside a cocoon-like bed. The bed resembles the children's toy known as Chinese handcuffs, and confines him inside a limited area to prevent him from drifting around the room while he sleeps.

Being a fan of the force of gravity, he has chosen to keep his gravity boots on while he's in bed. Even though he knows that the cocoon will limit his movement while he sleeps, he knows that he'll need them if he has to walk around the room during the night.

The final leg of Matt's trip, his shuttle flight to the Moon, is scheduled for nine o'clock the next morning. If everything goes as planned, he will be at Gabriel's Cave in the little Garden of Eden by late afternoon.

At the Sagan Observatory, Doctor Bell and his colleagues are staring anxiously at the sky, hoping to catch a glimpse of the imminent deep-space collision. After a long wait, a burst of bright light finally appears on one of the monitors linked to the giant telescope, and reports begin to spew out of the various printers around the room.

As Doctor Bell reads through the hundreds of lines of data, he rapidly becomes horrified when he realizes that the worst possible scenario has occurred! Although the Hades Comet has been destroyed in the interstellar collision that occurred almost 49,000,000 miles away, a fifteen-mile-wide piece of the once-majestic Prometheus asteroid has careened off into space, and is now on a potentially devastating collision course with Earth.

That chunk of rock is now speeding toward Earth at approximately 31,000 miles per hour, making impact with our planet a distinct possibility in only 66.666 days.

If it occurs, it would be an impact from hell.

Late in the afternoon in a field office in Siberia, Doctor Isadore Kirk is concentrating on reviewing several detailed documents. It is very cold outside, and with a continual snowfall, the excavations are moving along slowly. So far, they have managed to uncover the tops of three domes, and they are now digging trenches around each structure to see how far they reach into the ground.

When one of his associates barges into the room, excited and fearful at the same time, Doctor Kirk looks up from his studies.

"Doctor, you must come out to the excavation! The domes! They are humming and vibrating! And they are beginning to emit heat!"

A wake-up call from the front desk rouses Matt from a deep sleep. He stretches within his cocoon bed and then slowly pushes himself out of the small opening. His magnetic gravity boots anchor him securely to the floor, allowing him to walk almost normally to the bathroom area.

In the weightlessness of space, everyday activities inevitably become adventures. Remembering the way things work in space, Matt enters the small compartment, latches the door shut, and heads directly for the toilet area, which is located in a separate compartment and contains just enough room for one person to sit down.

In outer space there is no other option, so everyone must sit on the toilet. When he is properly seated the room begins to spin, which creates an artificial gravity field that prevents his "official business" from floating all over the room. When he is done, he exits into the main bathroom and washes himself down with disposable antiseptic wipes.

Brushing his teeth is another experience. The toothpaste provided by the hotel is edible, so he brushes, and then swallows. The taste is not exactly pleasant, so he does not linger over this activity.

When he has completed his morning routine, he retrieves his clothes from a webbed bag this is hanging on the wall, and makes his way back into the sleeping area. He dresses slowly and carefully, trying not to let his clothes float too far away.

Predictably, his stomach soon begins to rumble, and his thoughts turn to food. Since his shuttle to the Moon departs in only thirty minutes, he is happy that the flight includes a complimentary breakfast. However, he knows that eating during space travel poses its own challenges.

President Bush is once again in the Situation Room, looking at the faces of her cabinet members, the Joint Chiefs, and her Chief of Staff. Each of them is waiting for her to speak.

"People, we have a doomsday scenario in the making. I've been in contact with many of the world's leaders, and all of them have told me that they will be conducting meetings similar to this one today. The piece that broke off from the remnant of Prometheus is over fifteen miles wide, and impact with our planet is expected to occur in approximately sixty-six days. Therefore, we have very little time to devise a plan to defend the Earth. Complicating matters is the fact that the most effective plans are nuclear-based, and because all of the world's nuclear missiles have been destroyed, there isn't enough time for us to build a new device, test it, and deploy it with precision. Consequently, I fear this planet may be lost. Without a specific plan in place to defend ourselves against this deadly space rock, it will probably hit us and destroy life as we know it. I need each of you…"

"Excuse me, Madam President," interrupts Air Force General Allan Bradley. "Not all of our nuclear missiles were destroyed."

CHAPTER FOURTEEN

I t is still snowing lightly when Peter Matteo pulls up to the barn-style church of Saint John's. Walking quickly, he enters the building and is immediately greeted by the pastor, Father Quinn.

"Good morning! God bless you," says Father Quinn as he shakes Peter's hand. "You must be Mr. Matteo. You are not of this village, and we don't get many tourists here."

"Yes, good morning to you, Father. I am Peter Matteo." Peter glances around the church's interior and says, "From our phone call, you know that I'm looking for a statue of the Archangel Raphael that is supposed to be on display here."

"Yes, I know we talked but you ended our conversation before I could explain that there is no such statue here. It was here at one time, but that was a long time ago. You raised my curiosity, however, so I conducted some research before you arrived and I discovered what happened to it."

Noticing Peter's disappointment, the pastor guides him by the elbow and speaks in a soothing tone. "Come now, Peter, we can go to my residence. We'll have some tea while I explain where your journey will take you next."

Matt is happy to be on the last leg of his trip to the Moon. Strapped tightly into his seat so he won't float around the shuttle's cabin, he works the buttons on his personal video screen to get a clearer view of the scene outside the spacecraft.

There are no windows on Moon shuttles, so each seat is equipped with a personal video monitor that displays split-screen images from the forward and aft cameras. One side of Matt's screen is currently showing the giant blue marble of the Earth as it slowly decreases in size, while the other is showing the ever-enlarging and crater-filled Moon.

Concentrating on the image of the Moon, Matt searches the surface until he locates the tiny blue spot surrounded by wasteland that he knows is the Garden of Eden.

Within two hours, he will confront his destiny.

President Bush is staring at General Bradley in disbelief. "What the hell do you mean, 'Not all were destroyed?'"

"Madam President, everyone assumed that all the nuclear weapons were destroyed. However, within the last few days, several old records were discovered in the archives and brought to my attention. It seems that back in the 1980s, during the height of the Cold War, we built a satellite with nuclear-strike missile capabilities and deployed it into high Earth orbit. The satellite went silent at the turn of the century so it was not included in our disarmament treaty. It is still orbiting the Earth and is carrying three nuclear-armed missiles with payloads of fifty kilotons each."

All of the meeting's attendees raise their eyebrows at this news and begin to murmur excitedly but the General holds up his hand to silence them.

"You need to know that even though these nuclear weapons are at our disposal, there is a problem with them. They are not laser-or GPS-guided. Instead, they are preprogrammed with specific strike coordinates. We would need to rendezvous with the satellite and insert new programming into each missile before they could be used to deflect or destroy the asteroid."

"Is that feasible, General?" asks the president.

"Yes, ma'am, but there is still one other problem. The missiles will only detonate on contact, so even if we reprogram them, getting them to hit a moving target would be like aiming for an apple on a person's head with an arrow shot from fifty yards away. It would also take approximately two months to assemble and train a crew to fly up to the satellite and install new software and a new power source. And we would also need time to reactivate the satellite before we could launch the missiles from Earth. Now, if we decide to do all of this, we only have sixty-six days or so before impact, so we would need to get started immediately. Madame President, we believe this plan has about a twenty percent chance of success, but it may be the only means we have of defending ourselves against the asteroid."

President Bush lowers her head. "General," she says after a minute of contemplation, "I think twenty percent is an exaggeration. How do we know the missiles will fire after we reprogram them?"

"We don't."

An uncomfortable silence fills the room until the president walks over to where Bradley is sitting and places her hand on his shoulder. "General, you have my permission to get started on this mission immediately. I also want a full report on how we lost track of that satellite in the first place—but to be frank, I'm glad we did. I pray that you're successful."

General Bradley has his orders, so after he leaves the room to begin preparations, the president continues the meeting with the rest of the attendees.

"Now that we have a plan, I need to confer with the other world leaders on this situation. While I'm doing that, I want the rest of you to put together a backup course of action in the event the general's mission fails. Keep in mind, though," she says she looks around the room, "and this is something that I really must insist upon," she adds somberly, "we cannot tell the people of the Earth about the wayward piece of asteroid that is heading toward us. Not yet, anyway. May God have mercy on us. I believe that He is the only one who can help us now."

Pastor Quinn pours a cup of tea while Peter samples one of the hot scones before him.

"Thank you, Father. The tea is delicious, and it certainly helps to take the chill away. But it seems as though I've come a long way for a cup of tea."

"I'm very sorry you came all this way only to be disappointed. However, I do have some information that may help you." The priest settles back in his chair before continuing.

"For many years, stories have been told by the villagers in the surrounding countryside of miraculous cures attributed to a statue of Saint Raphael that was said to be located in the original church on this site. Now, before we won our independence from Great Britain, British officers were in charge of this area. One of them had ancestors who fought in the Crusades, and he said his family passed down tales of a battle that was won through the extraordinary influence of a staff that belonged to Saint Raphael. The family stories indicated that after the battle, the staff was placed in the hand of a statue of Saint Raphael for safekeeping. When the British officer saw a statue of the saint in our church, he ordered his soldiers to confiscate it, and he had it sent to London. Unfortunately, that is where my trail ends. However, I believe I can still help you. London's Westminster Cathedral has a private library that contains old documents and ledgers. If you can gain access to that library, you may be able to track down information that could lead you to the statue. It's unfortunate that knowledge of its whereabouts has been lost over time, but I hope I've been able to assist you in some way."

"Yes, you have, Father! This is great information. Thank you very much! I just hope that my superiors will allow me to continue with this quest." Peter finishes the last of his tea and rises from his chair.

"The tea and scones were wonderful, but I need to get back to my hotel. It looks like it may snow again, and it's a long drive to the city."

"Yes, I understand. Let me give you a blessing before you go, for safety on your drive back and for success in your future endeavors."

It seems that it never stops snowing in Siberia. With the temperature at -20°C, or -4°F, Doctor Kirk is shivering as he stands near the three domes in the Tunguska tundra, even though he is as bundled up as he could be in his protective suit and face mask.

While it is snowing in the general area around the dig, the ground near the domes is snow-free. In fact, that section of ground is quite warm. It seems that the heat being generated by the structures is melting the ice and snow.

Doctor Ivan Popov from the Russian Archeological Society is busily monitoring the excavation team. But when he notices Doctor Kirk nearby, he approaches the archeologist to brief him on the team's progress.

"It is quite remarkable, Doctor. The domes have suddenly become active. They are humming continually now, and there appear to be lights originating from below the ground. I had to pull the large earth-moving equipment away from the excavation, though, because the soil is becoming very muddy and unstable."

"Ivan, correct me if I am wrong, but do the domes appear to be protruding higher out of the ground, as if they are rising upward?"

"No, you are not wrong. They are about 35 centimeters higher than they were earlier today."

CHAPTER FIFTEEN

As she has done several times over the past few days, President Bush consults with as many world leaders as she can. She speaks to each of them individually and then places a call to NASA headquarters in Houston to check on their progress in choosing the crew that will awaken the Cold War satellite. Just as she ends the call, Levar Daniels barges into the room.

"Madam President, I have some good news for a change!"

"Excellent! Go ahead, Levar. Heaven knows I could use some good news."

"Yes, ma'am. Reports from the Gulf of Mexico indicate that the oil slick is moving up to the surface! Apparently, the cooling temperatures in the Northern Hemisphere have affected the waters of the Gulf enough to allow the slick to rise. Argon Oil has dispatched their oil recovery ship from Galveston and it should be at the site of the spill within three hours. An empty tanker is also en route to the site. When both ships are in place, they will begin to remove the oil. More tankers will be needed to hold all of the recovered oil, so Florida is sending two tankers from Port Everglades and Dubai is sending a super-tanker. Argon estimates that they will need about forty-five days to remove all the oil."

"Levar, that is very good news! But remember, if we don't divert that asteroid, it won't mean a damn thing if we remove the oil or not."

Matt has finally arrived at Moon Base Challenger. As he prepares to exit the shuttle, he thinks back twenty years to the last time he's seen his colleagues Joe Toteda, and James and Christine Reynolds, and he eagerly anticipates his first steps back onto the Earth's natural satellite.

The pull of the Moon's gravity is much less than that of the Earth's, so it's much easier for human muscles to work up there. That particular aspect of space travel is especially appealing to him this time around, because for as long as he's up in space, he will be able to essentially ignore the fact that he has a progressive neurodegenerative disease.

He's also happy that he's not footing the bill for this trip. Flights to the Moon usually cost twenty-five thousand dollars per traveler, but the Moon's diamond mining enterprise is subsidizing much of the cost of his flight and his room at the Empyrian Hotel. The balance is being paid by NASA.

The Empyrian Hotel offers rooms for temporary workers and for visitors who are interested in touring the Garden of Eden surrounding Gabriel's Cave. The shuttle's elevator places visitors directly into a portal attached to the hotel's main lobby. The entrance to the Garden is at one end of the lobby, and the entrance to Moon Base Challenger is at the opposite end.

When Matt steps out of the elevator, he heads straight for the front desk. As he waits for the check in process to be completed, he picks up a copy of the hotel's promotional literature to pass the time. Glancing through it quickly, he reads that although there are only ten rooms currently available, the hotel is advertising an expansion of its facilities in the very near future. Silently, he wonders whether that expansion will ever take place now that Prometheus has broken apart and all tourism travel to the Moon has been cancelled.

After he receives his lock coordinates, he heads to his room to drop off his bags and freshen up. When he feels more presentable, he walks back through the lobby toward the portal to the Garden area.

The portal is a walkway that separates the simulated Earth atmosphere of the hotel from the foreign environment inside the dome of energy that surrounds the Moon's holy sites. The most notable memory Matt has of this walkway is the feeling of passing through what he describes as an "energy curtain."

Before entering the portal, Matt reaches into his pocket and retrieves a small compass that his son, Peter, gave to him many years ago on his first trip to the Moon. His son gave it to him because he wanted to make sure that his dad wouldn't get lost on his journey. Holding back an emotional tear, he caresses the compass while he passes through the "curtain."

On the other side of the energy field, Matt sees the outlines of his buddies as they await the arrival of their friend.

The accumulating snow on the roads is making Peter's drive back to Dublin a slow one. On the way, he uses the extra time to think about what he needs to say to convince his boss to expand his overseas travel to England.

He is about to put together the final arguments in his imagined discussion when his thoughts are interrupted by his cell phone. A quick glance in his rearview mirror shows the way clear so he pulls off to the side of the road and takes a look at the display screen. The caller is his boss, Stanley Jameson.

"Mr. Jameson! You're up early this morning."

"Yes, it's necessary with the time difference. Listen, Peter, I need you to return home as soon as possible. I need to redirect you to Siberia."

Surprised by this turn of events, Peter launches into his request to continue on to England. "But, sir, I didn't find the statue in Ireland. It was moved to England, and I have some good leads…"

"I'm sorry, Peter," interrupts Jameson in a firm voice. "That investigation will have to be put on the back burner for now. Something is happening at the Tunguska dig and I need you there ASAP."

Dejected, but cognizant of his boss' tone, he answers, "Okay, I'll change my flight home. But what's going on out there?"

"The domes are becoming active. I'll give you the details when you get back to Washington."

Matt continues to walk through "energy field curtain." As he nears the end, he is surprised to see a dazzling light surround him and to feel tiny "fingers" thumping all over his body. He is puzzled by these sensations but has no time to analyze them before he breaks through the "curtain" and is grabbed by his friends into a group bear hug.

"Welcome to our Garden!" they all exclaim excitedly.

Knowing that Matt is on a special mission, the friends continue their cheerful chatter as they escort him toward the Garden's entrance. But an unusual sound stops them in their tracks just before they step onto the pathway. The sound is ethereal and mesmerizing, and it places each of them into a peaceful, trance-like state. It the sound of angels singing.

CHAPTER SIXTEEN

F inally back in his Dublin hotel room, Peter goes online to change the date of his return flight back to Washington. With only twenty-four hours before departure, he decides to forgo sleep in order to do more work on the scrolls before he has to return home. He knows that he can sleep on the plane, so he orders a room service meal, and gets busy.

Argon's oil spill recovery vessel, nicknamed the "world's largest wet-vac," has finally arrived at the site of the oil leak in the Gulf of Mexico. The ship earned its nickname from the action of the large tubes that are placed directly into spills to suck up oil and seawater.

The mixture that enters the ship through the tubes is directed into an enormous tank in the cargo hold. This recovery tank is split into two sections. The upper portion contains a Kevlar carbon filter supported three-quarters of the way into the tank by a grid of stainless-steel mesh. When the mixture of oil and seawater is pumped over the filter, gravity separates them into their individual components. The oil, which is lighter than the seawater, remains on top of the filter while the heavier seawater sinks to the bottom of the tank.

On the deck of the ship, special cutoffs and large bypasses are connected to the suction tubes to inhibit marine life and debris from entering the recovery tank along with the oil. Any detritus that manages to makes it through the process is sent back into the Gulf through openings on the opposite side of the ship. The filtered seawater that sinks to the bottom of the tank is pumped back into the Gulf, and the oil that collects at the top is pumped into a waiting tanker ship to be processed and refined.

Weather permitting, this process will continue around the clock, hopefully with only occasional downtime for maintenance, until all the oil is recovered. The Argon Oil recovery vessel is nuclear-powered, so the ship can continue operating indefinitely without any need to refuel. If the weather holds, the entire process is expected to be completed in approximately forty-five days.

While Argon Oil's disaster cleanup teams concentrate on completing their job as soon as possible, NASA announces to the world that the astronauts who will be sent on the most important mission in the history of the Earth have been chosen. The task of these brave souls, codenamed ANUBIS, is to reactivate the only nuclear-capable satellite that still remains in orbit after Judgement Day.

Major Ralston, Moon Base Challenger's commanding officer, is at NASA's Sonny Carter Training Center near the Johnson Space Center in Houston. This facility is where the astronauts are training for their spacewalk to repair the satellite and reprogram its missiles.

The major is seated in a conference room where he is receiving a briefing on the repair plan. An optimistic person by nature, he is nevertheless dismayed when he receives bad news.

Regrettably, NASA has determined that the hypersonic shuttle currently being used for space travel is not large enough to be retrofitted with the huge control arm that will be needed to secure the satellite while the repairs are being done. Frustrated by this development, Major Ralston places an emergency call to General Parkins, Chairman of the Joint Chiefs of Staff.

"Hello, Major Ralston. What can I do for you?"

"We have a problem, General. The hypersonic shuttle can't be used to get the astronauts up to the satellite. It isn't large enough to be fitted with the control arm necessary to hold the satellite in place."

"So, what the hell are you guys going to do about it?"

"We need to go 'old school.' We're going to use the Space Shuttle Atlantis."

"Isn't that the one that's on display at the Kennedy Space Center Visitor Complex in Florida?"

"That's the one. It's large enough to hold the control arm, and it's already at the Cape."

"Yes, but it's been deactivated for years."

"The techs say they can get it ready for launch in four weeks, well within our time frame."

"Well, if they say they can do it…Very good, Major. Go ahead with your plan, and Godspeed."

The snow that is falling outside of the Oval Office is providing a soothing backdrop for President Bush. She is worrying about the piece of asteroid that is still on track to impact the Earth, and about this season's winter weather, which is becoming increasingly bad. But even though the planet seems to be on a doomsday track, she knows that there is still a spot of good news—the oil recovery efforts in the Gulf are on schedule. The well has been capped, there is no more oil flowing into the Gulf, and the oil slick is slowly and steadily being removed.

Sighing, the president prays quietly and begs God and His Son not to abandon the human race in their hour of need. In the middle of her prayers, a bright light abruptly appears in front of the old Kennedy desk. Shocked by the unusual sight, Mrs. Bush is about to buzz for the Secret Service when she suddenly stops mid-action and stares at the glow with widening eyes. Forming within the light is the very recognizable figure of the Son of God! Stunned, the president drops to the floor and lays prostrate on the ground in front of her Lord.

"My little child, you are among the few who have retained their faith. My Father and I have not abandoned you, but man has abandoned Us. Pray that the ones We have chosen will succeed."

Jesus leaves as quickly as He appeared, but President Bush remains on the floor, sobbing.

Jennifer Matteo has been sitting near the video phone for a while waiting for a call from her husband. It is now late in the evening, and Matt was supposed to call when he reached the Moon. Jennifer is not worried. She knows that something important must have prevented him from calling when he said he would, so she decides to go to bed. If Matt calls during the night, she'll be only too happy to wake up to speak to him.

Before climbing into bed, she turns up the temperature on the thermostat in the kitchen. The evening weather forecast predicted dramatically colder temperatures overnight.

It is already the next day in Ireland, and as the early morning sun rises over the land, Peter stretches in his chair and closes his laptop. He has worked throughout the night trying to decipher more of the scrolls, and has made progress. He was able to translate a long passage that seems to indicate that Saint Paul, the scroll's writer, received a private revelation from God the Father. The passage says that God told Saint Paul, "I have placed in charge of protecting this little place where you live, the three angel guardians who stand behind Me at the Throne of Heaven—Michael, Gabriel, and Raphael."

Noticing the time, Peter rushes into the bathroom for some last minute preparations before his flight home. When he's ready, he grabs his already-packed luggage and walks down to the lobby to check out from the hotel, and to catch his ride to the airport.

By the time the plane takes off, he is sound asleep in his seat.

CHAPTER SEVENTEEN

In the morning, Jennifer takes a shower and eats a breakfast of warm oatmeal and coffee, all the while watching the time on the clock. Wondering for the umpteenth time why she hasn't heard from her husband, she gives in to a sense of unease and dials Major Ralston's number with a trembling finger.

"Hello, Major?" she says in a shaking voice. "This is Jennifer Matteo."

Ralston hears the agitation in her voice. "Good morning, Mrs. Matteo. What can I do for you? You sound a little upset."

"Yes, I'm very upset, Major. Matt was supposed to call me yesterday, after he arrived on the Moon. But I still haven't heard from him. Can you contact the Moon base to check up on him for me? This is not like him at all."

Wishing to sound reassuring, he responds lightly, "I don't think there's anything to worry about, ma'am, but I will call up there for you. I'll let you know what I find out as soon as I can."

"Please do, Major. Thank you."

After Major Ralston hangs up with Jennifer, he initiates a video call to Doctor Benjamin Gadh, manager of the moon's diamond mining and water recovery operations at Challenger Base.

"Hello, Doctor Gadh. I need a favor," explains Major Ralston. "Can you send me the whereabouts of Doctor Raphael Matteo? Check with the hotel and with the Reynoldses over at the Garden. His wife is concerned because he hasn't contacted her after he arrived there yesterday."

"Yes, I can do that, Major. I was on my way out to do a moonwalk this morning, but I'll check on him before I leave."

"Thanks, Doc. Contact me as soon as you have any info. And please ask Doctor Matteo to call his wife."

Doctor Gadh turns off the video phone and walks toward the Empyrian Hotel's reception area. He stops on the way to peer down the hallway containing the portal with the energy curtain passageway, but when he doesn't see anyone in there, he moves on to the front desk.

"Good morning," he says to the clerk on duty. "Have you seen Doctor Raphael Matteo since he arrived at the hotel?"

The desk clerk looks up from his paperwork but continues with his work while he responds to the doctor's question. "Mornin' Doc. I haven't seen him since yesterday, when he entered the portal. I only came on duty a little while ago, but when the maid came down a few minutes ago, she said he wasn't in his room."

"Thanks. I guess I'll need to go for a walk in the Garden."

Leaving the preoccupied clerk at the reception desk, Doctor Gadh walks through the energy curtain portal and enters the Garden. Seeing no one nearby, he continues on to the Visitor's Center, where he finds James, Christine, and Joe motionless and staring at the lake through the observation window. They do not hear him as he approaches.

Puzzled, the doctor reaches out and grabs James' shoulder. "Jim? Are you okay?"

At the doctor's touch, Jim suddenly awakens from what appears to have been a deep trance. "Doctor Gadh? What are you doing here?" he asks, a little confused to see the diamond mining manager.

"What the hell is going here, Jim?"

Instead of responding, James Reynolds looks around at the others who are still standing motionless. He walks over to his wife and shakes her awake. Then, he awakens Joe Toteda. Turning back to Doctor Gadh, he says, "The last thing I remember is that we were walking to the Visitor's Center with Matt when we heard angels singing."

"*Angels?* Where is Doctor Matteo now?"

The friends glance at each other questioningly until Joe replies, "We don't know where he is. Isn't he at the hotel?"

"No. I just got a call from Major Ralston. He wants me to find him because he hasn't contacted his wife since he arrived."

Well, if he isn't at the hotel," proposes Christine Reynolds, "he must be out in the Garden."

At that suggestion, all of them look out of the window for any sight of Matt around the lake or in the nearby botanical area. They don't see any sign of him, but they do see the golden Tree of God which is sparkling like silver and gold in the sunlight.

"Let's search the Garden," says Jim to Doctor Gadh. Chris and I will walk around the left side of the lake, and you and Joe can go around the right. We'll meet at the Tree. Matt must be off the path somewhere."

Within minutes of leaving the Visitor's Center, both groups meet at the Tree. Neither of them has seen any sign of Raphael, so Joe yells out his name. When he receives no response, he turns toward the others. "You know, I have a funny feeling. I bet he's in Gabriel's Cave."

Gabriel's Cave is hollow opening in a cliff in the Moon's Montes Apenninus Mountain Range. It is the place where God spilled out the water that first formed a lake, and where later, He produced the new Garden of Eden and the incredible domed energy field that surrounds the cave, the garden, and the lake. The altar in the cave is where Gabriel's Chalice was left for mankind and where Raphael Matteo was chosen to bring it to the world. It is also where the announcement of the Great Judgment was made.

The group heads toward the sacred cave, up the long, gradual walkway that was created on a slope leading up to the entrance. As they climb, they hear Matt's voice in the distance. It sounds like he's talking to someone.

When they reach the cave's entrance, they are stunned by the sight of a large being of light towering over Matt. The apparition looks at them, smiles, and calls out in a deep and penetrating voice, *"My name is Gabriel, and I have brought you Good News!"*

Following that declaration, the apparition disappears in a bright flash of light that leaves the humans beings shaken and speechless.

Until that time, Matt had been standing in front of the altar, but now he drops to his knees and crosses himself reverently, prompting Joe and James to rush to his side.

"Are you okay, Matt? What just happened here?" they ask in unison.

"I'm fine," responds their friend with a smile and a twinkle in his eye. "I was just having a little chat with the Archangel Gabriel."

Stunned at what they have just witnessed, James looks at the altar, and then back at Matt. "Matt, do you realize that you were taking to an *angel*?"

"Yes, I do," says Matt with a wide smile. Then, he stands up and walks out of the dark cave.

With questioning looks at each other, the foursome shakes their heads in disbelief and follows Matt out of the cave.

On the walk back down the pathway, none of them ventures to speak until Doctor Gadh breaks the silence. First, he introduces himself to Matt, and then he asks the question that all of them want to ask.

"Doctor Matteo, I'm Doctor Benjamin Gadh. I'm in charge of operations here at Challenger Base. Major Ralston asked me to check up on you. He said your wife is a little concerned that you didn't call her when you arrived yesterday. But can we put that aside for a moment? What did the angel say to you back there?"

Matt is quiet as he reflects on his experience. Then he says, "God the Father has a task for me, and it has something to do with the Earth. Gabriel said that God would tell me more near His Tree."

The group walks toward the golden tree at the lake, each of them pondering the meaning of the incident in the Cave. At their approach, God's Tree begins to shimmer brightly, and the sounds of whistling wind and singing angels fills the area. When they reach the base of the Tree, a thunderous voice fills the Garden of Eden and addresses Matt directly.

"I AM WHAT I AM. My little creature, I have chosen you to save mankind. Before My Son brought His Judgment upon the world, you were guided by My guardian, Gabriel, to complete a task. Now, I choose you again.

"My Son brought His peace and tranquility to the planet that I provided for your existence, but man has disrupted My creation. Man has caused chaos in the heavens and has initiated the impending destruction of your world. My little children, you have your faith. You have forgotten what My Son has done for you. You have chosen your fate through greed and lust for power.

"The events that mankind has set into motion must be corrected by man himself. I choose not to intervene in these events so that mankind will learn from their mistakes. My little creature, with the help of your own child, you have a journey to complete. You must go to the place where My Son was transfigured before His apostles. There, you will find understanding. But be forewarned; your lack of faith has emboldened the Malignant, and he will put Me to the test. I will not help you to find what you must seek, but I will protect you while you seek it. Know that although My guardians are charged with protecting the place you call Earth, you need to request that they do so. Be warned: they will only respond to My Commandments."

When the voice stops speaking, Matt finds the courage to break into the profound silence that follows the thunderous voice.

"My God, I am truly honored that you have entrusted another mission to me. I will do as You say, but You know that I am not in good health. How will I be able to accomplish this task?"

God reveals a touch of His anger with an intense voice that shocks them all.

70

"O, ye of little faith! With God, nothing is impossible! Your Major Ralston knows the Truth. I am growing weary of My creatures' insolence. I will show you My Power now, but do not test Me further."

In an instant, a powerful and penetrating light radiates from the base of the Tree and envelopes Raphael. He falls to his knees in intense pain, as if his entire body is being pricked by thousands of tiny needles. When he cries out, the light slowly recedes, and the Tree goes dark.

Matt is now lying on the ground in front of the Tree. Joe and Doctor Gadh help him to stand while Christine asks in amazement, "Did we really just hear from God the Father?!"

"Yes," answers Jim. "God is in control, and I guess we all screwed up again. He must have been talking about the Gulf oil spill and the asteroid that broke up because of our drilling up there. He said Major Ralston knows what's going on. We need to talk to him!"

When Matt is able to stand without aid, he looks around at the faces staring at him and knows they want answers. However, before he opens his mouth to speak, he realizes that something's different. He feels great; better than he has for weeks. His tremors are gone and he is no longer weak. In fact, he's feeling a surge of strength and stability throughout his entire body.

Surprised by what's happening, he declares in a quiet voice, "Guys, I think I'm cured. I think God cured me! I don't feel the way I did on Earth. I actually feel great!"

Tears begin to flow from Matt's eyes and the eyes of his friends as all of them gather around him and marvel at his newfound strength and well-being. Amid hugs and kisses, they begin the walk back to the visitor's center. On the way, Matt questions the doctor.

"Doctor Gadh, besides the severe cold weather on Earth, have you heard about any other threats to the planet?"

"Well, yes, I have. I've been told that a piece of Prometheus hit the Comet Hades."

"What?!" shrieks the group in unison.

"Do you think it will hit the Earth?" cries James.

Doctor Gadh attempts to dismiss the question, although he knows the answer. "Uh, you should really speak to Major Ralston about that," he says, and immediately changes the subject. "Are you sure you're feeling well, Matt?"

Matt responds with a smile a mile wide. "I feel wonderful! Absolutely wonderful! But what did you say about a comet? We really do need to contact the Major. It seems that he has a lot to tell us. And I should also call my wife."

"Yeah, and from what we just heard," interrupts Joe, "you better give your son a heads-up."

CHAPTER EIGHTEEN

Bidding each other goodbye, the group splits up after they exit the Garden. Joe Toteda and the Reynoldses enter their personal quarters in the hotel, while Matt follows Doctor Gadh to his office at Challenger Base.

"Doc, is it too late to call Major Ralston in Houston?" asks Matt.

"No, I don't think he cares about the time. He asked me to call him as soon as I had any information about you. I'll call him now."

Doctor Gadh establishes a connection to Earth and then waits for the video feed to go through. Soon, a familiar face fills the screen.

"Hello, Doctor Gadh. Oh, I see you found Doctor Matteo. Is everything okay up there?"

"I found him, Major, but the both of us have an important question for you. We need you to tell us what's going on down there. God gave Matt another message for mankind, and He says that *we're* causing the destruction of our planet! What's going on?!"

"You got another message? Wow!" The major falls silent for a moment. Then, he says, "Look. What I'm about to tell you is classified, on a need-to-know basis. You can't reveal it to anyone, and I mean *anyone*. Not family, not friends, no one. Do each of you understand that?"

The major pauses until he sees both Matt and Doctor Gadh nod their heads in agreement.

"Okay. I know you've heard about the oil spill in the Gulf of Mexico."

"Yes, we know about that," says Matt.

"Well, it's had a devastating effect on the planet's ecosystem. It stopped the flow of the Gulf Stream, and our best scientists believe that the last Ice Age, which occurred tens of thousands of years ago, was the result of a similar set of circumstances. Fortunately, we now have the technology to remove the oil, and we already have people working feverishly on doing just that. We hope that after the Gulf is cleaned up, the warm water will start flowing again in enough time to prevent us from entering another ice age. But that's not all. When the mining operation on Prometheus caused the asteroid to break apart, a piece of it collided with the Hades Comet. That collision caused another chunk of asteroid to break off, and that smaller piece is now headed directly for Earth. We put together a plan to try to intercept it before it strikes us, but that mission has about a twenty percent chance of success. So, while an ice age would bring disastrous consequences to our planet, it may not be of much importance, because if that asteroid hits us, all life on Earth will end in an instant."

Doctor Gadh is shocked and remains silent, but Matt reacts with unusual confidence.

"Major, God has chosen me to help the Earth because He won't intervene when His children deliberately cause their own problems. He said we have the free choice He gave us, but we consistently choose poorly. We have ignored Him and His Son, so we must solve our problems ourselves. He told me to go to the place where Jesus transfigured to receive more understanding of what I must do. How much time do we have before that piece of asteroid hits us?"

"We have about sixty days. If God has told you to do something, NASA will help you in any way we can. But first, take a minute to call your wife."

"Yes, I will. But Major, how are you going to intercept that asteroid?"

"I've told you too much already. Just pray that it works. Let me know what you need, Matt, and may God bless you. I thank God for His message to you. Without divine intervention, we're all certain to be doomed."

Major Ralston ends the call and leaves Matt and Doctor Gadh in open-mouthed astonishment.

"I can't believe it!" exclaims Doctor Gadh. "Not one, but two events that could completely devastate the Earth! You need to get ready to go back home immediately, Matt. Do you know where Jesus was transfigured?"

"No, but I'm sure my son does."

President Bush's secretary opens the door to the Oval Office.

"Madam President, Major Ralston from NASA is on line three for you. He says it's very urgent."

"Thank you, Marjorie," says the president as she picks up her desk telephone. "Hello, Major. How's the training going?"

"Madam President, the training is proceeding ahead of schedule, but that's not why I'm calling. It's about Doctor Raphael Matteo being called back to the Garden of Eden on the Moon."

"Yes, Major. Doctor Matteo brought us Gabriel's Chalice, and he has recently received another divine message."

"That's correct. The doctor is on the Moon right now and he has just been given another task by God. God says that He will not interfere in situations that we ourselves cause by meddling in His creation. I'm sure you'll agree that the standstill of the Gulf Stream and the collision of the comet were largely caused by our own deeds."

"Yes, I agree."

"Well, God has tasked Doctor Matteo with facilitating a correction of our actions."

A soft whimper escapes through the hand that is clasped to the president's mouth in shock.

"Madame President, I've assured the doctor of NASA's full cooperation with his mission. We'll provide him with whatever he needs to accomplish his task. Of course, I'll keep you informed at every stage of his progress. I'm convinced that because our Father in heaven is paying special attention to Doctor Matteo, we must assist him in every way. He may be the only one who can save our planet now."

"If God is behind him, there's no doubt about that, Major. Please be sure to keep me in the loop at all times. I will officially offer him the assistance of the entire federal government. And if necessary, I'll also enlist the cooperation of every other nation on the face of the Earth."

After Major Ralston ended the video call with Matt and Doctor Gadh, he called Jennifer to let her know that her husband is okay and that he will contact her via video phone as soon as he could. Matt couldn't call home himself because just as the call with the major ended, the Moon moved out of position in relation to the Earth. But now that conditions are favorable, he is anxiously waiting for a connection.

"Hi, Jenn! I love you!" he says with a smile when his wife appears on the monitor.

"Oh, Matt! What happened? I was so worried when you didn't call. Are you okay? You look different."

Matt is bursting with news, but he doesn't want to tell her anything until he can explain it all in person. "I have a lot to tell you, Jenn! I'm going to get on the next shuttle flight back. I can't wait to tell you what happened. I'll be home in a couple of days."

Curious, Jenn asks, "What happened in the Garden, Matt?"

"Everything is fine. I'll explain it all when I get home." Matt throws a kiss toward the image of his wife and wipes away a tear.

Jenn does the same.

CHAPTER NINETEEN

Pete's conventional flight has finally landed at BWI. A hypersonic plane would have shaved several hours off his trip, but he wasn't able to book one when his plans changed abruptly in Ireland. He makes a beeline for Customs, but by the time he goes through the process and is sitting in his boss's office, it is late afternoon.

"Welcome back, Peter." states Stanley Jameson. "Thanks for returning so quickly."

"Hello, Mr. Jameson. I'm glad you could fit me in this afternoon because I have great news for you. I've been able to decipher more of the scrolls, and I also have a lead on the location of Raphael's staff!"

"You know I told you that search has to stop for a while."

"Yes, I know. But I really do have good news."

"Hmm. What have you found out?"

"According to the scrolls, the apostle Paul received a revelation that three archangels have been tasked with the job of protecting the Earth—Michael, Gabriel, and Raphael. And I think the staff was taken to England—to Westminster Cathedral in London. I know you want me to go to Russia, but I think it's critical that I pursue Raphael's staff."

"I respect your opinion, Pete, but I need to remind you that you're going to have to put that investigation on the back burner."

With a sigh, Peter accepts his boss's order.

"Alright, alright. But what's so important about Russia?"

"The team in Siberia found metallic domes buried in the Tunguska tundra and they're rising out of the ground under their own power. You may be aware that the nomads who lived in that region at the time of the Tunguska blast claimed that what they described as 'beings of light' erected structures in the area long before the blast. They said the structures sent shafts of brilliant light into the sky, and they believe that the intense light is what caused the great explosion over the tundra, not a comet or an asteroid strike. This may be just what you're looking for, Pete. What you find in Siberia may give you some insight into the *Tres Archangelis* scrolls."

"There really are structures in the Tundra?" asks Peter.

"Yes, this is real, but the staff described in the scrolls may be just a myth. Go home and rest up for your trip; you leave tomorrow. I booked you on a hypersonic flight to Moscow so you'll be in Siberia twenty-four hours after you leave the U.S."

Matt is taking the next shuttle flight home to Earth, scheduled for the following day. He wasn't expecting to receive his instructions from God so soon after arriving so he's happy to have extra time to visit with his friends and take in as much of the holy sites as possible. This morning, he's having breakfast with James, Christine, and Joe at the restaurant near the Garden of Eden.

"Do you guys want to walk through the Garden with me after breakfast?" he asks. "I have to warn you, though. Today may not be as eventful as yesterday."

Agreeing to join him, the group chats amiably as they stroll down the Garden path. When they reach the Tree of God, they stop to gaze at its twinkling leaves.

"It's so peaceful here," remarks Matt. "I feel sheltered from all the chaos back on Earth."

"I know what you mean," states James. "All of us feel sheltered here, and we're blessed to be God's curators."

As they gaze at the tree, the sunlight strikes its leaves and causes it to sparkle brilliantly. But as beautiful as that is, their attention is diverted by something in the distance. From the direction of Gabriel's Cave, a strong beam of light radiates out into the sky and heads toward the Earth.

"*Uh-oh*," says Christine Reynolds ominously. "*Now*, what's going on?"

At that very same moment, similar beams of light are traveling outward from the altar sites at Yellowstone National Park in Wyoming and Kuril Lake in Russia. The light from Yellowstone is heading east while the light from Kuril Lake is heading west. Eventually, the two beams intersect with the beam of light that is traveling down from the Moon. They converge directly over Vatican City.

When the populace of Rome realizes that three beams of light are uniting over Vatican City, they head directly for Saint Peter's Square.

It was over twenty years ago when a similarly unusual event first occurred in the world, and that event was just before Judgment Day when a giant cross appeared in the sky over the Vatican.

The current occupant of the Chair of Peter is Pope Peter I. After the Great Judgment, when all of the world's religions came together as one, a new Church was formed with Pope Peter as its head. Arising from the Roman Catholic and Apostolic Church, the new Church is now called the Roman Universal and Apostolic Church. The word "catholic" was dropped because it literally means "universal," but the word "apostolic" was retained because the office of the pope is based upon the papacy's unbroken line to the apostle Peter.

Pope Peter I is unique in that he is the head of a new Church, but he is also unique in another way. When he chose the name Peter at the beginning of his papacy, he unknowingly fulfilled the prophecies of past centuries that suggested that the last pope of the Roman Catholic and Apostolic Church would be named Peter. Because that Church no longer exists, Pope Peter is indeed the last Pope of the Roman Catholic Church.

Informed about the phenomenon in the sky, the pope's secretary runs through the Vatican's vast hallways and barges into the pontiff's office. Breathing heavily, he shouts, "Your Holiness! You must look out of your window at the sky over the Square! There is a cross! AN IMMENSE CROSS IS IN THE SKY!"

Now close to eighty years old, Pope Peter heeds his secretary's request and makes his way over to the large window in his spacious office. Gazing skyward, he gasps and then drops to his knees.

The image of the giant cross in the sky is similar to the event that occurred before Jesus' return so many years ago. The cross is dazzlingly bright and illuminates the entire earth below it. Millions of people around the globe are also looking heavenward, and a great part of the human race is joining together in prayer.

Simultaneous with the event that is occurring on Earth, Matt, James, Chris, and Joe have stopped dead in their tracks in the Moon's Garden of Eden. They are transfixed by the bright light that is shining from Gabriel's

Cave toward their home planet. But while they are spellbound by that sight, another event astonishes them further. The Tree of God before them suddenly begins to speak again.

"I AM WHAT I AM," says a powerful voice. *"This is a sign for My children and a sign for My guardians, those who stand behind Me at the Throne of Heaven."*

On the Earth, Pope Peter is still on his knees, staring skyward at the sign from God. Suddenly, he turns toward his secretary.

"At first," he says thoughtfully, "I thought it was a cross, like the one that appeared before. But it is not," he declares firmly. "The vertical shaft is too long, and the horizontal shaft is too short. It is not a cross, it is a *sword*!"

CHAPTER TWENTY

“ *...in the Northern Hemisphere, which is falling deeper into a cold and grey winter. Snow is now on the ground in every continent across the globe. Average temperatures are down about twenty degrees, and environmentalists are blaming the oil spill in the Gulf. There are rumors that the Gulf Stream has halted, but no comments have been issued from the White House or the governing body of any other country.*

"On an encouraging note, the beams of light that traveled from the three "Judgment Altars" have converged over the Vatican to produce an immense sword in the sky. The image is so bright that it is visible during the day. More pilgrims than ever are flocking to the earthly holy sites, but the Garden of Eden on the Moon remains closed to visitors until further notice. We have tried to get an explanation from NASA for the termination of trips to the Moon, but their only comment continues to be that the visitor's center is under renovation.

"This is Gloria Johnson reporting for CNN News."

The pilot of a small twin-engine Cessna is navigating steadily toward the Siberian dig, with Peter Matteo as his only passenger. Wrapped in layers of cold weather gear, Peter is scrutinizing the countryside below them, impatient to catch a glimpse of the makeshift landing strip the archeological team created with their large earth-moving equipment.

The Tunguska excavation site is located in a remote area in the middle of Russia's vast Siberian province. It took two days of multiple cargo flights to get the entire research team from Moscow to Krasnoyarsk, the largest city in the region, and it took three more days to move all of their equipment to the actual dig site. The area is so remote that there is no cell phone coverage at the dig, so the team's only means of communication is through satellite phones and high-frequency single sideband (HF SSB) mobile radios. However, even with this technology, communication with the outside world is spotty at best because of the electromagnetic field that is being generated by the domes.

As the Cessna nears the dig, Peter is surprised to see the remnants of the large circular area where the mysterious explosion occurred in 1908. Inside that still barren area is the site where the three domes are beginning to protrude from the ground.

Noting that the makeshift landing strip is about five hundred yards away from the circle, Peter asks, "Why is the landing area so far from the dig?"

The pilot answers, "We cannot fly any closer to the excavation. The high EMF emanating from the domes interferes with all of the plane's electronics. That is why we must not fly over, or near, the excavation site."

After making a wide detour around the area, the pilot deftly lands the plane on the crude landing strip.

With thanks to the pilot, Peter bundles up and grabs his luggage before he steps out into the -30°C (-22°F) cold. When he's a safe distance away from the plane, the pilot taxis around and takes off again.

Matt is on his way back to Earth. He was fortunate to be able to catch a direct flight from the Moon, but because all space travel operates solely out of Houston, his trip home will not be completed when he lands on Earth. Mercifully, NASA has arranged for a private jet to fly him from Texas to Denver, and that will cut down on his total travel time considerably. He is anxious to talk to Jennifer.

When he arrives at Denver International Airport, he sees Jenn waiting near the luggage carousel. Wanting to surprise her with his renewed agility, he runs the short distance to her side. With her arms opened wide, Jennifer gathers her husband into a hug and a kiss. But soon, she stops and stares at her husband curiously.

"Hey, wait a minute… How were you able to run over here? What happened to you on the Moon?"

Examining her husband more closely, Jennifer realizes that he seems to be stronger and more youthful looking. His skin no longer has any pallor, and there is a fresh glow about him. Staring at him in astonishment, she asks, "What is going on?"

Matt struggles to speak through tears that are flowing freely down his face. "I…I'm fine, Jenn. Actually, I feel great! Look at me…I'm cured! I'm cured, Jenn! *God cured me!*"

Jenn gasps, and with another embrace, kisses away the tears that are continuing to run down her husband's face. While Matt's luggage circles the carousel again and again, the happy couple holds each other close, oblivious to their surroundings.

Doctor Isadore Kirk walks up to greet Peter as he trudges through the snow from the landing strip to the archeological excavation site.

"Welcome, Peter! We are most excited to have you here! First, we must get you to the central station where you can put on protective clothing. It is a necessary defense against the EMF."

Overwhelmed by the cold, Peter barely manages to speak a few words in response as they walk briskly toward a mobile office about 20 meters (65 feet) from the dig site. "Thank you. Can you bring me up-to-date? And can we walk a little faster? I'm *freezing*!"

When the men enter the portable office building, Doctor Kirk points Peter toward a rack of hanging garments. As he puts on his gear, Doctor Kirk describes recent events at the site.

"I know Mr. Jameson gave you basic information about what is happening here, but things are changing rapidly. By our measurements, the domes have now risen a half meter, or one and a half feet, out of the ground. And we have noticed that there is something engraved on the top of each dome. Each of the engravings is different, but we don't know what any of them mean. They could be letters, or perhaps they are pictograms."

Doctor Kirk hands Peter a drawing of the three different symbols.

"We are trying to decipher each of their meanings. And we are also trying to determine what the structures are made of. We have attempted to conduct several different tests to determine their composition, but we cannot even mar their surfaces enough to take a sample. They are much too dense."

While the doctor was talking, Peter was listening to him and examining the drawings at the same time. When the doctor pauses, Peter says, "You know, these symbols are unusual, but I think I've seen similar ones on the

Nazca Plains in Peru. Please take a photo of each of them and send them to the Smithsonian via your satellite phone. I'd like to see them up close, though. Can you take me to the site now?"

CHAPTER
TWENTY-ONE

After the historic collision in space between a piece of the Prometheus asteroid and the Comet Hades, the inhabitants of the Earth are going about their business. Most of them didn't know that the catastrophe occurred, and even less of them know about the possibility of a subsequent impact with the Earth that could end all life on the planet. As the smaller piece of Prometheus rushes silently through the cosmos with nothing to impede or alter it from its track, the people of Earth are deliberately being kept in the dark about the prospect of a cataclysmic disaster in their future.

The day after Matt returned home from the Moon, he called his neurologist to let him know that he's feeling better and that he believes he's been cured of his illness. The skeptical doctor urged him to come into the office for a checkup as soon as possible.

On the day of his appointment, Matt is subjected to several tests to determine his current condition. While the Matteo's wait in the doctor's office for the test results, the couple holds each other's hands and thinks back to the first time they met Doctor Senjali, and to the earth-shattering news they received at that time. This time, they are confident that they will be hearing much better news.

When the doctor finally walks into his office with Matt's files, he sits down at his desk and looks directly at his patient. "Matt, I don't know how this happened, but from everything I can see it certainly does seem that you are cured. There is no longer any indication of amyotrophic lateral sclerosis. In fact, your MRI shows that the areas of arthritis in your hips and knees are also gone. This is all highly unusual, to say the least. I could even call it miraculous!"

At the dig site, Peter immediately notices a low electronic hum that seems to surround the mysterious domes. As he ventures closer, he notices that there is a light shining from under the dome that he is standing closest to.

"Doctor Kirk, are there lights at the other domes as well?"

"Yes, they seem to be coming from under the surface of the earth. As you can see here on the far side of this one, we have begun to remove the dirt from around the domes to try to determine how large the structures are. The light seems to be coming from these large rectangular panels that resemble stained glass. And we are also noticing that the EMF surrounding the domes is diminishing as they rise higher out of the ground."

Peter walks around to the rear of the dome and looks into the pit created by the investigation team. "Hmm, this structure resembles a bullet, almost like a giant 9MM cartridge." Looking closer, he continues, "The surface of the structure is quite interesting. I've never seen anything like it."

"Nor have I. One of my men swung a pickaxe against the side of it, and not only did it not mar the surface, but the axe broke."

Taking a few steps backward, Peter gazes at the three domes and their relative placement in the ground. "Doctor Kirk, have you noticed anything strange about how these domes are positioned in the ground with respect to each other?"

"No, not really, but we have determined that two of them are located in a straight, southwesterly line relative to each other, while the third is located along that same southwesterly line, but a little north of the others."

"Precisely. It seems to me that the domes are mimicking the arrangement of the three brightest stars in the Belt of Orion in the constellation Orion. That placement is similar to the positions of the pyramids in Egypt and Mexico. The Egyptians associated the stars of Orion with the god Osiris, their sun god of rebirth and the afterlife, and the Incas of Mexico believed that all life came from the constellation Orion. I don't think the placement of these domes is coincidental."

Back at home after his appointment with the doctor, Matt is at his desk, surfing the Internet. He's trying to locate the site of the Transfiguration, the place where God said he needed to go. When he locates the Monastery of Saint Catherine at Mount Sinai, he shouts to his wife, Jenn! I think this is where I have to go!"

The Monastery of Saint Catherine at Mount Sinai is located in Egypt at the foot of Mount Sinai on the Sinai Peninsula. That mountain is where it is believed the Ten Commandments were given to Moses and where the burning bush is located. The patronal feast of the monastery is the Transfiguration, and it was built over what many believe to be the burning bush through which God spoke to Moses. It is the oldest continuously-inhabited Christian monastery in the world, and outside of the Vatican, its library holds the world's largest collection of ancient scrolls, icons, and tablets.

From the other room, Jennifer could barely make out what Matt was saying to her. Because she couldn't understand him clearly, she walks into his man cave to find out what had him so excited. "Matt, you know I can't understand you when you talk to me from another room. What did you say?"

Looking up from the computer, Matt considers what he needs to tell his wife. "You know, I haven't told you exactly what I have to do yet; what God tasked me to do. I did tell you that God gave me a mission, but you don't know why He gave it to me. Promise me that you won't tell anyone else what I'm about to tell you."

Jennifer grabs a small stool and sits down next to her husband. "Of course I won't tell anyone. What is it?"

"You know the asteroid that we were mining out in deep space?" Jenn nods her head. "Well, it broke apart, and it was our fault—humanity's fault—that it ruptured. It broke apart because we were mining on a foreign body in space. But that's not the entire story. After it split apart, a piece of it collided with a comet, and a large chunk of that piece is now going to hit the Earth."

Seeing Jennifer's eyes widen in alarm, Matt continues talking before she can say anything. "I received messages from both the Archangel Gabriel and God the Father. God told me that He won't intervene in our affairs when we deliberately screw up. Well, He didn't say it in those words, exactly. He said that His guardians, the archangels that Gabriel said stand behind Him at the Throne of Heaven, are supposed to protect His planet, but that it's man's responsibility to obtain their help. It's our responsibility to ask for their power when we need it the most."

Matt glances at his wife to gauge her reaction to this news, but with a wave of her hand she urges him to continue. "God said that I have to go to the place where His Son transfigured, and that Pete must go there with me. He says I must find the way to save the planet from the destruction that's headed our way."

"What?!" exclaims Jennifer.

"That chunk of asteroid is going to collide with the Earth in about six weeks. So I have six weeks to figure out how to save the Earth. If it hits us, all life on this planet will end. God said that it's our fault. It's the people of the Earth's fault that this is happening. It's because of our greed and our interference in His creation. When He told me what I had to do, I didn't think I'd be able to do it with my ALS, and He wasn't pleased about that. First, He scolded me, but then He cured me to prove His power. So, here I am. Or, here *we* are."

"We?" asks Jennifer.

"Jenn, I don't know exactly how I'm going to do what He wants, but I'm certain that I have to go Saint Catherine's Monastery in Egypt. Some people believe that the Transfiguration occurred on a different mountain, but my mind is telling me that that monastery is where I'm sure I'll discover how the archangels can help us. Pete needs to go there with me and I want you to come too, because if I'm not successful, I want my family nearby."

Jennifer places her arms around Matt's neck and together, they read over the information about the monastery on the computer screen.

"Matt, God and the Angel Gabriel are with you, and so am I. We'll do this together. But Peter said he's going to be in Siberia, so I don't know if we'll be able to get in touch with him."

"We don't have much time, so we'll have to do everything we can to reach him. Funny thing, though. Even if we do manage to prevent the asteroid from hitting the Earth, we'll still be in trouble because it looks like we're heading for an ice age. From what I saw of the Earth from space, the entire Northern Hemisphere is covered in white, so there's something else going on. I still have friends at NOAA. I'll cash in some chips to see if I can find out what it is."

"Yeah, the weather has really been strange lately," says Jennifer. "The exhibit hall at the Kennedy Space Center where the Space Shuttle Atlantis is located had to be closed when it was hit by a 'snownado.' "

"A what? What's a snownado? It sounds like a headline from *The New York Post*."

"Yeah, or the *Drudge Report*. It was a snow blizzard that contained a tornado. They said the roof was blown off the exhibition hall and the shuttle sustained damage. NASA has to transport it back to that large building near the old launch site for repairs. They say the exhibit will be closed down for at least two months."

CHAPTER
TWENTY-TWO

There is no signal when Peter tries to make a satellite phone call from the dig's command center, so Doctor Kirk turns to the backup HF radio. The unit, a Sunair Electronics RT 9000 model built in the 1990s, is a CB radio on steroids. With its thousand-watt amplifier, this old piece of technology is still reliable. Its signal reaches a Russian military base about fifty miles west of Moscow, where it is transferred to a land line.

After numerous clicks and beeps, the call to Stanley Jameson's house finally goes through, and wakes him up from a deep sleep. The three p.m. call from Russia reaches Washington at about four o'clock in the morning, eleven hours behind Siberian time.

"Mr. Jameson? Sorry to wake you. This is Peter Matteo."

"Peter? What time is it?" asks Jameson as he rubs his eyes.

"It must be about four o'clock in the morning where you are, sir."

"Hmph. This is the third phone call since yesterday that involved your name. I'm glad you called, though. I have some information to give you. But I'll let you talk first."

Surprised that anyone has been talking about him, Peter shrugs it off so he can give his report.

"Okay. Well, I'm at the dig, and I've been able to examine as much of the domes as we can see of them. They seem to be made of a metallic-like compound, but their exact composition is unknown. And there is a light coming from the ground below each of them. We're not able to determine exactly where the light is coming from because it doesn't look like the domes have completely risen out of the ground. Also, there is an engraving at the top of each dome. The designs look extra-terrestrial, but I think I've seen similar ones in photographs of the glyphs from the Nazca plains. We'll send photos of these as soon as we can."

Jameson is enthused. "I look forward to seeing them! Get them to me as soon as you can."

"Yes, we'll send them later today. Sir, I may have more to tell you after a meeting I've arranged with a descendant of Genghis Khan. His people have lived in this area since the Tunguska explosion and I was told that he has a great story to tell us. But to get back to the domes—at the rate they're rising out of the ground, we should know more in a week or so."

"That's great news, Peter, but unfortunately, you won't be there to see it. I received two phone calls about you yesterday. The first came from Major Ralston at NASA, and the second came from your father. I won't go into all the details now, but you're needed back here ASAP."

Upset and confused, Peter asks the first thing that comes to mind. "Is something wrong with my father?"

"No, no, he's fine."

"Then why do I need to return so quickly? You rushed me over here from Ireland, and you were right. This find is earth-shattering! I really think I should stay to..."

"I'm sorry, Pete," interrupts Stanley, "but what's happening at home is more earth-shattering than you can imagine. You need to return. *Now*."

"But…"

"No buts! Make arrangements to get back here ASAP!"

As an archeologist about to investigate a terrific discovery, Peter is dejected but also curious about what is going.

"Okay," he says, "my frequent flyer miles are really going to be piling up. It's going to take at least twenty-four hours to get a plane to come out here, so I'm going to conduct that interview before I have to leave. Mr. Jameson, why did my father call you? Is there anything you can tell me about the reason I have to rush back?"

"I'm sorry, but I can't say anything else, Peter. Due to security concerns, I can't give you any details now. But I can say that when Major Ralston called me, he suggested that I contact the White House to confirm what he was telling me. As for the reason your father called, I'll leave it to him to tell you. Your family is okay, but you do need to talk to him. Have a safe trip home, Peter. And bring those photos with you. I'd rather see the originals than the ones sent by sat phone."

The beams of light that have been shining from the Yellowstone National Park altar and the Russian Kuril Lake altar are continuing to head upward to meet the beam from Gabriel's Cave on the Moon. And the giant sword they created over Saint Peter's Square is still illuminating the sky. Each of these wonders is attracting pilgrims from all over the world, drawing record numbers of visitors who want to see them for themselves.

Meanwhile, alternative news websites and blogs from amateur astronomers are beginning to warn about an impending collision from a runaway asteroid, calling it a warning from God. But official government agencies around the world are dismissing those reports, claiming that the remnant of Prometheus will only come within 100,000 miles of the Earth.

The government agencies cannot explain away the sword in the sky over the Vatican, however. Church officials have begun to refer to the phenomenon as God's way of reassuring us of His presence, and millions of people are now praying for God's help and guidance amid the bitter cold and snow of the changing climate.

As these events continue to unfold, more and more of the world's population is coming to believe that prayer is the means by which things can change. The faith of many is increasing, and church attendance is on the rise; it is almost at the same level it was more than twenty years ago. God the Father and His Only Son are pleased, but also concerned. They know how fickle Their little children are. Our Heavenly Father, the all-knowing God, is fully aware of how things will turn out in the end, but because of His gift of free will, He doesn't know exactly how each of His children will react to the coming events.

Although Peter's flight back to civilization is scheduled for one o'clock in the afternoon, he wakes up early to take one last look at the domes, and to prepare for his meeting with Baras-Aghur Tomov, the descendant of Genghis Khan. Tomov's family has lived in the area since the days of the Mongol Empire. Peter is fortunate that Doctor Kirk will be able to attend the meeting as translator.

After breakfast, he suits up and heads out into the -30°C (-22°F) environment. But while the temperature outside the command center is glacial, it is a balmy 20°C (68°F) near the domes. The warmer air around the dig is keeping the ground from freezing, making it much easier for the excavation team to do their work.

Doctor Kirk is already there when Peter arrives. He informs Peter that the EMF field has just about vanished, but says the domes are emitting an ever-increasing hum. He also tells him that the domes are now one meter (three feet) out of the ground, and still rising.

As Peter studies the scene, he is stunned to realize that he is actually able to watch the structures rising out of the ground. The team estimates that the domes are surging upward at the rate of one centimeter, or about half an inch per minute.

Because the EMF has decreased and the location is so warm, Peter removes his protective gear and unbuttons his heavy winter coat. The electromagnetic field has disappeared, so there is no longer any need to wear protective garments.

He remains in the area until the time of his meeting, watching Doctor Kirk take photos of the earth-moving machines that are cutting deeper and deeper into the tundra to expose the base of each dome.

CHAPTER TWENTY-THREE

Sipping cups of strong coffee across the table from Peter and Doctor Kirk are Baras-Aghur Tomov and several of his companions. The men speak an old Russian dialect, a mixture of Mongolian and Russian, so Doctor Kirk's fluency in languages will be put to the test during this meeting.

The men exchange customary pleasantries, then Peter opens the discussion by posing a question regarding the reason for the gathering—the event at Tunguska. As the group's spokesperson, Baras-Aghur responds immediately.

As Doctor Kirk translates, Peter listens in awe at the unfolding of a tale that has been handed down through the generations by the nomadic Mongol tribespeople who live on the tundra.

"Late in the evening one spring day many years ago, bright lights awakened our tribespeople. Some of the men went to the area to investigate, and at the site where the lights originated, they saw three beings of light. The beings spoke to them and said they were sent there to 163 the Earth. My great, great, great uncle, Aghur Khan, asked the creatures where they came from, and to answer him, they pointed to three stars in the heavens. The creatures of light said they were going to build tools of protection, and they warned our people to move out of the area for their safety. When Aghur Khan asked them how far away they should move, they were told to go where all the animals will be waiting—to walk to the place where the sun sets.

"The men went back to their tents and awakened the rest of the people. Everyone packed up their belongings and they began their journey the next day. They walked for two sunrises, until they came to a rise in a plateau where they found bears, wolves, and deer all grazing together peacefully. The people and the animals remained there waiting for something, but not knowing what it was. They waited peacefully, each of them looking instinctively toward the east.

"After several days, they saw shafts of light in the east rising into the sky, and other shafts falling down toward the Earth. Then, there was a great explosion, and a large cloud in the shape of a wild mushroom rose high into the sky. After the explosion, a strong, hot wind shook them all and knocked down their tents. When the hot wind passed, there was nothing but silence.

"Some time later, one of the beings of light appeared to the people where they were waiting and said they could return to their land. The being said they would leave their machines here for future use. But he said special keys would be needed to unlock their power.

When the tribe returned to their land, they saw great destruction. All the trees were blown down and the ground was scorched. They also saw three structures arranged in a straight line on the ground but they could not get close to them, because those who did became sick. My people say that the outsiders who came to investigate the devastated area also became sick when they approached the structures. Eventually, the structures sank into the tundra. That is the story told by my people."

When Doctor Kirk ends his translation of Baras-Aghur's narrative, Peter exclaims, "I'm absolutely dumbfounded! That is amazing, totally amazing! Doctor Kirk, can you ask him if any of the beings told his people who they were? Ask him if they know their names."

Doctor Kirk translates the question, and with widened eyes, gives Peter the response. "He says, yes, his people know the name of one of them! The being of light who said they could return home was named *Gabriel*!"

Peter and the doctor are rendered speechless by the entire story, each of them staring at the other in open-mouthed astonishment.

"Holy crap on a cracker!" shouts Peter. "Don't translate that, Isadore. But—*angels*? If any of that is true, what in the world *are* those domes that we've been digging up?"

"Peter," says the doctor, "Baras-Aghur is requesting permission for him and some of his men to remain at the dig to help with the excavation. They want to see for themselves what their ancestors saw."

"Yes, yes, of course!" says Peter. Turning to Baras-Aghur and the others, Peter smiles and shakes their hands warmly. Then he asks Doctor Kirk to thank their guests for their time and their story.

After the doctor translates Peter's words, he asks an associate to guide the Mongols to the dig site.

As their guests are being led away, Peter says, "I'm sorry, Isadore, but I must leave now. My flight departs soon, so I need to get ready for the long journey home. I hope I'll be able to find out more when I get back there."

Dr. Kirk looks questioningly at Peter. "But why must you leave now? We don't know what any of this means yet. We have so much more to learn!"

With his hand placed on Doctor Kirk's shoulder, Peter confides, "When I was told that I must drop everything to come here, I was interrupted from pursuing another quest, which I now believe has become even more important than it was before. Don't be too surprised if I show up on your doorstep again, maybe sometime soon."

CHAPTER
TWENTY-FOUR

After almost twenty-four hours of travel, Peter is once again sitting in his boss's office at the Smithsonian Institution. He is exhausted, but is anxiously waiting to learn the reason he was called home so urgently.

"Before I fill you in on what's going on," begins Stanley Jameson, "I need to comment on the symbols at the tops of the domes. After I saw the photos you attached to the email you sent from Moscow, I searched through our archives and found some documents about the purported 'language of the angels.' And now that I've seen the original photos, I must tell you that this is remarkable!"

Peter begins to say something, but Stanley holds up his hand to stop him. "Please let me finish," he says. "As you know, we went through the Judgment from God a little over twenty years ago. At that time, the people of Earth were given a period of time to accept the Messiah before God and His Son came down to Earth on the Throne of Heaven. When that happened, the final Judgment Day occurred for those who had not made their choice. Being an atheist, I was one of the millions who had not made a final choice, and on that day, I found myself in the presence of the Heavenly Court. Thank the Lord that I finally chose wisely, but the reason I'm telling you this, is because I want you to know what I saw that day."

Enthralled, Peter is grateful that even though he was very young at the time, he was able to choose wisely before Judgment Day.

"Please go on, sir," he says to encourage Jameson, and with a faraway look in his eyes, Stanley continues.

"I found myself in a giant room with two large thrones at the far end.

God the Father was seated on one throne and His Son was seated to the right of Him, on the other throne. A beautiful woman was standing next to the Son, and I believe She was Christ's Holy Mother, Mary.

"Now, what I really want you to know is what I observed behind the thrones. I saw two rows of angels standing behind God the Father and Jesus. In the front row were three angels and behind them were four more. The four in the rear were only visible to me as figures of light, but the three in the front were very clear. Peter, each of those three angels in the front row wore armor that shone like gold, and on each of their golden breastplates was a unique symbol, the same symbols that are on the domes!"

Stanley leans over his desk to explain a drawing that he is showing Peter.

"Here are the symbols on the angels as I saw them in my vision. This one, the one that has one semicircle at the bottom and three smaller circles at the top, represents Raphael. The one with two semicircles and three smaller circles represents Gabriel, and the final one with the triangle represents Michael. This is what I saw on the breastplates of each angel in my vision, and they are identical to the symbols on the domes at Tunguska!"

Peter is amazed, but wisely remains silent.

"The four beings of light that I saw behind Raphael, Gabriel and Michael were the lesser-known archangels—Uriel, Remiel, Sariel, and Raguel. After I read the report on your meeting with the Mongol tribesmen, I believe those domes at Tunguska were placed there by the archangels, and that Orion is where they're from. Many ancient civilizations believed that life came from the stars—specifically, the stars in Orion's Belt. This brings me to why you were called back home."

Stanley pauses, and smiles weakly. "As you know, the Archangel Gabriel called your father to the Moon and gave him a task from God. Now, I'm sure your father wants to fill you in on the details of his mission himself, but I can tell you that we're in serious trouble. An asteroid has recently moved into a trajectory that puts it on a collision course with our planet."

"*What*?!" sputters Peter.

"Yes, it's true, and I can only imagine your shock. But there's more. I showed the symbols on the domes to several others and we all re-read the report on your meeting with the Mongols. We think that your father may be the one who needs to find the 'keys' the angel said are needed to unlock the power of the domes."

"Holy cow! How in the world could he do *that*?"

"I don't know. Go home now, Peter. Talk to your father, and then get some rest. I notified Major Ralston about our theory, and he agrees that it's plausible. He said the president is giving your father her full support and that all federal agencies are offering whatever assistance he may need to do what he has to do. But we only have about five more weeks before that asteroid impacts the Earth."

"Holy cow," says Peter again, this time in a more subdued manner. "I don't know about any of this, but I do know that I need some sleep. I'm thoroughly exhausted. And I *really* need to talk to my dad."

"Yes, get a good night's sleep; you're going home tomorrow. At eight a.m., a driver from NASA will pick you up and take you to BWI, where a private jet will fly you to Denver. From there, another driver will take you to your father's house. The driver and the private jet will remain in the city at your father's disposal."

Peter sits back in his chair, completely lost in thought. Mr. Jameson attempts to get his attention, but a bright light suddenly appears in the room and startles them both. Temporarily blinded by the brightness, all they can do is listen to the forceful voice that pierces the light.

"I am Gabriel," the voice declares, *"and the Good News has been given."*

Under the guise of being "repaired," the Space Shuttle Atlantis is slowly making its way to the VAB, the enormous Vehicle Assembly Building at Kennedy Space Center. When it arrives there, it will be placed under intense security and prepped for the space flight that will enable a team of astronauts to reawaken the ANUBIS satellite and its nuclear missiles. With luck, those missiles will destroy the asteroid that is threatening the planet.

Only time will tell if this plan will succeed.

In Denver, Matt and Jennifer are prepared to begin their quest as soon as their son arrives home the following afternoon. Peter still doesn't know that God has instructed him to be part of his father's mission, though.

With their luggage packed and set in the hallway, everything is ready for their journey. Eager for their mission to begin, they climb into bed early and pray a Rosary together before nodding off to sleep.

While they sleep, the Archangel Gabriel stands in the corner of their room and smiles as he watches over them. And in Washington, D.C., the Archangel Raphael silently guards a softly-snoring Peter.

As nighttime falls over the northern hemisphere, the wayward piece of Prometheus is relentlessly coming closer to the Earth for its rendezvous from hell.

Still deep in space, it is slowly beginning to speed up, which will change the experts' current estimate of five weeks until impact. When the change in speed is detected, alarms at deep-space observatories around the world suddenly scream out their warnings, and a phone rings insistently at the White House.

While this is happening, the Malignant smiles wickedly in the bowels of Gehenna as he reflects upon his plan to obstruct Matteos' mission. Although he and his minions have been forbidden from interfering directly in the lives of the detestable human beings, he has nevertheless been able to devise a scheme that he hopes will delay or perhaps even stop God's chosen ones from fulfilling God's plan.

At the time of the Great Judgment, the being formerly known as Lucifer, the once-proud angel of God, was exiled to an underworld prison. Now, with his hate-filled scheme about to be unleashed, his haunting laughter fills the charred halls of fire and torture and drowns out the horrible sounds of wailing and grinding of teeth from the tortured souls who chose poorly.

Staring angrily toward the heavens, the Malignant howls, "I *will* put You to the test! And this time, I will not back down, for *I* am the power and the glory!"

The Devil's evil plan is to use the asteroid from hell to destroy all of God's creation. It is a plan that he hopes will be his ultimate revenge on the God who banished him from glory.

CHAPTER TWENTY-FIVE

"I've called this emergency meeting because we have bad news. The asteroid's speed has increased, and we now only have three weeks to destroy it. Major Ralston, I'm giving the Joint Chiefs authorization to place the full resources of all branches of the military at your disposal. What can you tell me about our plans at this time?"

"Madame President, by the end of the day, the space shuttle will be in the VAB at the Cape. We will be able to fit it with two booster rockets and send it to the launch site pretty quickly. The team of astronauts still needs more training, but they're professionals. By next week we'll get them on board the shuttle, and then proceed with the launch. As you all know, Doctor Matteo has been chosen by God to help us save the planet. I just hope he has enough time to complete his task."

"Don't we all, Major. Now…" President Bush suddenly stops speaking and stares at her team. "Okay, this is not an amusing discussion! Who is laughing?" President Bush has heard a deep-throated cackle of laughter, but so far, she seems to be the only person who has heard it, because faces around the table are turning to each other with expressions of surprise and concern.

"Madam President," inquires General Parkins, "are you all right? No one is laughing."

Immediately following his question, the General abruptly rises from his chair with an expression changing from disbelief to alarm. With sharp turns of his head, his eyes follow a dark shadow that only he can see moving around the meeting room. As he watches the shadow flit from corner to corner, the temperature in the room drops by twenty degrees. Then suddenly, the shadow passes through a wall with a loud and haunting laugh that is heard by everyone present.

Doctor Kirk is coatless as he stands near the three domes. The ambient temperature is a balmy 4°C (39°F), even though the temperature on the surrounding tundra is -58°C (-72°F).

The domes are now three meters, or almost eleven feet high, and are still rising. With their positions on the tundra in the same pattern as the three brightest stars on the Belt of Orion, they appear as if they are rising toward the heavens.

As the structures continue to reach for the sky, narrow, illuminated panels resembling stained glass are now becoming visible on the outside of each unit, and the humming noise is becoming louder and louder.

Walking around the domes, Doctor Kirk notices that the strange symbols on their tops is repeated on each side panel. Since a large part of the objects is still below the surface, Doctor Kirk hopes that their mysteries will be revealed when all of their features are discernible.

Severe weather over Denver International Airport has forced Peter's plane to be diverted to Houston. He is anxious to get home to see his father and find out what he has to do, but an unusually harsh blizzard, complete with lightning and tornados, has hit the area—another so-called snownado. Appearing to come out of nowhere, the storm has completely covered the city, a strange occurrence for the region. When he deplanes in Houston, a Marine sergeant greets him in the terminal.

"Mr. Matteo, I am Sergeant Gonzalez. I have been sent by Major Ralston to escort you onto a flight to Colorado Springs. Denver Airport is closed so you are being sent to the Air Force Academy there. Don't worry, we have notified your father, and he will meet us at the Academy. Please follow me, sir."

Peter is puzzled by all the attention he is receiving, and wonders if it's related to his father's important mission.

"Matt! Come in here and take a look at the TV!"

Entering the family room, Matt asks, "What is it, Jenn?"

"Denver Airport was hit by a snownado like the one at the Space Center in Florida! That's why they diverted Pete's flight to the Air Force Academy. They say the airport is going to be closed for a while. Look at the pictures—the place is a wreck! Planes were tossed all over the place, and there are hundreds of injuries. Luckily, no one has died."

"That's awful! But tornados are not supposed to occur in the snow! It's almost as if someone doesn't want Peter to come home." Turning off the TV, Matt continues, "Let's leave now. The roads are covered with snow, and if there are no other weather delays, Peter should arrive in Colorado Springs in about an hour."

Bundled up in their thick coats, Matt and Jenn head out to their SUV for the trip to the Air Force Academy to pick up their son. It is snowing and the roads are slick, but it is not a situation that a native Coloradan can't handle. It is getting late, though, and they have lost most of the day due to Pete's diverted flight. Since they now have only three weeks to save the planet, a day lost here and an hour lost there makes it more urgent for them to start their task as soon as possible.

Matt and Jenn are waiting for Peter in a hangar near the end of a runway at the Air Force Academy. His private NASA jet has just landed and is taxiing to a stop outside of the building.

As they watch, the aircraft's door opens and the steps swing out, allowing Pete's head to poke out into the cold night air. Bundled into a heavy coat and gloves, he grasps his luggage and walks briskly down the steps, then runs toward the hangar to get out of the cold.

As he greets his father, he notices that something is different. His dad seems a lot stronger and much more stable on his feet than he was during his last visit home.

"Dad? What the hell happened? You look great! What's going on here?"

"Yes, I'm doing well, Son. I'll tell you everything about it when we get home."

"Aw, come on, Dad, give me a hint! I've been through a lot in the past few days! I was pulled away from my original quest in Ireland and sent in a rush to Siberia. Then, I was yanked back home, and NASA sent a private jet and driver to bring me here. As Grandpa used to say, what's the skinny?"

"Just have patience, Son. We'll talk about it when we get home."

With a sigh and a questioning look at his mother, Peter gives up for now and gives his Mom a hug and kiss. The family walks outside the hanger together and climbs into Matt's SUV, which is parked nearby. It is no longer snowing, so the drive home will be much easier than the drive there.

CHAPTER TWENTY-SIX

Peter Matteo is sipping a cup of hot chocolate in the kitchen with his mom while he waits impatiently for Matt to pour himself another cup of coffee and re-join them at the kitchen table.

"Okay, Pete," begins Matt warily. "You told us about your trips to Ireland and Russia and about that fantastic conversation you had with the Mongol tribesman. Now it's my turn to let you know what's going on here. I just hope you're ready to hear it."

"Go ahead, Dad. I can take it."

Grasping Jennifer's hand for comfort, Matt closes his eyes for a minute to focus on what Pete needs to know. "Okay, Son, here goes. You heard about the oil spill in the Gulf of Mexico, right?"

Peter nods his head, so he continues.

"Well, that oil spill stopped the Gulf Stream from flowing northward. That's why we're having such a horrible winter. And if it doesn't return to flowing normally, we'll soon enter conditions that may put us into an ice age."

The look of astonishment on Peter's face tugs at Matt's heart, but he knows that Peter needs to hear it all, so he ignores his paternal feelings.

"That's not the worst of it. As you know from the recent news reports, the deep-space mining operation on Prometheus was halted because it split the asteroid in two. That's what the public has been told so far. What's being withheld from them is that after it split in two, one of the pieces smashed into the Comet Hades and wasn't completely destroyed. A small piece of the asteroid survived and is now on a collision course with the Earth."

Peter is so surprised by that news that he chokes on his hot chocolate.

Mid-swallow, the hot liquid burns the back of his throat and exits his nose. Amid forceful coughs, he manages to yell, *"What? What are you saying, Dad?"*

Jennifer hands Peter a napkin and pats his back comfortingly while Matt resumes speaking.

"All of that happened about two weeks ago. At that time, the experts said we had about two months to figure out what to do before that piece of asteroid hits us. But Major Ralston called me today and said the asteroid's speed has increased. So now, we only have three weeks before impact. Peter, when God summoned me to the Moon, He commanded me to help this planet. Even though He can do it Himself, He won't directly intervene to correct things when we screw up His creation so badly. He said we must tend to those mistakes ourselves as punishment for our lack of faith and respect. Now, after listening to what you said about the domes, and putting it together with what God told me about the archangels, I believe that we need to find some 'keys' that will unlock those devices you saw in Siberia. I think we're supposed to use them to protect the planet."

Staring at his father, Peter says, "That's the same thing my boss said!" But what do you mean, 'we'? Your health…I mean, you know…"

Both parents reach out to their son. Jennifer grasps Peter's right hand while Matt takes his left.

"Peter," says Matt, "I put God to the test. I questioned Him about my illness. I doubted His power, but He let me know that He understood why I was saying that. Then, He cured me! I'm completely free of all disease! I don't even have arthritis anymore!"

Matt squeezes his son's hand with tears in his eyes. "Peter, God said that you must go with me to the place where Jesus was transfigured. He said I would get more information there about what I need to do. I believe that place is in Egypt, at Saint Catherine's Monastery in the Sinai. God also said that His three archangels—*Tres Archangelis*—are protecting the Earth."

For what seems like an eternity, Pete stares at his father in disbelief. Then, in a soft voice, he asks, *"Tres Archangelis,* Dad? And you and I are supposed to protect the Earth?"

"Yes—with the help of the archangels," interjects Jennifer.

A thoughtful silence ensues until Peter's internal conflict between faith and science takes control and causes him to erupt with questions.

"We have to go to *Egypt*? How are we supposed to protect the Earth, Dad? And what in the world are those 'keys' that we have to find?"

Staring into Peter's eyes, Matt replies calmly, "All of us need to have faith in Almighty God. I don't know how we're going to do this, but I hope we can do it soon. We only have three weeks to find those keys, whatever and wherever they are."

At Matt's words, a bright light enters the kitchen and shines on Matt, Jennifer, and Peter. From within the light, a being appears and speaks to them all.

"I am Michael. You will be protected on your quest, for we will join you. You will be challenged by dark forces, but we will be by your side at all times. We cannot help you find what you search for, but we will not allow anything to stop you. I am Michael. I bring you this good news."

After the being stops speaking, the light fades and the kitchen returns to normal, leaving three very surprised people looking at each other in astonishment.

"Dad!" gasps Peter. "Did you see Michael's chest? One of the symbols from the domes was on his breastplate! And there was a belt around his waist that had three stars on it—like Orion's Belt!"

Unknown to the Matteos, an event occurred halfway around the world at Saint Catherine's Monastery in Egypt at the same time the Archangel Michael was speaking to them in their Colorado kitchen. The bush where God spoke to Moses, now enclosed by the monastery, began to glow, startling the monks and their visitors. At the sight, everyone dropped to their knees in reverence as a loud voice proclaimed, *"I AM WHAT I AM. Prepare for a visit from the one I have chosen."*

In Gehenna, the Malignant curses and cries out in frustration.

"My brother Michael haunts me and Gabriel and Raphael taunt me! But I will not fail! I must not fail! This is my final charge, and I will prevail! HAHAHAHAHAHAHA!!"

The sound of the Evil One's fiendish laughter fills the halls of the underworld while the godless souls around him suffer their unrelenting tortures.

At Cape Kennedy, the Space Shuttle Atlantis is finally ready to be moved to the launch pad. Teams of engineers have been working around the clock to prepare it for the most important flight of its career. Nestled securely on the Crawler-Transporter, a giant 18-wheel platform, the shuttle's 3.5-mile journey to the launch pad is scheduled to commence within twenty-four hours. At a maximum speed of only 1 mph, the short distance will take about five hours to complete.

The Matteos' journey will also commence within twenty-four hours.

As the time for solutions ticks down for the inhabitants of Earth, everyone involved in the planning of these two separate missions fervently hopes that at least one of them will reach a successful conclusion.

The astronauts in Houston are going through last minute training for their critical space mission. The ones who will exit the spacecraft to awaken ANUBIS are at NASA Johnson Space Center. The remaining astronauts who will remain in the spacecraft are going over their flight instructions in a separate facility.

To be sure their mission is an absolute success, the astronauts who will be working outside the space shuttle are repeatedly rehearsing their specialized jobs. To simulate the weightlessness of space, they are currently in an enormous tank of water, practicing the tasks involved in replacing the batteries and guidance software on the Cold War era nuclear missiles. They have also practiced with a replica of the large control arm that was recently fitted onto Atlantis to hold the ANUBIS satellite steady while they work on its weapons.

At fifty feet high, the satellite is the platform that holds the three missiles that were sent into orbit years ago as part of the United States' defense shield.

It is expected that the astronauts will need about three hours to complete their tasks. In the event of unexpected trouble, their space suits are equipped with four hours' worth of air regeneration capability before they will need to be recharged. If recharging is necessary, the astronauts will have to return to the space station and wait for twenty-four hours. Since time is critically short, NASA has urged them to complete their jobs as quickly as possible.

Without warning, unusual events are occurring across the Earth. In Italy, the celestial sword over the Vatican has suddenly burst apart in an explosion of light like a giant firework in the sky. The crowd that witnessed the celestial fireworks in Saint Peter's Square is now loudly begging for God's mercy.

At the same time the celestial sword burst apart, the beams of light from the sacred altars on the Earth and the Moon stopped shining. The pilgrims who flocked to the two earthly altar sites are confused by the now-darkened altars, but they are maintaining their vigils and wondering aloud about what may come next.

And in the Garden of Eden on the Moon, the leaves of the Tree of

God have changed color. When James, Christine, and Joe noticed that the light that had been shining from Gabriel's Cave had disappeared, they started off toward the cave, but never made it there. When they came upon the Tree of God, they were surprised by its dramatic change in appearance. The tree's leaves, which were previously shaded in variations of silver and gold, are now pure gold.

"Major Ralston? This is Doctor Matteo. You told me to contact you if I needed resources or support. Well, I need to get to Saint Catherine's Monastery on the Sinai Peninsula in Egypt. That is, *we* need to get there. What can you do for us?"

"By 'us,' do you mean you and Peter?"

"Actually, there are three of us now. My wife will be traveling with Peter and me. So, can you help us? You know—*tempus fugit.*"

"Yes, I know, time flies. But I'll have to call you back in the morning. We need to get authorization from the Egyptian government before we can use military transportation to get you there quickly. With any luck, we'll get permission overnight. Why that particular monastery, Doctor?"

"I don't know, but that's where I was commanded to go."

Confident in the Major's ability to get things done, Matt hangs up the phone and turns to his waiting family. "Time to turn in, guys. Our adventure starts tomorrow."

"...and here's the latest from Rome. The giant sword disappeared from the sky yesterday in a huge explosion. The crowd at Saint Peter's Square is still quite large, but it is beginning to thin out as the snow and freezing temperatures force the people indoors.

"In other news, officials from around the world are still disputing the multitude of internet postings that claim an asteroid is on a collision course with the Earth. Possibly related to this are reports from a news station in Orlando, Florida that there is unusual activity at the Vehicle Assembly Building at Kennedy Space Center. NASA officials claim they are only repairing the Space Shuttle Atlantis from damage it sustained in recent storms but that building was last used over forty years ago, at the end of the space shuttle program.

"Could all these stories be connected to each other in some way? Our reporters are trying to get to the bottom of it. This is Jenna Stark, Fox News."

CHAPTER
TWENTY-SEVEN

The next morning, Matt rises early. He makes a pot of coffee, and then turns on the TV to listen to Fox News.

"Yesterday, Jenna Stark reported on the unusual activity at the Vehicle Assembly Building at Kennedy Space Center. During the early years of this century, that building was used to prepare the shuttle orbiters for space flight. That entire area is now cordoned off, but our Jenna Stark and her camera crew were able to take these photos from a helicopter just outside the perimeter. Visible in the distance is the Space Shuttle Atlantis on the enormous Crawler-Transporter, and it looks like it's headed toward Launch Pad 39A. The shuttle appears to have been fitted with solid-rocket boosters in preparation for flight. When we contacted NASA about what we've seen, we were told that a press conference will be held this morning at eleven o'clock Eastern Standard Time.

"What we want to know is this: Why would a relic of past space exploration programs go up into space now? Is there a connection between this activity and an approaching asteroid? Perhaps we'll have some answers at eleven. This is John Jennings reporting. Now, back to Fox & Friends.*"*

As Matt's instant oatmeal breakfast spins in the microwave, he ponders the news report and wonders what NASA is up to. When the bell rings, he takes the hot bowl out and carefully places it on the kitchen table while Jennifer pours two cups of coffee. Before he can begin eating, the phone rings.

"Doctor Matteo, this is Major Ralston. We made arrangements for your family to fly to Cairo with the full cooperation of the Egyptian government.

When you arrive, they will supply you with a car and a ground escort to the monastery, which is about six hours from the city. The monks at the monastery will provide sleeping quarters and meals for you and your family for as long as you need to remain there. The hypersonic flight we chartered to Cairo leaves at twelve noon, so we'll send a car to pick you up at eleven. You should be at the monastery by late this evening our time, early tomorrow their time."

"Thank you, Major! That's great! I have one unrelated question for you, though. What's going on at the Cape?"

On the other end of the line, Matt hears a sharp intake of breath, and then, "As the saying goes, if I tell you, I'll have to kill you."

"Crap! Is it that bad?"

"Look, all I can say is that an official statement will be given at a press conference this morning. Doctor Matteo, we're both working hard to solve this crisis. You'll find out what's going on there in due time. Good luck, Doctor. Sergeant Gonzalez will pick you up at eleven."

Peter walks into the kitchen just as Matt ends the call. "Who was on the phone?" he asks.

"Mornin', Son. That was Major Ralston. NASA chartered us a flight to Cairo. A car will pick us up at eleven for a noon flight. We should be at the monastery twelve hours later."

Jennifer pours Peter a cup of coffee as more news reports from Fox are heard over the TV.

"Why is there going to be a news conference by NASA today?"

"I don't know; we're just hearing about it now," replies Jennifer.

"Actually," answers Matt, "I heard a report about it before you guys woke up. They're transporting the old space shuttle Atlantis to one of the launch pads, and they're supposed to tell us why at the news conference. I have a feeling that it has something to do with the asteroid. I asked Major Ralston about it, but he wouldn't, or couldn't, tell me."

At Denver International Airport, a Hypersonic Boeing 800 is being prepped for flight. This aircraft typically holds eighty-five passengers and crew, but for its next flight, it will carry only four passengers—the Matteos, and their military escort, Sergeant Gonzalez.

The Matteos will soon begin their journey to save the planet, but not if the Malignant has anything to do with it. Knowing this, the Archangels Gabriel and Raphael have stationed themselves around the aircraft to provide divine protection for their crucial mission.

The crew of the Crawler-Transporter is on high alert. The massive vehicle is continuing its slow march to Launch Pad 39A, but the persistent snowfall is a problem. The crew is meticulously removing all the snow from the vehicle's path while trying not to think about what happened the last time a shuttle took off in cold weather. After the disastrous launch of the Shuttle Challenger, the rubber seals and O-rings of the shuttle fleet were weatherized, but there is still a chance that the cold air may cause a different type of deadly failure.

The shuttle's five-man astronaut crew, currently on their way from Houston, will board the vehicle tomorrow. Knowing that the astronauts are on their way is putting extra pressure on the NASA engineers who are busily making final adjustments to the replacement software for each missile. Because of the increased speed of the approaching chunk of Prometheus, new coordinates will have to be programmed at the last minute to ensure that each missile makes an accurate strike.

In the Gulf of Mexico, the process for removing the oil is way ahead of schedule, but its progress may be slowed by an urgent need for an additional empty tanker.

The only empty super-tanker available to help in the crisis is currently in the Pacific Ocean, and it will take some time before it reaches the newly-built Costa Rican Canal, the only waterway that can accommodate a ship of its size. The oil removal procedure may be halted until the ship arrives in ten days. But as soon as it's in place, the rest of the oil will be separated from the water.

The world hopes that maybe, just maybe, after all the oil has been removed, the Gulf Stream will regenerate and start flowing again normally. However, if the runaway asteroid is not destroyed before it hits the planet, it won't matter in the least.

Sergeant Gonzalez is driving the Matteo family to a seldom-used area at Denver Airport to board their chartered jet because the main terminal is still closed from the damage caused by the snownado.

Sitting in the back of the car, Peter shares his android cell phone with his parents. The family is watching the NASA press conference from Cape Canaveral on the phone's tiny screen. In the background of the image they can just make out the shuttle with its attached booster rockets.

When the press secretary for NASA operations begins speaking, the snow stops falling and the sun pokes through the clouds. The air temperature, which is currently about 50°F, begins to rise.

"Good morning. As you can see behind me, the Space Shuttle Atlantis is on its way to Launch Pad 39A. We have taken Atlantis out of retirement for a critical space flight. The story we circulated earlier about the shuttle sustaining damage in the recent storm was designed to conceal what is happening now.

"After the Great Judgment, when we entered the one thousand years of peace, the world's leaders ordered all nuclear weapons in their arsenals to be dismantled and destroyed. At the time, it was understood that every nation complied with those orders. However, we have recently learned that here in the United States, several of those weapons were not destroyed. Archived files and radar confirmation have revealed that an American relic from the Cold War is still circling the planet.

"Some of you may remember the old ANUBIS Project, which placed nuclear weapons on satellite platforms in Earth orbit. All this time we believed that we had de-commissioned and destroyed all of those satellites, but we did not. One satellite is still in Earth orbit, but it has gone dark after all these years. It has no power and is not responding to commands. The ANUBIS satellite carries three nuclear missiles with payloads of fifty kilotons each. It would be extremely dangerous to try to bring those payloads back to Earth, so we have decided that the best course of action is to re-activate the weapons and fire them out into space. In order to do that, we must first send new batteries up to the satellite to power it up. Then, we need to neutralize the warheads before we can send the missiles harmlessly into deep space.

"At this time, the Shuttle Atlantis is the only vehicle in our fleet that has a control arm large enough to hold the satellite steady while our astronauts work on it. We have scheduled this space flight for next week.

"Thank you. This concludes my statement. I will not be taking any questions at this time."

When the press conference ends, Peter turns off his phone. "Dad, do you believe what he said? Do think this space flight has something to do with the asteroid?"

"Yes, I do. My guess is that they're going to try to shoot it down. But those old missiles don't have onboard guidance systems. They can only be fired at predetermined coordinates. Because the asteroid is moving, that would be like skeet shooting with a bow and arrow. Look, I believe it's up to us. I think those domes are here for our protection."

"You know, I have about a million questions about those domes, but here's one for starters. If it's true that God directed His archangels to protect the Earth, and if the story the nomads tell on the tundra is true about the archangels building the domes, then why would God want to prevent people from getting close to them? The nomads and the scientists who went to the area all got very ill from being there."

"Good question, but I don't know the answer. But maybe it's like the Ark of the Covenant. Remember the passage in the Bible about the persons who touched the Holy Ark and died? Not everyone was allowed to touch it. If you weren't one of the chosen ones, you died if you had contact with it. Perhaps we can ask one of the angels about that if we get the chance.

CHAPTER
TWENTY-EIGHT

"This is Spiritair Flight 2103 requesting assistance from CAI."

Responding to the request, the air traffic controller at Cairo International Airport announces, "This is CAI Control, Flight 2103."

"CAI Control, we are at 50,000 feet, just off the coast of Gibraltar. We are observing what looks like a large, dark cloud. It's blocking the Moon just east of us. Can you confirm?"

"Flight 2103 that is negative. We have nothing on radar in that area."

Breaking into the chatter, the controller at Lisbon International Airport declares, "Flight 2103, this is LIS Control. We show an anomaly in your path 15 kilometers out."

"10-4, LIS. We'll take proper measures to avoid it. We'll descend below..." Before the captain can complete his sentence, something hits the windshield, and he jerks his head back in an involuntary reaction.

"What the hell was that?" he asks.

"Don't know; looks like some kind of insect," responds the copilot.

"An insect? At 50,000 feet?"

As the pilot sends the jet into a sharp dive to avoid the dark cloud, the cloud responds by following the plane downward.

In the passenger compartment, the Matteos and Sergeant Gonzalez are surprised by the aircraft's sudden descent. Jennifer gasps and grabs Matts arm. "What's going on?"

"I don't know, Jenn."

The Matteos and Sergeant Gonzalez stare out of their windows in horror as the Moon disappears behind the darkness that is moving toward the aircraft.

50,000, 40,000, 30,000. As the altimeter spins off the numbers in rapid succession, the dark cloud suddenly engulfs the airplane like a wide-opened mouth.

"Holy shit! It's LOCUSTS!" erupts the normally cool and collected pilot.

As thousands of insects hit the plane like bullets, the pilots pull on their oxygen masks and goggles in case of windshield failure, and the copilot broadcasts a mayday message. "Mayday, mayday! Spiritair Flight 2103 has encountered a cloud of locusts off the coast of Gibraltar. We are attempting to out-maneuver it."

The Control Tower at CAI responds, "Flight 2103, we are clearing your area. Status, please."

While the air traffic controller in Cairo frantically clears the skies around Flight 2103 to keep other flights out of harm's way, hundreds of locusts continually slam into the aircraft. And as the plane passes through the dense cloud, the hypersonic jet engines suck up thousands of the insects.

"Control, we have flameout! We lost all power! Water impact is imminent! Repeat: we have lost all power, and we expect water impact!"

As the copilot methodically goes down his checklist to seal the aircraft before they hit the water, he flips the switch for the plane's intercom. "Prepare for water impact! Prepare for water impact!"

Momentarily paralyzed by fear, the four passengers quickly scramble to put on their flotation vests. Jennifer begins to cry when the lone attendant describes the crash procedures, and Peter tries to comfort his mother.

Staring out of his window, the only thing Matt can see are bugs hitting the glass. He prays silently, *Archangel Gabriel, the ball is in your court. Someone or something wants to stop us."*

20,000, 15,000, 10,000, 5,000 feet. The Boeing 800 plunges like a rock—this delta-wing jet has little to no glide ratio.

Without the roar of the engines, the flight crew is desperately trying to level the plane off in an eerie silence. When the aircraft reaches 4,000 feet, it emerges from the swarm of locusts, but the pilots are still struggling against the controls, frantically trying to pull the nose of the Boeing 800 up. They know that if they can slide the aircraft into the water tail first, the flotation devices in the fuselage and wings will deploy and the plane will remain buoyant. But if it lands nose first, the fuselage will probably fail and water will enter the plane, eventually drowning everyone.

With impact imminent, the Matteos are deep in prayer for deliverance from whatever is trying to stop them, when they suddenly realize that the plane is no longer descending. Jennifer calls aloud, "Have we stopped falling?"

"I think so!" responds the flight attendant. "But there is still no power. I don't think the engines are working!"

No sooner has the woman stopped speaking, when an urgent sensation suddenly overcomes Peter and causes him to remove his oxygen mask, unfasten his seatbelt, and move to the left side of the plane. When he looks out of the window, the sight that greets his eyes fills him with jubilation. Gesturing wildly, he shouts, "Come quick! You need to see this! Come quick! Oh, my *God*!"

Hearing the excitement in Peter's voice, Matt, Jenn, Sergeant Gonzalez, and the flight attendant quickly free themselves and hurry to join him. What they see when they gaze out of the windows is, well…miraculous.

Under the wing, a giant being of light seems to be flying horizontally under the plane, holding it upon its shoulders. While the others remain mesmerized by that sight, Matt rushes to the other side of the plane and finds a similar being holding up the aircraft on that side. Smiling widely, he proclaims, "There's another one on this side, and I know who it is! It's the Archangel Gabriel!"

At CAI, the air traffic controller notices that Flight 2103 has leveled off at 3,400 feet.

"Flight 2103, have you regained power and control?"

"This is 2103. You're not going to believe this. *We* don't believe this! The engines are still not functional, but we have regained control. We request an emergency landing. We're 100 kilometers out. Airspeed is 300 kilometers per hour."

"Flight 2103, you are clear for approach. Land on runway three."

At the airport, air traffic personnel and ground maintenance crews look skyward, trying to catch a glimpse of Flight 2103 as it approaches the runway. When it comes into view, all of them are stunned into disbelief. Two archangels are supporting the plane and guiding it to a perfect landing.

When the plane comes to a gentle stop at the end of the runway, the two archangels disappear from view. The pilots remain in their seats for several minutes, staring uncomprehendingly out of a bug-splattered windshield.

"What the hell just happened?" asks the captain after he regains his composure. "How the hell did we manage to pull this landing off?"

Crossing himself, the copilot says, "We have some very special passengers. Hell may have sent the bugs, but I'm certain that Heaven had something to do with the landing."

In response to the plane's safe landing, a loud, guttural cry is heard in Gehenna as the Malignant pounds the walls in malevolent disgust.

The crew and passengers of the Boeing 800 slide down the emergency chutes as emergency vehicles circle the aircraft, which is covered in dead locusts.

When the captain exits the plane, he takes a quick walk around, examining each engine as he goes. To his astonishment, he finds that all of the air intakes are packed full of insects.

Noticing the captain's puzzled expression, Matt walks over to let him know how the plane made it safely down to the ground. Listening to Matt's tale, the pilot crosses himself and responds with surprise and admiration. "So that's what happened? Now, I understand! I couldn't figure out how we could have landed safely when the engines weren't working. Thank God for those angels! We couldn't raise the nose up! The impact with the water would have been catastrophic!"

Egyptian government officials soon arrive on the scene. They meet with Sergeant Gonzalez to discuss their arrangements to transport the group to their destination. Placing Matt and Jennifer in one Land Rover and Peter and Sergeant Gonzalez in another, the two-car caravan promptly speeds off to Saint Catherine's Monastery.

Hopefully, the final leg of this trip will be less eventful. Hopefully.

CHAPTER
TWENTY-NINE

"Doctor! You must come out to the domes immediately!" Doctor Isadore Kirk's assistant pushes him to the door of the dig's control center and yanks him outside.

Now that the three domes have risen higher out of the ground, their shapes have changed and more sections are visible. They are now six meters high and three meters wide (20' H x 10' W), and appear more like giant silos than domes. The top of each of tube is now shining in the sunlight with a golden metallic sheen. Their sides are still black in color, except for the panels that encircle each tube and look like illuminated stained glass.

Also visible on the side of each structure are unusually-shaped recessed areas. On the silo that contains the symbol that Stanley Jameson said is for the Archangel Gabriel, the indented area looks like the outline of a chalice, and the silo for the Archangel Michael contains a recessed area in the shape of a sword. A long, rectangular niche marks a similar area on the silo for the Archangel Raphael. Also, under each of these hollow areas, is a phrase in Greek: Από τις Εντολές του Θεού, which Doctor Kirk translates as meaning, "From the Commandments of God." The strange symbols that were originally seen only at the top of each structure are now visible just above each of these recessed areas.

These unmistakable and significant changes prompt the doctor to take photographs of each structure from all angles so he can send them to the Smithsonian. As he walks around, the heat they are giving off raises the air temperature high enough to cause him to discard his coat and roll up his sleeves.

Commander Richard Stallings was able to leave the Houston area before the big snow storm hit, so he is the first of the five astronauts to arrive at Cape Canaveral. The other four are scheduled to arrive the following day.

The launch team is relieved that Florida is now experiencing warmer weather than the rest of the Northern Hemisphere. Temperatures in the state are rising during the day into the low fifties, and at night they are only dipping down into the low thirties. This warming trend is predicted to last about one week, so they are rushing to launch the shuttle as soon as possible. If they launch too early to enter the correct orbit to dock with ANUBIS, they will dock at the International Space Station and wait there until the time is right.

But even though the weather is warmer, the reliability of the rubber seals and O-rings is still a concern. Emergency escape pods have been incorporated into the shuttle but they are only a feel-good feature. If there is an explosion or any other type of catastrophic failure, none of the astronauts will survive no matter what they do.

The two-car caravan carrying the Matteos and Sergeant Gonzalez to Saint Catherine's Monastery is now about one hour away from their destination. The vehicles are following an old trade route across the Sinai Desert. Matt and Jennifer are in the lead car with a corporal from the Egyptian army at the wheel, while Peter and Sergeant Gonzalez are following behind them in a car driven by a representative of the Egyptian government.

As they round a turn, both vehicles are buffeted by high winds, and a dark brown wall suddenly appears before them. Matt and Jennifer, who have been looking out of their windows at the passing scenery, cry out in alarm. "What the heck is that?" they ask the driver.

"Looks like a *khamaseen*," replies the Egyptian corporal. "A sandstorm."

In front of the cars is a giant wall of sand that is approaching them like a tsunami. The wind is so strong that the cars have to come to a complete stop.

"This is bad, Doctor. I have never seen so much wind and sand. This could last for days."

The sand wall is about 500 meters, almost one third of a mile high and is approaching them at 50 kilometers, or 31 miles per hour. At that speed, the wall should hit them in about five minutes. The drivers slip out of their cars to confer with each other and then quickly climb back into their respective vehicles.

"There is an outcropping of rocks just to the left," the corporal tells Matt. "We will drive behind them and wait. We cannot drive through the storm; the sand will ruin the engines."

Before the corporal re-starts the vehicle, Jennifer screams out, "Look at the wall! There's a face in the sand!"

As the churning sandstorm moves closer and closer, a shape has abruptly formed on its leading surface in the form of a skull with a wide-opened mouth. The skull looks as if it's ready to devour anything in its path.

"First locusts, and now this!" moans Matt. "Jenn, I'm so sorry that I brought you and Peter out here!"

There is no time left for either vehicle to make it to the rocks, so all of the passengers and drivers brace for impact with the approaching wall of sand. But as they look toward the swirling mass with a growing sense of fear, a tall being, about fifty feet in height, unexpectedly appears in front of them, holding a shield and a sword in its hands. The being is clothed in white and its shield, which is a radiant gold, contains one of the symbols from the silo structures in Siberia. When Peter sees the symbol, he opens his car window and yells as loud as he can to the other vehicle, "THAT'S THE ARCHANGEL MICHAEL!"

Overwhelmed by that information, the travelers watch the scene that is dramatically unfolding before them. The Archangel Michael confidently walks toward the ever-enlarging sand wall and holds out his shield, which grows immensely in size and forms itself into a tunnel-like tube that penetrates the wall of sand. When Saint Michael reaches the churning sand, he turns toward the caravan and waves his sword, beckoning them to follow him.

With complete trust in their deliverer, the drivers maneuver their vehicles into the miraculously-formed tunnel. As they pass through it, they are able to hear distressing sounds, almost like the wailing and grinding of teeth, in the tunnel's dark interior.

After fifteen minutes of nervous travel, the caravan finally emerges into the light on the opposite side of the enormous sand wall. When the travelers realize that they have once again been freed from the clutches of the Evil One, they turn around just in time to see the wall of sand collapsing behind them. At that moment, each of them is reminded of the Jews who walked unharmed through the miraculously-parted Red Sea during their escape from Egypt.

With the vehicles' safety now assured, the Prince of all Angels bows his head and rises into the sky, leaving the travelers in a state of stunned wonderment and awe. When they regain their senses, they are amazed to see Saint Catherine's Monastery just ahead of them.

The travelers are sufficiently encouraged by these unexplained events to continue on their quest with a renewed sense of purpose. But they still wonder aloud to each other about the divine protection they have just received—as if two angels carrying their plane was not enough proof of Heaven's assistance.

Looking down on them, God shakes His head at His creatures' lack of faith.

The Malignant has been foiled again, and he is enraged. A foul, sulfuric stench fills his throne room while the wails of millions of tortured souls echo throughout the room in a continuous drone of despair. This once-proud, majestic angel of God now looks more like a half-man, half-dragon monster. His formerly golden wings are tattered and dark like the wings of a bat, and his skin is ugly and scaly.

Crouching on his throne of rock, he is contemplating his next move when the sound of a strong and powerful voice fills his tortured halls.

"I gave you power, and you abandoned Me—you fell from My grace. You were at My side, and you betrayed Me. I gave you reign over My creatures for over one hundred years, and you failed to destroy them. The Queen of Heaven smashed the head of the serpent, and My Son banished you for one thousand years. DO NOT PUT ME TO THE TEST AGAIN."

CHAPTER THIRTY

With renewed faith, Stanley Jameson is studying the photos that Doctor Kirk took of the three black structures that are continuing to surface in Tunguska. The doctor sent fifty shots that he took at various angles.

When Jameson translates the Greek text that appears on each of the monoliths, he immediately tries to contact Peter Matteo, but there is no telephone service in the Sinai. Frustrated, he relays the Greek text and its translation to Major Ralston, who forwards it to his contact in the Egyptian government.

Eventually, Peter will get the message.

The caravan has finally reached the monastery. One of the monks meets the group at the gate and silently escorts them into the compound. He brings Matt and Jenn to one room and shows Peter and Sergeant Gonzalez to another room that they will share. There are no regular communications with the outside world, so the two Egyptian military drivers will also remain there in the Matteos' service.

Each room is simple and contains only one or two beds with a small table and oil lamp. There are no bathrooms adjoining these small living spaces. The entire monastery shares a single bathroom with one toilet and one shower.

When Peter and Gonzalez enter their small room, they are dismayed to see that there is only one bed. Not wanting to offend their hosts, they look at each other questioningly until a different monk enters their room with an air mattress. Their relief soon gives way to a new concern when they are told that they must inflate the air mattress with an old bicycle pump.

The spartan lifestyle of the monastery's inhabitants prohibits electricity from being used anywhere in the compound, and it also limits their ability to communicate with the outside world. The hermits' only means of contact is through a generator-powered ham radio housed in a small closet-like area they call their "radio room." The radio is used sparingly—for pre-scheduled official business and emergencies.

The travelers set their bags in their rooms and then gather together in the center of the compound, in the area where the burning bush is located. They surround the bush and gaze at it in wonder. The flames engulfing it are about six feet high, but they are producing no heat.

As it is almost time for the monks' daily meal, the brothers recite some prayers and begin to prepare a simple dish of rice and boiled lamb that they and their guests will share. When it's ready, one of the monks enters the common area and gestures for the travelers to follow him to the dining hall, but none of them is ready to leave the holy bush. A few moments later, the first monk is joined by a second one who insists in English that they come to the dining area, adding, "Tomorrow is another day."

Pleased that someone there speaks English, Peter asks for directions to the library where they have been told they can do some research. "Be patient, my son," replies the monk. "The information you seek has been here since the beginning. Another day presents no concerns at all."

The English-speaking monk is from Great Britain, and has spent the last fifty years of his life at Saint Catherine's. He is an elderly man, about eighty years old. As the only one who speaks English, he has been assigned to be the group's guide.

The supertanker *Exxon Maru* is the largest supertanker in the world and the only one that is nuclear-powered. It has barely made it through the newly-opened Costa Rican Canal, even though this canal was specifically built to accept the larger ships that will not fit through the Panama Canal. The seaway's workers had a tough time guiding it through; they had to ease the ocean leviathan slowly and carefully through each lock so that it wouldn't scrape its hull.

Navigating through the canal was the slowest part of the supertanker's journey to the Gulf of Mexico. Now that it's free of the locks, it will increase its speed as it passes south of Jamaica and west of Cuba on its way to the Gulf, where the final batch of oil will be pumped into its massive hull. By the following week, the world may know if the Gulf Stream is able to resurrect itself, or if frigid temperatures will become the norm.

As worrying as this situation is, it is the only set of circumstances that the world's leaders will allow the unwary public to focus upon. Except for a privileged few, the majority of the people of Earth have no idea that life as they know it may soon be cut short by another, more threatening disaster from the sky.

Jennifer has awakened early from a much-needed sleep. With no windows in the small room, she fumbles her way over to the table and feels around for the matches that were left near the oil lamp. When she ignites the wick, the darkness is replaced by a warm, yellow glow.

Turning around to awaken Matt, she is surprised to see that his cot is empty. Thinking that he is probably in the communal bathroom, she pulls on her slacks beneath her nightshirt and walks down the hallway, guided by the yellow hue of the oil lamps that are hanging from the ceiling.

When she reaches the bathroom door, she knocks softly and calls Matt's name. In response, the door opens and she hears, "Morning, Mom. Sleep well?"

"Oh, sorry, Pete!" she answers. "I was expecting your father. Have you seen him this morning?"

"No, isn't he with you? Well, that's obviously a 'no', or you wouldn't have asked. Maybe he went to the dining area."

"Yes, that's possible. Are you finished here? I'll freshen up a bit and get dressed. Then, I'll meet you at your room and we'll go find your father."

A few minutes later, mother and son are heading over to the dining hall, which is in a separate building, past the common area. When they enter the courtyard, they are struck by the sight of a man kneeling in front of the royal blue flames of the blazing burning bush.

"Mom, it's Dad!" shouts Peter.

When they approach the holy bush, they notice that Matt seems to be talking to someone but they don't hear anyone responding. As they watch, the blue flames rise higher into the air and a set of eyes becomes visible through the dancing colors. A thunderous voice that all of them perceives abruptly declares, *"I AM WHAT I AM. The keys to your salvation lie within your grasp. This is your quest. You must seek the one who guards My library, for he is the only one who will help."*

Unbelievably, Matt speaks to the powerful voice. "Almighty Father, may I be so bold as to ask two questions? I must ask them, if You would allow me to do so."

"Proceed, My child, but be aware. These are the only questions I will answer."

Taking a deep breath for courage, Matt asks timidly, "My Lord and My God, can you reveal the significance of the Constellation Orion? And may I ask, who, or what, is trying to stop us?"

When the Almighty responds, the blue flames rise even higher.

"My once-great guardian, the one who has fallen from grace due to his greed and pride, is the one who wants you to fail. So far, he has not succeeded, but he will try again and will put Me to the test. But ye of little faith, did you not see your protectors?"

The blue flame dances higher.

"As for the place you call Orion, there are many levels in the heavens. I have created the heavens, and I have created life in My image on your tiny planet in the universe. Across the heavens, many other such places exist. These are the objects My little creatures stare at in the night skies. I have appointed My guardians to protect all of My creation. The guardians are stationed at the place you call Orion. Know this, little one: The seven major stars harbor the seven archangels. As you explore My endless frontiers, heed My warning to mankind: ORION IS A SPECIAL PLACE. DO NOT GO TO ORION."

"Thank you, My Lord." Emboldened by God's response, Matt risks asking another question. "Father in Heaven, as Your humble servant, I beg to ask just one more question. Please."

The flames grow brighter and taller while a profound silence engulfs the onlookers for several minutes. Then, the voice resumes.

"Proceed, My little creature. But there will be no responses apart from this final one."

"Thank you, Heavenly Father. My question is, why are we harmed we come too close to the instruments your guardians left here?"

"Akin to the Ark of the Covenant, they contain My great power and the power of the guardians—the power of the universe. Only the chosen ones who have the keys to your salvation are able to control what I have given to Moses, David, Solomon, and the protectors of the Holy Land. If this power was commanded by the undeserving, havoc and destruction would envelop the human race."

The voice stops speaking and the flames surrounding the bush return to their normal appearance.

"Wow, Dad!" gushes Peter as he helps his father rise off his knees.

"You just had a conversation with *God*! *And* He confirmed our theory about Orion! Many ancient civilizations claimed that life originated from there, and those domes in Siberia are arranged just like the stars in Orion's Belt! So are the Mayan and Egyptian pyramids. And now we also know where the sandstorm and the locusts came from! But, and no pun intended, God only knows what else is going to happen!"

"Matt, what are the 'keys to our salvation'?" asks Jennifer in a quiet voice. "And why did you leave the room so early this morning?"

"The Archangel Gabriel appeared to me while I was sleeping, and directed me to come out here. He said the Holy Mother had a message for me. When I arrived at the burning bush I began to pray, and the Virgin Mary appeared to me and said, 'Be patient, My little one.' I have no idea what She meant by that or what 'the keys to our salvation' are, but..." Matt stops speaking and slaps his forehead when a sudden thought comes to mind. "Wow! I can't believe it! It has something to do with the *library*! Now, we know why we're here! But we still have no idea what we're looking for!"

CHAPTER
THIRTY-ONE

More than one hundred twenty-two feet above Launch Pad 39A, Commander Richard Stallings sits at the controls of the Space Shuttle Atlantis. Alongside him are his copilot, Captain Jane Tingsdale, engineering Captain Lou Sinorelli, Colonel Andrew "Andy" Jones, and civilian Lance Sutherland from Martin Marietta, the company that manufactured the ANUBIS satellite.

The shuttle's payload consists of a five-hundred pound battery pack that the astronauts will use to resurrect the satellite, and an aluminum case that contains the three printed circuit boards that will reconfigure and reset the missiles' targets.

As Stallings and Tingsdale go through their preflight checks, the shuttle's giant orange fuel tank is filling up with fuel.

With built-in holds for system checks, the countdown to lift-off usually takes forty-eight hours. But due to the time crunch, NASA plans to launch in only twenty-four hours. If the weather holds and the temperature doesn't drop, Atlantis will take flight again, more than forty years since its retirement.

The stillness in a roomful of people is eerie. The monks at Saint Catherine's have pledged a vow of silence; therefore, none of them are talking during their morning meal. None of them except Joshua, that is. Since he is the only one of their number who speaks English, he is allowed to communicate with the outside world on their ham radio, and he has been given singular permission to interact with their special guests.

As their communications liaison, Joshua is allowed to make one radio transmission per week to the office of the Archbishop of Egypt in Cairo. His next scheduled communication is in two days, and that is when officials in Cairo will pass along the latest information from the Tunguska dig to Peter and Matt.

Matt is enjoying the simple breakfast meal, but thoughts of his mission are never far from his mind. Leaning his head close to Joshua, he whispers, "I have been tasked to research your vast library for information, but I don't know what I'm looking for."

Joshua smiles. "You will know it when you see it. To begin, I will help you find information about the archangels, but you must be prepared to review a vast amount of documents that are written in Latin, Aramaic, and Greek."

Matt turns to Peter, who is sitting beside him. "Son, I know you can read Latin, but how are you with Greek and Aramaic?"

"I can read Aramaic passably, and fumble through Greek with the translation software on my laptop. But without electricity, that's going to be a problem. The laptop's battery only holds a charge for a few hours."

Matt turns back to Joshua. "We're going to need your help in two more areas, please. First, we need to recharge our computers. I know that you have a radio here for communicating with your Archbishop. Can we charge our devices off your generator? We will pay for your fuel and make a donation to the monastery for our visit here. Also, can you assist in translating Greek?"

"Yes, you should be able to charge your devices with our generator. We normally contact Cairo only once a week, but due to your visit here, the Archbishop's office is keeping their radio on so we can get in touch with them whenever you wish. If we begin to run low on fuel, we can call them right away. The Archbishop provides our fuel, so a donation would be welcome, but it isn't mandatory. However, if you insist, you can make a donation with him."

The monks conclude their meal with morning prayers, so Matt, Jenn, Peter, Sergeant Gonzalez, and the two Egyptian drivers listen and wait patiently. After an hour, Joshua escorts Matt and Peter to the monastery's library while the others return to their rooms. Jennifer intends to spend the morning catching up on reading some of the books she brought with her on the trip, but later in the day she wants to join her husband and son in the library.

In the Caribbean Sea between Central America and Cuba, the *Exxon Maru* is gliding past Jamaica and making a turn toward the north. Within a couple of days, it will begin to take on its new cargo.

In space, the threatening chunk of Prometheus is altering its movements once again. It is now tumbling and rotating as it heads toward the Earth. This unbalanced gyration is causing its trajectory to fluctuate wildly, which is going to make it even harder to hit. At just a little over two weeks from impact, this leaves NASA with zero room for error.

In Gehenna, the Malignant laughs with joy.

Matt and Peter are quietly taking in the vast collection that surrounds them in the monastery's library. Established in 381 AD, the library at Saint Catherine's contains the second-largest collection of ancient scrolls and books in the world, and as the librarian and caretaker of these treasures, Joshua has unlimited access to it all. The monk points his guests toward chairs at a large table that appears to be as old as the monastery itself, and then he disappears behind a large bookcase.

As the travelers gaze admiringly at all the ancient books and scrolls, they become aware of an exquisite essence of paper, parchment, and papyrus mixed with dust, mold, and knowledge. This essence evokes the existence of times gone by that no modern ebook reading device could ever achieve.

While Matt and Peter are still taking in the sights and smells of this archive of human knowledge, Joshua begins to bring out document after document of writings that refer to God's guardians, the archangels. But by early afternoon, hours of searching for a needle in the haystack of antiquity have produced nothing but headaches and backaches. Tired and frustrated, Peter exclaims, "Dad, I already need to recharge my laptop, and we still have hundreds of documents to go through! This is hopeless!"

"Yeah, it seems to be quite daunting, but 'ye of little faith,' I'm confident that we'll prevail in the end. We *have* to."

Glancing around, Matt looks for the monk. When he doesn't see him, he walks over to the other side of the room and finds Joshua reaching up to a high shelf to grab more manuscripts.

"Excuse me, Joshua. Peter needs to recharge his laptop. Can we do that now?"

"Yes, certainly. Please follow me to our radio room. I'll start the generator for you, and while I'm there, I'll call Cairo. I'll ask them to send more fuel now so we don't run out. We should be restocked by later today or tomorrow."

"Where are you all going?" asks Jennifer as she arrives in the library.

"Oh, hi, Mom," responds Peter. "I need to recharge my laptop. Come with us; we're going to the radio room."

"Good idea. While we're there, we should also recharge dad's laptop and all the cell phones," says Jennifer.

Mrs. Matteo," interjects Joshua, "if you would like some refreshments, please feel free to help yourself in our kitchen. I've asked my brother monks to give you all the assistance you may need while you're here."

"Thank you," says Jennifer as she follows Joshua and the others to the radio room on the far side of the compound.

On the way, Joshua spots a monk who is doing some grounds keeping in the courtyard. Motioning toward Jennifer, he asks him in Arabic to assist her in the kitchen. Nodding in agreement, the monk uses hand motions to signal Jennifer to follow him.

When they arrive at the radio room, Joshua stops to start up the generator. Then, he guides Peter and Matt into the small room.

Outside, the rumble of the large diesel engine startles the other monks. They are accustomed to hearing that sound interrupt the quiet of the desert only on the appointed day and time once a week, so hearing it on this day is unusual. Oblivious to how their presence is affecting the monastery's inhabitants, Matt and Pete plug their chargers into international power adapters before inserting them into the room's electrical receptacles. While they wait for the devices to be charged, Joshua places a call to the Archbishop.

"Hello," he says in Arabic, "this is Saint Catherine's." Receiving no response, he waits a few minutes and then transmits again. "This is the monastery. Is anyone there?"

Sitting at his desk in Cairo, the Archbishop's secretary hears the transmission from another room and runs over to answer the call.

"God bless you, Joshua. We are pleased that you have called earlier than usual. We have urgent news for Peter Matteo."

CHAPTER THIRTY-TWO

"This is Peter Matteo," says Peter into the radio's transceiver.

"God bless you, Peter. I am Father Kazan from the Archdiocese of Cairo. A message was received for you at one of our military bases. It's from Mr. Stanley Jameson in Washington. Let me read it to you. It says, 'Peter, Doctor Kirk sent me new photographs of the structures at Tunguska. They have risen out of the ground to a height of over 4.5 meters, or 15 feet, and there is no longer any EMF radiation in the area. Because of the structures' increased height, Doctor Kirk is now describing them as large silos instead of domes. He says the multicolored panels are more visible now, and there are recessed areas on each silo that he is calling "keyways." The symbols that you saw at the top of each structure are repeated on their sides, and for ease of description, he has named the silos based upon the symbols displayed on each one. The middle silo, with the symbol for Saint Michael, has a keyway resembling a sword about three feet in length. The silo to the right of it is for Saint Gabriel, and it has a keyway resembling a chalice or another type of serving cup. The silo to the left of Saint Michael's is for Saint Raphael, and that keyway is a rectangular slot about five feet long and two inches wide. Doctor Kirk says that under each of these recessed panels is an inscription in Greek. The translation is, *From the Commandments of God.* I wish you and your family well, and I hope to see you soon.' That is the end of the message from Mr. Jameson." Hearing only silence on the other end of the line, the priest asks, "Are you still there, Mr. Matteo?"

"Yes, Father, I'm here. Thank you *very* much for reading me that message from Mr. Jameson. What he said is wonderful!"

"Yes, it sounds amazing! But what is it all about?" asks Father Kazan.

"I'm so sorry, Father, I can't explain it to you now. But let me put Brother Joshua back on the line for you. Thank you again!"

Joshua speaks to Father Kazan for a few minutes and then ends the transmission. Sensing that the Matteos would like to converse in private after receiving so much information, Joshua leaves the radio room so they can be alone.

When the door closes, Peter turns to his father and exclaims, "That's it, Dad, that's it! We now know what we're looking for! We know what the keys are!"

Matt is all smiles. "Yes! One of the keys must be the chalice that Gabriel left on the Moon! But what about the other two?"

"Well, Raphael's key may be the staff I was looking for in Ireland. And Michael was holding a sword when we saw him in the desert."

"You know," muses Matt, "they say there was a sword in the sky over the Vatican."

"That's right! That must be why Michael's keyway is shaped like a sword. Those recessed panels must be where we need to insert the keys to activate the structures."

"Hmm, that's a great deduction, Pete, but it presents a problem. How do we get all of those keys? The only one we have access to is Gabriel's Chalice at the Vatican. We'll have to search for the others, and there are only two weeks left to do it."

Peter begins to pace the room, deep in thought. "Right, right," he says after a moment. "Okay, here's what we should do. You and Mom remain here to search the library for information about the location of Saint Michael's sword. It's obvious now that we were sent here to find it, so the information we need must be here somewhere. Since we already know where the chalice is, I'll go back to England to search for Raphael's staff. Before I leave here, I'll download my Greek translation software onto your flash drive so you can access it while I'm gone. You're going to need it to understand a lot of the documents in the library. The Greek inscription on the structures is proof that God commanded his guardians to protect the Earth. It validates what God told you, and it also validates the passage from the scrolls I found that were written by Saint Paul, remember? In one of the scrolls, Saint Paul said that God told him that He placed His three guardian angels, Michael, Gabriel, and Raphael, in charge of protecting the Earth."

Matt agrees with his son, but is unwavering in his sense of urgency.

"Yes, I remember," he answers. "That's a good plan, Pete, but there isn't much time. If you're going to go to England, you need to get started right now. Let's talk to Joshua."

Matt opens the radio room's door to look for the monk, but the pair sees that he has been waiting for them in the garden. Matt asks, "Joshua, can you coordinate a flight out of Cairo between the Archdiocese, our consulate, and the Egyptian authorities so Peter can get home as soon as possible?"

"Yes, let me call Cairo right now. I'll do my best to arrange it for you."

"Thank you, Joshua," says Peter. "My driver and I will pack our things and be ready to leave whenever you give us the word."

"Good," says Matt. "Let's go tell your mother."

Matt and Peter walk to the kitchen while Joshua sets up another call to Cairo.

After Peter leaves the monastery, Matt will have the daunting task of searching through hundreds, if not thousands, of scrolls and parchments without the help of his son. He hopes that Joshua has access to a catalog of the library's contents that lists the documents pertaining to Saint Michael the Archangel and his sword.

In Florida, the countdown for the Shuttle Atlantis and its crew has begun. The large fuel tank has been filled and the payloads are secure. With the temperature in the low fifties, the weather is good for launch. At T-minus twenty-four hours and counting, the astronauts are going through their preflight checks, each of them hoping that none of the F.R.E.D.s on board— those f---ing, ridiculous, electronic devices—gives them any trouble.

Amazingly, Joshua was able to arrange for Peter to leave that afternoon. On his trip through the desert back to Cairo, Peter watches for unusual incidents like the ones that occurred on the way to Saint Catherine's, but notices nothing. What he doesn't know is that high above his speeding SUV, the Archangel Raphael, in full body armor, is providing him with divine guidance and "air support."

The plane that NASA chartered to get the Matteos to Egypt is still out of commission after its unusual encounter with locusts a few days ago, so the Egyptian military has agreed to fly Peter to the U.S. airbase in Aviano, Italy. From there, he will take an American military flight to Andrews Air Force Base in Washington, D.C.

He has a long journey ahead of him. First, he needs pick up all the information he left at his office in Washington about his search for Raphael's staff, and then he must get to the cathedral in London to try to track the object down.

That will give the Matteos and the world less than two weeks to avert disaster.

At the monastery, Matt has enlisted Jennifer's help in sifting through a multitude of ancient texts for clues about the location of Saint Michael's sword. Together, they look through document after document, book after book and scroll after scroll, as often as Joshua can place them at their disposal.

Since Peter is no longer there to help, Matt's job has become even more difficult. Neither Matt nor Jennifer can understand much of Latin, and neither of them understands any Aramaic or Greek. Luckily, Joshua can read Aramaic.

After working for a time to organize the documents by language, Matt abruptly stops and sighs deeply. Turning to his wife, he mutters, "I know God has sent us here, and my faith in Him tells me that we will succeed, but this is overwhelming, Jenn. I can't read Greek, and neither can anyone else."

"Mr. Matteo, that is not entirely true."

Matt turns his head toward Brother Joshua, who is sitting at the far end of the table. "What is not true?"

"Brother Theo is from Athens. I believe that under these circumstances, I can obtain permission for him to waive his vow of silence. Let me speak to the Holy Council. I'm sure they will allow him to help you."

The remnant of Prometheus is continuing its unstable tumble toward Earth. It is currently 14,880,000 miles away and is traveling at 62,000 miles an hour. In order to keep the missiles' impact with the asteroid far enough out in space so that it won't affect the Earth, NASA has re-calibrated the optimal time to launch the missiles. If there are no further changes in its speed or trajectory, impact will occur in ten days, therefore, the missiles must be launched in six days and eighteen hours. The weapons will need to travel at 5,000 miles an hour to ensure that the collision and resulting explosion will take place 360,000 miles out in space.

With the assistance of the White House, Major Ralston has obtained the cooperation of government agencies all over the world to coordinate all of Peter's flights. He has arranged for Peter to board a small Egyptian Air Force cargo jet to fly from Cairo to Aviano Air Base in northern Italy. That flight will last just shy of three hours, and as soon as he arrives at Aviano, a

Gulf Stream Jet owned by the CIA will take him to Andrews Air Force Base in Washington. A U.S. military aircraft will then take him to London.

As Prometheus looms ever closer to a potential rendezvous with Earth, all of God's children seem to be cooperating with each other. They know that time is running out.

CHAPTER
THIRTY-THREE

"Madame President," states Major Ralston. "We moved up the launch date for the missiles. Atlantis will be taking off later today and the missiles will be launched four days later. That will place their impact with Prometheus far enough away in outer space so it won't affect us here on Earth. But as you are aware, the asteroid is still tumbling and rotating, and that will make the missiles' strikes even more difficult. I pray that we're successful."

"So do I, Major. Let's also pray that the Matteos are successful in their mission and that God has not forsaken His people on Earth."

Matt and Jennifer have been in the old library for hours, reviewing document after document for references to Saint Michael's sword. Thankfully, Brother Joshua was able to obtain permission for Brother Theo to join them, so now there are four persons poring through the dusty archives.

Brother Theo is currently reading some scrolls about Saint Paul and his followers that contain details about Saint Paul's apparition of the three archangels. However, he has not found much more information than Peter Matteo did, except to read that Saint Paul says the Archangel Michael is in charge of all the archangels, and that there are seven archangels, not three.

As Matt listens to Brother Theo read a passage about the seven archangels, any doubts about his mission disappear in a flash, for he realizes that it confirms what Peter said his boss, Stanley, saw on Judgment Day. His joy at this revelation infects the others, who are reassured that they are on the right track.

When Matt returns to reading a 500 AD document that he has been studying for a while, he notices something interesting. and calls for the others' attention.

"Hey, listen up everyone. It says here that Saint Michael appeared to a bishop on a mountain on the Gargano Peninsula in Italy, and that the Saint placed an altar that he consecrated himself in a cave on that mountain. There is also a footprint in that cave that was left behind by Saint Michael, along with a crystal cross. Let me read to you what this says; it's supposed to be from Saint Michael: 'I am Michael the Archangel, and I am always in the presence of God. I chose the cave, as it is sacred to me. There will be no more shedding of bull's blood. There, where the rocks open widely; the sins of men may be pardoned. What is asked there in prayer will be granted. Therefore, go up to the mountain cave and dedicate it to the Christian God.' "

"Is there any reference to a sword in that document?" asks Jennifer.

"No, no sword. It says that Saint Michael appeared there because they were slaughtering bulls and hoping that those sacrifices would stop an epidemic of some kind."

Brother Joshua has heard about another appearance by Saint Michael, so he speaks up to add that information to the discussion.

"Mr. Matteo, Saint Michael also appeared during a plague in Rome in the year of Our Lord 590. He was seen over the Tomb of Hadrian, which had been converted into a fortified castle where the popes could take refuge via a secret, covered passageway called the Passetto di Borgo. That passage links the popes' living quarters in the Vatican to the castle. After Saint Michael appeared at the top of the tomb, the plague in Rome ended, so Pope Saint Gregory the Great renamed the former tomb Castel Sant'Angelo in honor of the Archangel. But there have been many rumors that Saint Michael appeared to Pope Gregory again. Perhaps we can find information about that in our archives. It may prove useful."

"Thank you, Brother Joshua, that's very helpful," says Matt with a yawn. "Why don't we all take a break now? We need some sleep."

"You and Mrs. Matteo can get some rest, but Brother Theo and I will remain here and gather together all the scrolls and documents we can find about the Castel. We will continue working with the stamina we receive from Our Lord."

Grateful for the monks' dedication, Matt and Jennifer retire to their room. They hope that after a few hours of sleep they will be refreshed when they return to the library later that day. Before they nod off, they spend a few minutes talking about their son and praying that his search for Saint

Raphael's staff is going well.

Peter's flight is now one hour away from landing in Washington, D.C. It has been a smooth ride, due to the protection of the Archangel Raphael, who has been flying over the aircraft the entire time. When the air traffic controller's screen at Andrews Air Force Base captures the plane coming in from Egypt, the controller notices a small blip directly over the airliner, and calls the pilot.

"CIA Flight 123, this is Andrews Tower."

"This is Flight 123. Go ahead."

"Flight 123, do you see an anomaly, anything unusual, around you?"

"Negative, Andrews."

"Flight 123, please descend to 20,000 feet."

"10-4, Andrews."

The plane descends along with its protector, who is now joined by the Archangel Gabriel.

"Andrews, this is 123. It seems that we have 'visitors.' "

"Flight 123, we see your 'visitors.' Do you want to make a formal report?"

"Umm...no...we don't want that headache. It must be a temperature inversion. Yeah, that's the ticket."

"10-4, Flight 123. Come to think of it, it sure does look like a temperature inversion. Tower out."

Peter looks out of the window and also sees one of the "visitors" alongside the plane. Happy to see his guardian, Peter smiles and waves at the Archangel Raphael, who looks over at him and smiles back.

At Cape Canaveral, the final countdown has begun.

Flight Director: "4 seconds to lift off..."

PAO (Public Affairs Officer) #2: "The solid rocket boosters have ignited, and... We have LIFT OFF! Atlantis has cleared the tower."

CAPCOM (Capsule Communicator): "The tower has been cleared. All engines look good. Beginning roll maneuver."

PAO #1: "One hundred twenty-degree roll into heads-down position has begun."

CAPCOM: "Roll maneuver complete. Atlantis, you're looking good."

Commander Richard Stallings: "Control, this is Atlantis. Main engines at sixty-five percent. Over."

CAPCOM: "Roger. Out."

PAO #2: "Atlantis has reached Mach 1, the speed of sound, and the space shuttle's main engines have been throttled down from one hundred percent to sixty-five percent."

Stallings: "Control, this is Atlantis. Max Q, maximum dynamic pressure. Over."

CAPCOM: "Roger, Atlantis. Out."

PAO #1: "Maximum dynamic pressure has been reached, and the space shuttle's main engines have been throttled back up to one hundred percent."

Stallings: "Control, this is Atlantis. We have SRB burnout. Ready for SRB sep. Over."

CAPCOM: "Roger. Out."

PAO #2: "The computer indicates that the solid rocket boosters have burned out in preparation for their separation from the orbiter."

Stallings: "Control, this is Atlantis. We have SRB, solid rocket booster, sep. Over."

CAPCOM: "Roger, we see it. Atlantis out."

PAO #1: "The solid rocket boosters have separated from the orbiter."

CAPCOM: "Atlantis, you are at negative return. Do you copy?"

LAB #1 (Laboratory Monitoring System; Captain Lou Sinorelli): "Roger, Mission Control. Negative return. Out."

PAO #2: "Mission Control has reported that a Return to Launch Site Abort is no longer possible."

Captain Jane Tingsdale: "Control, this is Atlantis. We are single engine press to MECO. Over."

CAPCOM: "Roger, Atlantis. Out."

PAO #1: "The commander has reported that Atlantis can reach orbit even if two main engines fail."

CAPCOM: "Atlantis, this is Control. Main engine throttle down. Over."

Stallings: "Roger. Out."

PAO #2: "Mission Control has instructed the pilot to throttle down to keep acceleration at less than three g's."

CAPCOM: "Atlantis, this is Control. Go for main engine cut-off. Over."

Stallings: "Roger. Main engine cut-off on schedule. Out."

PAO #1: "The three main engines have shut down."

CAPCOM: "Atlantis, this is Control. Go for ET separation."

Lab #1: "Roger, we have external tank sep. Over."

PAO #2: "The external tank has separated from the orbiter."

Stallings: "Beginning minus Z translation. Out.

PAO #1: "The crew is preparing for Orbital Maneuvering System burn number one."

CAPCOM: "Atlantis, this is Control. You are go for OMS-one burn. Over."

Tingsdale: "Roger, OMS-one. Out."

Stallings: "Control, this is Atlantis. We have OMS cut-off. Over."

PAO #2: "The Orbital Maneuvering System burn has ended."

CAPCOM: "Roger, we copy that. Please advise when ET umbilical doors are closed. Over."

Stallings: "Umbilical doors are closed. Over."

CAPCOM: "Roger. Out."

PAO #1: "The auxiliary power unit has been shut down and the external tank umbilical doors have been closed and latched. The pilot will now enter OPS105 into the computer system to update the program."

CAPCOM: "Atlantis, this is Control. Coming up on OMS-two. Over."

Lab #1: "Roger, OMS-two."

Tingsdale: "Orbital Maneuvering System burn number two has been initiated."

Stallings: "OMS-two cut-off. We have achieved orbit. Over."

CAPCOM: "Roger, Atlantis. Out."

PAO #1: "Captain Tingsdale will now enter OPS106 into the computer to update the program."

CAPCOM: "Atlantis, begin On-Orbit Operations."

Stallings: "Roger, Control. Out."

CHAPTER
THIRTY-FOUR

All of the Matteo family members have now gotten some much-needed sleep and are returning to their tasks at hand.

Peter has a quick breakfast of dry cereal, the only edible food he still has in his pantry, and then heads to his office at the Smithsonian Institution to meet with Stanley Jameson. He needs to pick up his files about Raphael's staff and he wants to find out if there are any updates from Tunguska. While he's there he will contact Major Ralston to get details on his flight to England.

With a ten-hour head start on Peter, Matt and Jennifer have been back in the library for several hours. They have been working diligently with Brother Theo and Brother Joshua to try to complete their mission as soon as possible, but things aren't looking good.

"Jenn, I think we've hit a wall," sighs Matt. "There doesn't seem to be any information here about Saint Michael's sword. We've found numerous accounts of his apparitions around the world, but there's no specific information about a sword. Brother Joshua, can you suggest any other places around the world where we could do more research?"

"Mr. Matteo, I mentioned earlier that there are stories about a personal encounter that Pope Gregory the Great had with Saint Michael when the plague ended in Rome. They say Saint Michael gave the pope a gift in gratitude for his faith that the plague would end. There is no information about what that gift was, or where it may be now, however, I have located some letters from a priest who was at the Vatican at the time of the plague. He left his diocese when the plague ended and became a brother here at Saint Catherine's.

The letters mention a gift that Pope Gregory received from Saint Michael, and indicate that the pope hid the gift in the Passetto di Borgo to protect it, hoping that a future pope would be able to honor it in some way. I've already mentioned that Castel Sant'Angelo was originally built as a tomb and that it was later converted into a refuge for the popes."

"Yes, I remember."

"Well, there are lavish living quarters for the popes on the fourth floor of the Castel, and in the sixteenth and eighteenth centuries, the building underwent vast renovations. Mr. Matteo, I believe that you need to go to Rome to conduct further research at the Vatican. You should look into the writings of Pope Saint Gregory the Great. I have a feeling that his documents from the eighteenth century will prove to be the most valuable to you. May I radio Cairo to set up your journey back?"

Agreeing that they should head to the Vatican, Matt and Jennifer return to their room to pack their things. The next morning, they thank the monastery's Holy Council for their support and many kindnesses during their stay, and then follow Brother Joshua to the SUV that will take them to the airport.

While their driver starts the vehicle, Sergeant Gonzalez climbs in to ride shotgun, and the Matteos say goodbye to their new friend, Joshua. After giving the monk a hug, Matt reaches into his laptop case and pulls out a photograph of God's Tree.

"Joshua, this is for you," he says. "It's a photo I took on the Moon."

Joshua tries to refuse the gift but Matt insists. "Please accept this small token of our gratitude. You've been a great help to us."

Joshua looks at the image reverently, and sighs deeply. "My dear friends, thank you very much for the honor of assisting you on this critical mission. I will share this photo with my brothers, and then we will preserve it in a special place in our library so the world will have access to it forever."

The Matteos wave at Brother Joshua from their departing vehicle, and then settle back into their seats for the long trip to Cairo. On the drive, the husband and wife take turns watching their phones for a strong signal so they can make a few phone calls. They need to ask Major Ralston to make arrangements for them to fly to Rome, and they also want to reach Peter to fill him in on their current plans.

As the sun begins to set over Mount Sinai, the Shuttle Atlantis crosses over their vehicle high above them in Earth orbit, with the ANUBIS satellite within sight.

So far, all is quiet and all is calm. If nothing changes, tomorrow will mark ten days until potential disaster.

Peter is sitting in Stanley Jameson's office, waiting for his boss to join him. After a few minutes, Stanley walks into the room with Peter's airline tickets and the recent photographs from Tunguska.

"Peter, here are your tickets; you leave for London in two hours. It's a hypersonic flight so it will arrive there in less than four hours. A car and driver will be waiting for you at the airport. The driver will take you directly to the cathedral where a room has been reserved for you in the rectory. The cathedral administrator is expecting you."

"Okay, great," says Peter.

"Now take a look at the photos that Doctor Kirk sent from Siberia."

Shuffling through the images, Peter quickly becomes aware of their significance. "Wow! Those things have changed significantly! And now I see the 'keyways' you described. I hope we can find the staff and the sword soon so we can find out what those silos are for."

"Remember, you'll have a little less than ten days after you arrive in London to do what you need to do. Impact is expected to occur on the thirteenth day of this month. No pressure, eh?" He smiles grimly.

"Yeah, no pressure."

Peter studies one of the photos of Doctor Kirk standing next to Michael's silo, with Raphael's silo in the background.

"Stan, those structures look a lot taller than fifteen feet. Doctor Kirk is six-feet tall, and the silos appear to be taller than three people of his height."

"Yes, I noticed that, too. And look, he's not wearing a coat, and he has even rolled up his shirt sleeves. Those structures must be giving off quite a lot of heat. But you know what? They still look as if they're partially sunken into the tundra. They don't look like they're resting completely on the surface yet."

"I think that may just be an illusion," answers Peter. "The ground is pretty muddy around each base, and perhaps the weight of the structures has pushed them slightly below the surface again."

"Well, that's possible." responds Stanley.

Peter hands the photos back to his boss. "You know, I could study those images for hours, but I really need to get to London. Please call me if anything else occurs at the dig."

Peter retrieves the files he needs from his office and heads out of the building to walk back to his apartment a few blocks away. He will wait there for the driver who has been sent to take him to BWI.

On the way to Twelfth Street, his mind drifts to his mom and dad, so when he sees the name that pops up on his ringing cell phone, he smiles. "Dad! I was just thinking about you and Mom. How are things going?"

"Hi, Pete! Your mom and I are in Cairo, and we're just about to board a flight to Rome. We have to research Pope Saint Gregory the Great and Castel Sant'Angelo. Apparently, Pope Gregory received a gift of some type from Saint Michael after the archangel appeared in Rome around 590 AD. We're hoping that it was the sword. As soon as you can make it here, we need you at the Vatican."

"Okay, I'll head there after I'm finished in London. But our time is running out. Impact is on the thirteenth."

"Son, are you still without faith? Remember, we will prevail. I have to hang up now, but Mom sends kisses. Godspeed, Peter!" Matt sighs as he ends the call.

"Do you really believe we will prevail?" asks Jennifer.

"Yes. God would not have put me…us…through all of this if it wasn't important. I believe it's a trial. Maybe it's our purgatory on Earth or a test of our faith, but it's going to be a close one. With the travel time alone between England, Rome, and Siberia… Well, say a prayer, Jenn. Say lots of prayers."

All of the Matteos are in the air at the same time, but at opposite ends of the Earth. Peter is headed to London while Matt, Jenn, and their escort, Sergeant Gonzalez, are headed to Rome. None of them is flying completely unescorted, however. The Archangel Raphael is accompanying Peter, and the Archangel Gabriel is flying alongside the senior Matteos' plane to Rome.

As events continue to unfold on Earth, the Malignant persists in plotting his strategy in Gehenna. He knows that he has nothing to lose, and his greed and lust for power make him fearless. He is not afraid of anything, not even his ex-Boss.

The Malignant wants all goodness on Earth to cease. His ultimate goal is to take control of the planet and to open the gates of hell there, so he can rule over a brand-new world of hate.

Meanwhile, one hundred fifty miles above the Atlantic Ocean, the shuttle Atlantis is about to capture her prize. Commander Stallings radios Mission Control in Houston to give them Atlantis' speed and proximity to ANUBIS.

Commander Stallings: "Ten feet, three feet per second…eight feet, one foot per second…four feet, one foot per second…two feet, three inches per second…eight inches…five inches…three, two, one… We have captured ANUBIS, Houston. Engines are off. ANUBIS is tethered."

CAPCOM: "10-4, Atlantis. Houston out."

Miles below the drama in space, the Matteos have reached their respective destinations. Peter's flight has landed in London, and Matt and Jenn are going through Customs in Rome.

Because of the mission that God has entrusted to them, the Matteo family is continuing to experience unfamiliar situations. The senior Matteos have been told that they will be picked up at the airport by a high-ranking representative of Vatican City and that they will be guests of Pope Peter in the Vatican apartments. Meanwhile, their son, Peter, will be met at the airport by a senior member of the clergy in London, who will personally escort him to Westminster Cathedral.

CHAPTER THIRTY-FIVE

"**M**r. Matteo? Mr. Matteo?"

With his mind still enveloped in a morning fog much like the one hanging over London, Peter climbs out of bed and moves toward the door.

"Yes?" he asks without opening it.

"Mr. Matteo, the cathedral administrator requests your presence at breakfast. It is after eight a.m. I am quite sure you would like to start your day, sir."

"Oh, no, I didn't realize it was so late! Please give my apologies to the Administrator. I'll be ready in fifteen minutes. Thank you."

Peter had intended to rise earlier in order to get a quick start on today's search, but it seems that sleep was what he needed more. Mentally kicking himself for oversleeping, he rushes to get ready for the day. When he finally darts out of his room, he finds the cathedral administrator's personal assistant waiting for him in the hallway. Apologizing again, he follows the man to the dining area, where Father Gregory Thompson is sipping his morning tea.

"Oh, there you are, Peter. Did you sleep well?"

"Yes, Father. I'm so sorry to keep you waiting. Thank you once again for allowing me to be your guest here at the rectory."

"It's my pleasure. Now, please take a seat. We'll say Grace, and then you can enjoy Mrs. Windom's cooking. She has been my cook ever since the Great Judgment."

The priest says Grace and then fill Peter's teacup. "You must taste our traditional English tea. It's quite good. After breakfast, I'll take you to the archives in the cellar. There is a journal there that you may be interested in."

The implication that there may be something important in written format is so heartening that Peter nearly chokes on a scone. Father Thompson raises his eyebrows at Peter's reaction, but continues talking. "I've taken the liberty of doing some research on my own, and I flagged some entries in that book that may help you find Saint Raphael's staff. I'm happy that the Smithsonian Institution has taken an interest in it. We know about the power it displayed during the Crusades, and we know that it was brought to England from Ireland. But we shall go into all of that later."

This morning, Matt, Jennifer, and Sergeant Gonzalez had the distinct honor of sharing a private breakfast with Pope Peter. At the conclusion of their meal, the pope introduced them to Domenico Bertulli, caretaker and librarian of the Vatican Archives.

As instructed by the pope, Domenico is escorting the trio through Saint Peter's Basilica on the way to the hermetically-sealed and temperature-controlled Vatican Library. The vast library's rooms were made airtight about five years after the Judgment in order to preserve their contents from environmental pollution.

Domenico stops the group before a glass coffin in the basilica. "*Signore* Matteo, *il Papa,* the pope, has told me about the item you are searching for. We feel that your research should center on three of our past Popes. One of them is *San Gregorio Magno*, Saint Gregory the Great. His body is here in this glass casket. He is the one who saw *San Michele* at the top of Castel Sant'Angelo."

Matt and Jenn scrutinize the uncorrupted Saint and his coffin for anything related to Saint Michael or his sword, but find nothing associated with their mission.

When they are finished with their inspection, Bertulli says, "Come. Please follow me to the Vatican Grottoes below the basilica. There, I will show you the tombs of two more Popes—Clement XI, and Benedict XIV. They had much influence in renovating Castel Sant'Angelo. Your journey may end with one of them."

The group descends the steps in front of the high altar of Saint Peter's Basilica to the grottoes, a series of underground passageways that contain many ancient burial sites including that of Saint Peter himself—the first Pope. In these underground chambers, visitors with special permission from the *Fabbrica di San Pietro*, the Excavation Office of Saint Peter's, can visit the tombs of several Popes

Following closely behind Signore Bertulli, the group arrives at the tomb of Pope Clement XI, where their guide points out a fresco depicting Saint Michael. A few minutes later, they reach Pope Benedict XIV's tomb, where they immediately notice a sword carved into the wall outside of the tomb.

"Signore Bertulli, that sword. What does it represent?"

"Pope Benedict XIV was excellent with the sword. How you say it? Ah, yes. He was a good swordsman. We believe it represents the sword he is buried with."

"Could it also represent Saint Michael's sword?"

"Sì, perhaps, Signore, but we cannot be sure of that. Come; let us go to the archives now. You have much to do, and little time to do it."

"Houston, this is Atlantis. We are preparing for EVA."

"10-4, Atlantis. Godspeed."

Astronaut Captain Lou Sinorelli, Colonel Andrew "Andy" Jones, and civilian engineer Lance Sutherland are ready for their extra-vehicular activities. They leave the relative safety of the shuttle's airlock and journey out into space, each of them keenly aware of the importance of the tasks at hand. With ANUBIS towering before them like a giant silver monolith, they fully realize that even though the satellite's three missiles have stood ready to deliver hell on Earth for over fifty years, the weapons' new mission is to save the Earth from total destruction.

Allowing themselves to float out into the void, Andy and Lance cautiously guide the heavy battery pack between them. Alongside them, Captain Lou Sinorelli grips the aluminum case containing the three printed circuit boards they will insert into each of the nuclear missiles as a replacement for their outdated guidance programs. If the battery pack successfully powers up the old ANUBIS space platform, the satellite will be ready for its new and more beneficial role in the planet's survival.

Tethered to the shuttle for safety, the three brave astronauts venture onward toward ANUBIS. When they reach the platform, Lou grabs hold of the leviathan and moves himself upward, toward the top of the first missile. The access panel he needs is near the weapon's nose.

The first thing Lou must do is unfasten each of the eight fast-bolts that keep the cover to the access panel closed. Turning each of them a half turn, he lets them fall from his hands, secure in the knowledge that they are attached to the cover and won't float away. After all the bolts are released, he takes the cover off and places it into a large satchel attached to his suit.

At the same time, Andy Jones and Lance Sutherland place the large battery at the base of ANUBIS. The conditions of space make it weightless, but because of its size and shape, it is still cumbersome to maneuver into position.

While Lou continues to work on the first missile, Lance begins to remove the access panel at the base of the ANUBIS satellite.

If all goes well, ANUBIS will return to life well within the three hours of oxygen available in their suits for each spacewalk. If they cannot get the satellite powered up within that time, they must return to Atlantis, recharge their suits, and continue with their task the following day.

Although they still have nine days until the asteroid hits the Earth, they must complete their work as quickly as possible. The missiles need to be launched in only five days and eighteen hours so they can intercept it while it's still 360,000 miles away. If they miss that window, impact with Earth will occur six to seven hours after the window expires.

Three hundred miles below the astronauts, Peter sits at a seventeenth-century desk, reading the old journal that Father Thompson has made available to him. In the diary, Peter reads that Raphael's staff was brought to Westminster Cathedral by British soldiers in the 1500s, and that it remained on display in the cathedral for hundreds of years. He continues to read that for many years after that, the spiritual treasure was loaned to churches around England for veneration by the faithful, and after a period of time, it was given a permanent home in a church dedicated to the Saint.

Unfortunately, that is where the journal's story ends. There seem to be no entries about the location of the church, only to note that it was named for Saint Raphael.

Leaving the book on the table in the cellar, Peter climbs the stairs to search for Father Thompson. He wants to ask him whether the cathedral archives contain a list of the old Catholic churches in England. He knows that many of the parishes' names are different now that the world's religions are united.

After the Great Judgment, when various Christian denominations merged into the Catholic Church, a new name was selected for the newly-united Church, and many individual churches around the world changed their names at the same time. The new names reflected their congregations' willingness to be accepted under the dominion of the new Roman Universal and Apostolic Church.

"Peter, our records before the Great Judgment are incomplete, but I know of three churches in London where you can search for the location of the staff. There is a former Anglican church in the Gordon Hill area, once known as Saint Michael & All Angels, and two old Catholic churches named for Saint Raphael—one in Yeading, and another one in Surbiton.

"I will be glad to drive you to each of them. I only hope that the weather holds out, because it looks like it will start snowing soon."

"Thank you, Father, that's very generous of you."

"Think nothing of it, my son. But now, let's take a moment to pray that your search is successful."

In the depths of Gehenna, the king of darkness sits on his throne and stares into the Flame of Discernment. Through this flame, he can perceive the events from which he has been banned in the world of God's creatures.

Staring at the astronauts working in space, he reflects on his next move. He considers scenario after scenario for destruction of their mission until his thoughts are interrupted by one of the tortured souls he has elevated to second in command of his demons. Hungarian Countess Victoria Bokor, a thoroughly evil human being who tortured and killed hundreds of people during her lifetime, arrived in hell after her execution by guillotine. Unwisely, Satan has chosen to ignore the words she spoke before she died, when she warned Satan that she would be coming to him soon, and that she would be taking over from him in hell.

"You are pathetic! You cower and hide, and do not act! You *are the power and the glory! What are you afraid of? What can HE possibly do to you that He has not already done? You have nothing to lose!"*

"SILENCE! He is what He is, and I am what I am. Remember that I can send you back to the fires and the flames and let your pathetic soul rot there. Do not forget what I can do! I am not through with HIM, or with anyone! Get out of my sight!"

CHAPTER
THIRTY-SIX

In lightly-falling snow, Father Thompson drives Peter northward, to the church of Saint Michael & All Angels in Gordon Hill. After about an hour on A10, they arrive at their destination.

Most of the original church was destroyed in the great London fire of 1666. With only the tower remaining, the church was rebuilt in 1672 and then renovated in the early 1980s. When Peter and Father Thompson enter the rectory office, they introduce themselves to the elderly lady at the front desk, who leaves them to find the pastor. Within a few minutes, an older man enters and greets Father Thompson warmly.

"Gregory! It's good to see you! What brings you out on this snowy morning?"

"Good morning, Tim! How are you?" Father Thompson shakes the hand of his friend, Reverend Timothy Marles, the church's rector. Gesturing to Peter, he says, "I'd like you to meet Mr. Peter Matteo. He has come to us from the Smithsonian Museum in America, and he's here to search for the staff of Saint Raphael the Archangel. I hope you can help him. I found several documents at the Cathedral that say that the staff was lent out many years ago to various parishes around London. I selected three churches as most likely ones the staff may have visited in the past. We hope that one of them is where it is still residing. Saint Michael & All Angels is our first stop."

"Well, that's quite a mission, Peter!" says Reverend Marles as he shakes Peter's hand. "Welcome to Saint Michael & All Angels! I'm sorry to inform you that we don't have the staff, but I know that it was on display here when the church was rebuilt after the Great Fire. Come with me. We'll have some tea, and I'll tell you more."

The Vatican Library's research room is a hermetically-sealed vault enclosed by bullet-proof glass. Sergeant Gonzalez, Matt, and Jennifer are sitting inside this room, waiting for Domenico Bertulli to retrieve certain documents for their review.

After about thirty minutes, Domenico appears out of a long hallway with the personal files of Pope Saint Gregory the Great. Laying the box of historical documents on the table in front of the trio, he says, "Matt, here are some of the letters and personal documents of Pope Gregory the Great. I have not read through them, but there have always been tales told at the Vatican that Pope Gregory received a gift from Saint Michael after the angel appeared at the top of Hadrian's tomb, which is now known as Castel Sant'Angelo. The archangel's appeared there to show Heaven's appreciation to Pope Gregory for holding a procession around Rome to encourage the people to pray to end a plague. When Saint Michael appeared on the tomb and sheathed his sword, the plague ended. Many stories suggest that Pope Gregory left behind an artifact of some kind that he received from Saint Michael."

Jennifer stops Domenico to ask, "Can you tell us anything else about the Castel?"

"*Sì*. The building was built about 139 AD as a mausoleum for the Roman Emperor Hadrian. In 401 AD, it was converted into a military fortress, and then in the fourteenth century, it became a *castello*, a castle, where the popes could take refuge when Rome was attacked. The Vatican is located outside of the city walls, so it had no protection. The popes fled to the castle through the Passetto di Borgo, a raised and enclosed corridor that leads from the Vatican to the fortress. The Passetto is about eight hundred meters long, or about one-half mile." Looking around at his guests, Domenico concludes, "I will leave you to your research. I will lock the gateway behind me, and a member of the Swiss Guard will stand at the entrance. If you have need of anything, press the blue button on that wall. The guard will talk to you through the intercom, and you can place your requests with him."

"Thank you, Signore Bertulli," reply the Matteos.

When Domenico exits the vault, the trio realizes that for all intents and purposes they are now locked into an elaborate, but comfortable, "jail." But they quickly put aside any apprehensions they may have and immediately get to work.

As they sift through the papers Domenico left them, Matt quickly realizes that the majority of them are written in either Latin or Italian.

"Please look for these two words," says Matt to Jennifer and Sergeant Gonzalez. "In Latin, the word for sword is *gladius*, and in Italian, it's *spada.*"

"Mr. Matteo," declares the sergeant, "I'm fluent in Spanish, which helps me to read Italian fairly well. Let me review the Italian documents."

"That would be great!"

"I don't know any other language but English," offers Jennifer, "but I can take notes. Would that help?"

"Yes, that would help. But Jenn, having you here with me is a great comfort, so don't worry if you can't do too much. Okay, guys, let's pray before we get started. And let's hope that we can find something…anything."

Inside the shuttle, Captain Tingsdale floats into her command chair and stares at the controls in wonder.

"Commander Stallings, can you come over here and take a look at this?"

In the middle of enjoying a snack break, the commander grabs at the M&M's circling his face and floats over to his co-pilot.

"What's up, Jane?"

"Look at the proximity indicator. It indicates that we're moving into a slightly higher orbit, but I haven't done anything to change course. It's almost as if we're being 'pushed.' "

"Must be a malfunction. Check with Houston."

Captain Tingsdale calls NASA Control but they confirm the unusual readings on her instrument panel.

When knowledge of this unplanned, upward movement spreads through mission central, NASA scientists and engineers discuss several theories, and endlessly speculate about why the shuttle and the connected ANUBIS satellite are moving into a higher orbit. The higher orbit is a problem because the higher they go, the further away they move from the Earth, and that will jeopardize the mission.

But deep in the bowels of Gehenna, the Malignant is continuing to blow into the Flame of Discernment and directing it toward the mated shuttle and satellite.

Unaware of the shuttle's change in orbit, Lou has finished retrofitting the first missile and is floating over to the second. On the way, he activates his radio.

"Guys, call me crazy, but I feel as if someone is watching me."

"Yeah? We were just saying the same thing. It's a weird feeling. How are you coming along? We just replaced the battery in ANUBIS and are now connecting it to the platform."

"I'm on point, Andy. I just reached the second missile, and except for this creepy feeling, everything is a Go."

CHAPTER THIRTY-SEVEN

"Well, Peter, as you may already know, Saint Michael & All Angels was an Anglican church before all the churches united, so it was very rare for an artifact that was treasured by the Catholic Church to be shared with our members. However, it *was* here for a while, and the feeling among the Anglican community has always been that the Catholic Church shared Raphael's staff with us to try to promote conversion. I know that while it was here, it was displayed on the wall behind the altar, but that's the only thing I know. After a period of time, it was moved to a different location, but there is nothing written to indicate where or when that occurred. It's interesting that there are two separate churches dedicated to Saint Raphael in the south London area. I'm sorry I can't be more helpful. Would you like more tea?"

"No, thank you, Reverend. I appreciate your hospitality, but we need to get back on the road before the snowfall becomes any heavier. Thank you for your time."

Peter and Father Thompson take leave of Reverend Marles and then head south to Saint Raphael in Surbiton, the next church on their list. Before returning to the Cathedral, they will also stop at the church in Yeading.

As Father Thompson navigates the snowy streets, Peter notes that it is now close to twelve noon. *Tempus Fugit*—time flies.

Taking a break from reviewing file after file, Matt rises from the table and walks around the small research room, staring through the glass wall at rows and rows of documents, books, and other material. They seem to go on forever.

"This is a daunting task, guys. I hope the archangels can give us a hand."

So far, the group's review of hundreds of documents has not produced anything of significance. It seems to them that Pope Gregory may not have made a notation in any of his writings about a sword from Saint Michael. But after another two hours of fruitless research, Sergeant Gonzalez announces a breakthrough as he reads through several of the pope's personal journal entries.

"Mr. Matteo, I think I may have found something! In this entry, Pope Gregory refers to a gift he received. He writes that he will leave a 'holy symbol of power' to his successors, and he hopes they will 'venerate it as much as he does.' He does not say what the gift is, but he mentions the tomb of Hadrian and says that he will place the gift there. He also writes that he hopes that sometime in the future, the Catholic Church will use the mausoleum for religious rather than military reasons."

"And that's exactly what they did!" exclaims Jennifer. "So now we should probably review all the information we can find about the tomb's transformation from a burial place, to a military fortress, and then to a sanctuary for popes."

Agreeing with Jenn's suggestion, Matt walks over to the call box at the entrance to the research room. With the push of a button, he summons the Swiss Guardsman and asks him to contact Domenico Bertulli.

Thousands of miles away, the process of cleaning up the Gulf of Mexico is almost complete. The last of the spilled oil is gradually making its way into the hold of the giant supertanker *Exxon Maru* while the world waits with bated breath for the Gulf Stream to return to normal.

Meanwhile, NASA scientists are still trying to come up with an effective fix for the shuttle's mysterious change in trajectory. The ship and the attached ANUBIS satellite are still moving further and further away from the Earth. If the shuttle continues on this path, it will bring the satellite and its missiles out into deep space, and any attempt to intercept Prometheus will be lost.

So far, all of NASA's attempts to correct the orbit creep have failed. At one point they tried to use the shuttle's retro-stabilizing thruster rockets to return it to its original orbit, but the rockets placed too much strain on the large control arm that is holding the two crafts together.

Oblivious to that drama, the astronauts outside the shuttle are continuing with their repairs as if nothing else is happening. Lance has successfully powered up the giant platform and Lou is now working on the third missile. All three spacewalkers need to return to the shuttle within the hour, whether their work is finished or not.

It is cold in London, about -5°C (23°F). It seems that the Earth's cooling has gone into overdrive. If the asteroid doesn't kill everyone outright, the cold will surely contribute to many deaths when crops across the Northern Hemisphere cease to grow.

Father Thompson slips his car into a parking spot near Saint Raphael's rectory in Surbiton, grateful that they won't have to walk far in the freezing weather. As soon as they enter the building, the reverend approaches the receptionist at the front desk.

"Good morning. I am Administrator Thompson from Westminster Cathedral. Is Pastor Muldoon available?"

"Good morning, Father. He is in the church. You can join him there, if you like."

With thanks to the elderly woman, Father Thompson motions for Peter to follow him outside.

Saint Raphael's Church, located near London's Kingston University, was originally built in the early 1800s as a Catholic chapel. It is a beautiful church—large columns line the center aisle, statues of saints and archangels look down from either side of the altar, and stained-glass windows encircle the entire building.

The men walk down the center aisle past row after row of wooden pews until they see Pastor Muldoon kneeling in the first row.

Respecting the pastor's prayer time, the men genuflect and slide into the pew behind him. They will wait quietly until the pastor is ready to speak to them.

A few minutes later, Pastor Muldoon sits back in his seat and turns around with a smile for his visitors.

"Good morning, gentlemen. Are you here to see me?"

"Yes, Father," answers the priest. I am Father Gregory Thompson, Cathedral Administrator for Westminster Cathedral, and this is Peter Matteo from the United States. He has come to London to search for the staff of Saint Raphael, which many believe the archangel gave to a commanding officer of the Crusades for divine assistance in battle. There are documents in the Cathedral archives that indicate that at one time, the staff may have been on display in this church."

Arching an eyebrow, the pastor asks, "Mr. Matteo, what is your interest in this staff?"

Peter knows that he cannot divulge any information about the impending asteroid strike and his role in preventing it, so in a bid to stall for time, he glances at the administrator and the pastor while trying to devise a story that will deflect the men from the real reason he is there.

"I'm with the Smithsonian Institution in Washington, D.C., Father, and I have been working at an archeological dig in Jerusalem. I recently discovered some information about Saint Raphael's staff and the Vatican asked me to search for it and bring it to Rome."

"Really? I happen to know from the history of our parish that when the original chapel was built in the early 1800s, the nearby parish of Saint Raphael in Yeading sent us a wooden statue of the Saint to honor our founding. That statue was sent to us as a loan, but because it was still here when we renovated the church in 2012, they granted it to us in perpetuity. It is now in the chapel next to the parish center. The image depicts Saint Raphael holding a walking staff, but I don't know if that is the staff you're looking for."

A visibly-excited Peter asks, "Can we see the statue now, Father?"

"Yes, if you wish. Come with me."

In the center of the Belt of Orion, Saint Michael the Archangel unexpectedly hears a thunderous voice.

"My trusted guardian, you must visit your fallen brother. He is trying My patience. I charge you to warn him of his pride and arrogance. I will not tolerate any further interference."

CHAPTER THIRTY-EIGHT

Back from a restroom break, Matt, Jennifer, and Sergeant Gonzalez continue to review the journals and manuscripts that Signore Bertulli has been able to provide them about Castel Sant'Angelo. Boxes and boxes of files, scrolls, and documents form a stack almost four feet square. It is a compilation of information covering over six hundred years, and Signore Bertulli and his associates are continuing to bring them even more.

"Signore Matteo, you have a tremendous task ahead of you. I will leave you my assistant, Francesco Scarpone, to help you find how you Americans say, 'a needle in a haystack?' "

Matt stares at the mound of documents that are stacked neatly on the floor next to the table the four of them will be sitting at for quite some time. He lowers his head, shakes it slowly, and announces with a deep sigh, "God help us."

The chapel at Saint Raphael in Yeading is fairly small, only about 84 square meters, or 900 square feet, wide. There are two sections of pews divided by an aisle down the center that leads to a hand-carved wooden altar.

Upon entering the chapel, Peter and Father Thompson immediately notice a life-sized wooden statue of Saint Raphael standing in the corner on the right side of the altar. The statue's left hand is raised and looks like as if it is waving, while the right hand holds a walking staff. As they approach the image, Peter notices that the staff is a separate object and is not directly connected to the sculpture.

"Father Muldoon, may I remove the staff to get a closer look at it?"

"Yes, please do whatever you feel is necessary."

Peter walks up to the five-foot-six-inch high statue to inspect the staff. He estimates the object to be about five feet long—the correct size, if it is indeed the staff that needs to fit into the silo at Tunguska.

The moment he reaches out to take the object into his hands, a bright light flashes in front of him and engulfs the statue and the staff in a light that becomes brighter and brighter by the minute. The light quickly becomes so overpowering that the men in the chapel have to shield their eyes from its brightness. Confused by what's happening, Peter begins to step away from the statue, but when a being appears in the light, he stops.

"Peter, this is my staff," says a voice. *"This is your key to salvation."*

Without understanding how, each of the men instantly realizes that the being is Saint Raphael. Awestruck, they watch as the being grows larger and larger and then disappears through the ceiling of the chapel.

When their eyes readjust to their surroundings, they notice that the statue is gone, and the staff that Peter is holding is now gleaming with a golden patina. Now on their knees, the priests and Peter stare at the staff for what seems like hours.

Eventually, the three men awaken from spiritual trances, and without a word between them, file out of the chapel.

Outside in the snow, Pastor Muldoon turns to Peter, who is tightly clutching Saint Raphael's staff. "I don't know why you were given that treasure, my son, but I pray that you use it wisely."

Father Thompson speaks quietly with Pastor Muldoon while Peter dials his dad's cell phone number with a shaking hand. When there is no answer, he calls Major Ralston.

"Major, I have the staff! The second key! I can't get through to my dad, so can you please call him for me? I also need to get back to Rome as soon as possible. It may take a while to get there, though. It's snowing quite heavily here, and I'm afraid the airports may be closed."

"That's fantastic, Pete! I can't believe you found it so quickly! I'll get word to your dad as soon as possible, and I'll also start trying to get you out of England."

In the halls of Gehenna, the Malignant is gazing intently into the Flame of Discernment. No longer a noble prince of Heaven, his appearance over the years has taken on the look of a mangy and emaciated-looking fiend. His legs are thin and lizard-like, and his long arms end in sharp talons that extend upward and outward from bony fingers. The ears on the sides of his dragon-like head expand backward like shiny, black fins, and the golden-feathered wings of which he was once so proud are now blackened, leathery, and ragged. The torso that supports this beast is permanently bent over at the waist and causes him to wobble unsteadily as he walks. The monster is startled when he hears a familiar voice in his chamber.

"Lucifer, my brother."

Not having heard his former name in eons, he asks suspiciously, *"Michael?"*

"You are in disfavor again. This is your final warning. Do not interfere, for the banishment you now suffer will pale in comparison to the punishment you would then receive."

With a quick slash of his sword, Saint Michael puts out the Fire of Discernment.

"You were once a proud guardian of Almighty God. I have been sent to warn you. Remain quiet, my brother."

Departing as suddenly as he appeared, Saint Michael leaves the Malignant howling throughout hell in a voice so loud that it drowns out the pitiful sounds made by the millions of souls that are suffering infinite and unrelenting torments.

The three astronauts have finally finished their tasks. The ANUBIS satellite and its missiles have been reawakened and are now awaiting instructions to begin their new missions.

When all of the space walkers are safely back inside the shuttle, Lance Sutherland, the civilian member of the team, notices an unfamiliar object through one of the spacecraft's windows that seems to be approaching them rapidly. Calling out to the crew, he shouts excitedly, "Hey, everyone, take a look outside! What do you think that is? Could it really be a *cloud* out here in space?"

Andy and Lou immediately float over to a window where they observe the same phenomenon. Surprised at what they're seeing, Andy asks, "Commander, do you see it? It's on our starboard side."

Commander Stallings and Captain Tingsdale are also at the window when the large, cloud-like object forms into a pair of giant "hands" that encircle the mated satellite and shuttle and grab it with a sudden, but gentle, jolt.

"NASA Control," radios the Commander, "this is Atlantis. We, ah… have a problem…or…something."

"Or *'something'*? Go ahead, Atlantis."

"You're not going to believe this, but two giant 'hands' are pushing us back into our original orbit."

"Repeat."

"Two giant hands seem to have surrounded us and are pushing us back into orbit! Do you detect a new trajectory?"

"We do...we thought it was your doing. Umm...Atlantis, are you sure you want to report this as stated?"

"Uh...Okay, 10-4, you are correct. Our thrusters are working now. EVA is complete, and ANUBIS has been reactivated. Uh... We're back in our original orbit now. Out."

CHAPTER
THIRTY-NINE

"Signore Matteo! Your son, he finds the staff of *Santo Raffaello*, Saint Raphael! He will arrive in *Roma* tomorrow!" exclaims Domenico Bertulli as he bursts into the Library.

A round of applause erupts in the room amid an outburst of laughter and smiles.

"Now we have two of the keys!" cheers Sergeant Gonzalez. "The chalice *and* the staff!"

"Yeah!" responds Matt with a wide grin. "It's a great accomplishment! But the third one...I don't know. I hope we have enough time. My faith is strong, but I'm still worried. We have less than eight days."

"Madam President, you have a call on line three."

"Thank you," answers Mrs. Bush as she picks up the phone.

"Madam President, this is Major Ralston. I have some good news for you! Peter Matteo found Raphael's staff! Now they have two of the three keys they need to unlock the structures in Russia!"

"That's terrific, Major! Where was it?"

"In a small church in England. Peter is on his way to Rome right now, and he has the staff with him. He needs to help his dad find the final key. But I have even more good news! The ANUBIS satellite has been released from the shuttle, and it is now active and awaiting new instructions!"

"That is excellent!"

"Yes, it is, Madam President. The shuttle is now on its way to the International Space Station to deliver supplies, and then it will return to

Florida."

"Good work, Major! Please pass my congratulations on to the Matteos."

"Thank you, I will."

The president is all smiles as she looks around at the others in the room.

"Ladies and Gentlemen, we are all set to fire up ANUBIS, and the Matteos have found the second key! But with any luck, our missiles will save the Earth before we need that third key."

Now that the last of the oil has been removed from the Gulf, the *Exxon Maru* is steaming toward Galveston Harbor. It will dock with a pumping station about a mile offshore, and then begin the process of transferring its liquid cargo to the refineries that have been waiting for it.

With the oil spill cleaned up, the world is also waiting. With a laser-like focus, the international media has shifted its attention from the recent climate changes to the scientists who are looking for any signs that the Gulf Stream has re-awakened.

While the world waits, the Earth is continuing its dramatic cooling. The cold has caused the Arctic Ocean to freeze completely, and ocean ice is now forming as far south as Greenland, Iceland, and most of the North Sea. The Bering Strait is so firm that people can now drive between Alaska and Russia.

Large bodies of water in northern locations are also completely frozen over, preventing oil tankers from delivering critical fuel. The freeze has prevented crude oil from being delivered to many of the world's refineries and is crippling the production of oil and gas, forcing spikes in the prices of gasoline and heating oil.

The rising price of gasoline is causing motorists around the world to rush to natural gas. Those who are willing and able to pay a three thousand dollar premium are buying the newer cars that are manufactured to run on natural gas, while many others are paying upwards of five thousand dollars to convert their current vehicles. More and more persons are rejecting fossil fuel-run transportation altogether, and are buying electric cars and trucks.

The average cost of heating oil is now over five dollars a gallon, when it's available at all. The excessive cost and extreme cold is forcing homeowners to install fireplaces and cast-iron stoves in their homes. They have had to abandon the previously-popular solar panels because of the snow that frequently covers them and the consistently cloudy and overcast skies that prevent them from working properly.

If the Gulf Stream does not awaken from its sleep, the Earth will continue its intense cooling, and its inhabitants will become trapped in the middle of an ice age that could kill millions.

For the inhabitants of the Moon, the drama on the Earth is a non-issue. The crew at Challenger Base is still mining diamonds and converting moon water into hydrogen and oxygen, and Joe Toteda and James and Christine Reynolds are still maintaining the biosphere, God's Garden of Eden. God's Golden Tree is still growing rapidly, and it is now the tallest object inside the sphere.

With tourism and extra supply runs to the Moon temporarily halted, lunar residents have learned to become even more self-sufficient than they were before. They are planting more vegetables and fruit trees, and are now are raising goats for milk and meat in a remote area of the Garden.

The longer the biosphere's inhabitants are cut off from the Earth, the more critical their small farm and gardens become. Their farming skills will need to sustain them completely if resupply shipments from Earth are not resumed soon.

James has been keeping tabs on the ever-expanding areas of ice on the Earth through a large telescope installed on a patio outside the visitor's center. When he returns from one of his Earth-checks, Joe and Chris ask him about what he is seeing.

"It doesn't look good. It appears that the Earth is going into an ice age, so we need to draft a plan to conserve our remaining resources up here. The extremely cold weather will most likely affect all of the Northern Hemisphere, and may even extend as far south as twenty degrees latitude. The Southern Hemisphere is currently going into summer, so that area shouldn't be affected yet. However, if the northern half of the planet doesn't heat back up, well, we could soon become more secluded than usual up here."

CHAPTER FORTY

There are now only seven days before the possible annihilation of our planet. In ninety-six hours, NASA will launch the ANUBIS missiles. Their rendezvous with Prometheus will occur about three days later and about 360,000 miles out in space.

The team at the library is down one man today. Sergeant Gonzalez is suffering from the flu and hasn't been able to leave his hotel room. However, Francesco Scarpone, Signore Bertulli's assistant, is now working with Matt and Jenn in the Library.

While they work, they are keeping an eye out for Peter, who is on his way with Raphael's staff. The collaborators are trying to find references to the Latin word *gladius,* which means "sword" in English. But as they examine document after document and find no relevant information, the pile of unusable material increases by the minute.

Matt is concentrating on official papers that were written about the construction of the Passetto di Borgo, the covered passage between Castel Sant'Angelo and the Vatican.

With everyone engrossed in their individual research, a sudden knock on the glass wall causes them all to look up. In unison, three heads turn toward Peter, who is standing at the door with a golden-hued staff in his hands.

The shuttle crew has completed their delivery of much-needed supplies to the International Space Station. They have undocked from the ISS, the largest habitable satellite in orbit, and are now preparing the shuttle to fall out of orbit on its return trip to Cape Canaveral.

However, the weather in Florida, as well as at the alternate landing sites in California and Houston, is not cooperating with the timing of the shuttle's return. Therefore, Atlantis and her crew have been directed to spend another day circling the globe.

With unscheduled time on their hands, mission control has directed the crew to take photographs of the Earth's increasing ice and snow cover. The crew has decided that they will slip the digital photographic records they took of the "Hands of God" that pushed them back into orbit into this stack, even though none of them wants to submit a formal report about that event.

At the excavation in Siberia, the silos of Raphael and Gabriel have changed dramatically. They are now vibrating and humming and exhibiting an ever-increasing display of flashing lights. But Michael's silo is silent. Doctor Kirk surmises that when the key to Michael's silo is found, it too, will come to life.

In the Vatican Library, Matt, Jennifer, and Signore Scarpone take turns holding Raphael's staff. As they do, each of them perceives an unexplainable presence about it. The object seems to exude some kind of "power."

"Dad, did Gabriel's Chalice have a similar sensation attached to it?"

"Yes, it did. These artifacts may be emitting a power of their own. I wonder what would happen if we brought the chalice and the staff together."

"I wonder what will happen when we bring them both to Russia!"

"Guys, nothing is going to happen if we don't find the sword," interjects Jennifer. "Except…"

Peter nods. "You're right, Mom. You always have a way of bringing us back to reality."

Peter takes the staff and places in the center of their work table, hoping that it will encourage them to persevere in their search for the last key. After offering a quick prayer, all four investigators return with renewed energy to the massive amount of information available to them in the Library.

They are now concentrating on the writings of Pope Nicholas III, who completed the passage to Castel Sant'Angelo in 1277. Hours go by as they read and re-read plans, ledgers, manuscripts, and diaries.

When Peter returns from a rare break, Francesco Scarpone asks for the group's attention.

"I have found something in one of the personal diaries of Pope Nicholas. He mentions a gift that a previous pope received from a 'guardian,' and he says he moved that gift to the Passetto to protect the popes who walk through the passageway."

"Really? Perhaps we should make a field trip to the Passetto," pronounces Matt.

"That's a good idea," agrees Peter. "But before we do, we should bring the staff to the Basilica of the Chalice so the Swiss Guard can protect it. Besides, I'd like to see if anything does happen when we bring those two artifacts together."

"Signore Matteo, I will guide you through the Passetto," offers Signore Scarpone. "From the Vatican to the Castel, it is an eight-hundred-meter long walk."

Calculating quickly, Peter offers, "That's almost half a mile, correct?"

"Yes, that is correct," states the signore, as he opens the Library's door.

It is a cold day in October, about 5°C, or 41°F, with an overcast sky and a chance of snow flurries. The outside entrance to the Passetto is not far from the buildings of the Vatican, but before the team goes there, they are making a detour to the Basilica of the Chalice. In anticipation of their needs, Signore Scarpone has called ahead and asked the Swiss Guard to clear the church of visitors so the group will have privacy when they arrive with the sacred object. They are grateful for the signore's forethought, for as soon as they enter the basilica, unusual things begin to happen. The chalice in the glass case on the altar and the staff in Peter's hand begin to glow at the same time, and two bright lights on either side of the altar rapidly coalesce into majestic beings of light.

Although these events are becoming somewhat familiar to them by now, they are still amazed. And they are further amazed when one of the beings speaks.

"My name is Raphael," the being says with authority, *"and I bring you Good News. We will stand guard. We will protect."*

Raphael beckons toward Peter, who approaches him cautiously. When he reaches the angel, Raphael holds out his hand and requests the staff. The angel takes it and reverently places it next to the chalice in its display case on the altar.

Raphael takes up a position at the right of the altar, and the second being, who has been standing at the altar's left, proclaims with firm resolve, *"This is a holy place. It must remain closed to all. I am Gabriel, and I bring you Good News."*

Bowing to the divine guardians, the participants in God's plan begin to make their way out of the basilica. Halfway down the aisle they stop briefly to allow Matt to snap a photo of the scene with his cell phone. But when an intense light flashes at the moment the shutter clicks, they know that the photo will be unrecognizable. With a sigh at the missed opportunity, Matt steers the group toward the massive church doors but just before they reach them they find their path blocked by another intense light, which they instantly recognize as the Son of God.

Speaking quietly, Jesus announces, *"Man's lack of faith has sent you on this quest. My children have abandoned My Father and Me, but We have not abandoned you."*

When Jesus disappears, the group remains spellbound until several Swiss Guardsmen enter the church. When they find that the team is about to leave, they conduct their usual search of the church interior to make sure no one else is there and then they lock the doors for the evening. When they have completed their tasks, one of the guards takes up a protective position in front of the main entrance.

In the square outside the church, Francesco Scarpone places a call to his superiors. He informs them in breathless words about the incidents inside the basilica, and recommends that guards be placed at all of the doors twenty-four hours a day, seven days a week, to comply with the angel's order.

"I must also go to Pope Peter to let him know what has happened," declares Francesco. "I am afraid that I will not be able to accompany you through the Passetto di Borgo, but I will take you to the entrance."

At the Passetto's entrance, Francesco has a brief conversation with the Swiss Guardsman on duty. Complying with his request, the guard unlocks the door and permits the Matteos and Sergeant Gonzalez to enter.

While Francesco hurries away to talk to the pope, the group enters the unlit passageway. But with no electrical lighting and only small openings to allow occasional rays of sunlight to penetrate the darkness, none of them feels confident enough to walk through the tunnel unescorted. As they mill about the entranceway discussing the feasibility of making the trip in the semi-darkness, Peter notices several battery-powered lanterns in a niche in the wall. Grateful for the assurance of light, each of them takes a lantern and turns it on. When they are assured they are all in working order, they splay their lights over the nearby walls, surprised to see that they are plain and unadorned. None of the Vatican's elaborate frescos or beautiful statues and paintings appears to grace this corridor. However, Peter notices a small Latin inscription scratched into the concrete above the entranceway.

"Dad, look at this above the archway. It says, *Septem archangelis, protege nos—Gabriel,* which means, Seven archangels, protect us. It seems to be attributed to Saint Gabriel."

"Is anything else mentioned there? Are there any other comments?"

"No, just that statement."

In silence, the team begins their trek toward Castel Sant'Angelo, searching along the way for clues relating to the location of Saint Michael's sword. But there is nothing on the walls, the floors, or the ceiling. The Passetto seems to be only a stark, elevated corridor with tiny windows overlooking Rome through which they can hear the passing traffic and the Roman people going about their daily routines, oblivious to what is in store for them.

The team is beginning to feel discouraged until Jennifer notices something on the floor after 100 meters, or 109 yards, of walking. A word is scratched into the rocks on the floor.

"Hey, everyone!" she shouts. "There's a word here! It says '*Uriel*!' It's the name of one of the seven archangels! Maybe we'll find the others' names in different places. Let's keep an eye out for 'Michael!' "

Renewed, they continue forward and begin to find other names at intervals of equal distance. The next one they find is Raguel, then Raphael, Remiel, and Sariel.

After forty-five minutes of walking, the Passetto ends at a large hallway in front of the entrance to the Castel. There, they find the name they've been searching for chiseled into the wall—Michael, the prince of all angels.

Happy to see that name at last, they nonetheless note that they have not found any signs of his sword. Separating, they search the hallway further until Matt stops in front of a small section of wall.

"Why are you staring at that wall, Matt?" asks Jennifer.

"This section is different than the area around it. It looks like it may have been repaired. Over here, where the concrete is flaking off, I can see a pattern of layered stones underneath that may be covering up a hole. Maybe the sword is in there. We need to get permission to break through this wall."

"Break through which wall?" a voice asks quietly.

Turning around, the group is astonished to see Pope Peter and Francesco Scarpone standing behind them.

"I ask again, break through which wall?"

"Your Holiness," answers Matt, "we found some records in the Vatican Library about an object that Saint Michael gave to Pope Gregory the Great for use by future popes. We also found one of Pope Nicholas III's diaries, where he wrote that he placed a gift from what he calls a 'guardian' in this passageway. It may be that Saint Michael's sword, the final key that we're searching for, is inside this wall. I ask your permission to remove these stones."

The group is silent while Pope Peter walks toward the area where the ancient stones are visible on the wall. Reaching out, he places his hands on the stones and bows his head in prayer.

A few moments later, he says, "I will arrange for someone to expose this area for you. For the sake of the world, I hope what you seek is here."

CHAPTER FORTY-ONE

In Houston, NASA Mission Control has started the countdown to launch the ANUBIS missiles. At T-minus seventy-two hours, it is a countdown to a future that most of the world's inhabitants have no knowledge of.

Thanks to Ceptofane X, a new wonder drug, Sergeant Gonzalez is soon well enough to function after his bout with the flu, even though he is still a little weak. Knowing that his assistance is critical, he joins the Matteos for breakfast the next day to catch up on the team's developments. While everyone is finishing their coffee, Domenico Bertulli and Francesco Scarpone walk over to their table.

"Signore Matteo, the work is complete in the Passetto. Signore Bertulli and I will accompany you there as soon as you are ready. The Holy Father, he is busy this morning, but he offers his prayers for the successful completion of your mission."

"What did they find?" interrupts Peter. "Did they find the sword?"

"Unfortunately, there is no sword, but I think you want to see what *is* there."

At 0°C (32°F), the morning is cold, so the group hurries on their way from the Vatican dining room to the Passetto and the long walk to Castel Sant'Angelo.

When the end of the tunnel finally comes into view, Peter's impatience gets the better of him, and he breaks away from the group to sprint the rest of the way. Stopping at a small chamber that has been cut into in the wall near the Castel's entrance, he pants to catch his breath and look through the opening. Noticing that there is a small alcove in the wall beyond the opening, he enters the chamber and finds two pegs protruding from the wall about seven inches apart from each other, with a plaque beneath them that reads, *Gladium Sancti Michaelis.*

Understanding that the English translation is, "The Sword of Saint Michael," Peter gingerly reaches out to touch the plaque, as if it might give him some insight as to the location of the sword.

When the rest of the team finds him, he is on his knees with his head resting against the plaque. Concerned, Jennifer rushes over and asks, "Peter, are you all right?"

Looking up at his mother, Peter states sadly, "It was here, Mom. The sword was here. We're getting close, but we're not close enough."

Peter is heartbroken that they haven't found the sword, but Domenico Bertulli is ecstatic. He turns to Francesco Scarpone and shouts, *"Gladium Sancti Michaelis! La Spada di San Michele! É vero, Francesco! San Michele dato la sua spada a Papa Gregorio Magno!"*

When he notices the blank faces around him, he apologizes with a smile. "I am so sorry! I am very happy! I say to Francesco that it is true Saint Michael gave his sword to Pope Gregory the Great! Signore Matteo," he continues, "let us concentrate on the renovations of Castel Sant'Angelo. The sword, it may be here somewhere!"

At T-minus six days until impact, the Matteos are running out of time. They must locate the final key and then bring all three of them to the guardians' silos far out on the Siberian tundra. With travel time to Siberia likely to take up to twenty hours, it is T-minus five days for the Matteos. Knowing that it's crunch time, the team returns to the Vatican Library to renew their research on the Castel.

With winter continuing its relentless creep over the Earth and the menacing chunk of the Prometheus asteroid drifting ever closer to the loathsome humans, the Malignant has become positively gleeful over the steady advancement of his plans.

Hours and hours of research have come and gone, but no new information has come to light. The group now knows that the sword did exist at one time; however, they still don't know what happened to it.

Late in the evening, Jennifer comes across some interesting facts. "Listen to this," she states. "It says here that there are many statues of Saint Michael around the Castel. Two of them are made out of metal and the others are either marble or stone. The most well-known statue is the metal one on top of the Castel, but it is huge. The other metal one is in the Hall of Perseus in the residential area of the Castel reserved for the popes. Pietro Bracci created it in 1736, and its dimensions are about right to hold our elusive sword. Could Pietro Bracci have incorporated Saint Michael's actual sword into his statue?"

"Well, there's only one way to find out," responds Matt. "Let's take a look at that statue."

Peter activates the intercom near the locked Library entrance to speak to the Swiss Guardsman on duty. "Sir, please call Signore Bertulli."

At almost eleven that night, Domenico Bertulli is awakened by an urgent knock on his door. Because Vatican City encompasses a very small geographical area, it only takes about fifteen minutes for him to arrive at the Library vault.

"The Guardsman say you have emergency request," he says sleepily to Matt.

"Yes, we need to go to the Castel, to the popes' living quarters. There is a statue of Saint Michael in the Hall of Perseus, and we think it may contain the sword."

"Signore, no one has entered those quarters since the Great Judgment. In fact, I do not think any pope has been there since Pope Francis died earlier this century. I do not know the condition of the living quarters, but we will find out soon. You like to go there now, or you want to wait for light of dawn?"

Behind his father, Peter's voice is urgent. "Dad, I think we need to go now. Time is getting short."

"Yes, you're right. Signore Bertulli, we would like to go now."

Grabbing their coats, the group follows Domenico Bertulli back to the Passeto di Borgo. It is very cold in the tunnel, and as the light from the lanterns cuts through the darkness, the vapor from their breaths can be easily seen in the air around them.

When they arrive at the end of the Passetto, they follow Domenico into the dark Castel. He leads them down a hallway and up a stairway to the papal residence on the fourth level. With an ancient key, he opens a door and switches on a light to reveal a large greeting room with paintings and frescos on the walls, and white cloths covering all of the furnishings.

"Follow me. That door, it opens to the room of Perseus."

Before entering the room, Jennifer takes out a book that she brought with her from the Vatican Library. It contains a photograph of the room with the statue of Saint Michael in it. When she enters the room, she identifies everything in the room except for one thing. The statue is missing.

"Dammit! Where's the statue?"

"Peter James Matteo!" scolds Jennifer at her son's crude language.

"Sorry, Mom," apologizes Peter. "Signore Bertulli, *where* is the statue?!"

"I do not know. There was much activity here at one time, but no one documented anything. It was a very confusing time. We need to look into Church events after the Great Judgment, and perhaps ask Pope Peter. He may know what happened to the statue."

"Let's hope that Pope Peter has some information because after today, there are only four more days. The world has only *four* more days!"

CHAPTER FORTY-TWO

It is now T-minus forty-eight hours. NASA officials have reviewed all mission data and have declared that everything is proceeding as planned. And outside the Basilica of the Chalice, thousands of people are still standing vigil in the snow, hoping that the archangels will make an appearance. With snow now falling across the entire northern half of the planet, it seems that winter has established itself quite firmly on the Earth, and that it may remain in place for a long time to come.

With only four days left, the team agrees that some of them should talk to Pope Peter while the rest of them look into Church activities prior, during, and after the Judgment. Jennifer and Sergeant Gonzalez volunteer to return to the vault with Francesco Scarpone while Domenico, Peter, and Matt ask for an unscheduled meeting with the Pope.

Thanks to Domenico's influence, the trio has been granted a few minutes with the pontiff, but they need to wait until he finishes celebrating morning Mass. When the service ends, the pope enters his office and greets his visitors warmly.

"Doctor Raphael Matteo and Mr. Peter Matteo! It is so nice to see you in a warmer and more comfortable place. God bless you both."

At Pope Peter's greeting, Matt kneels before the successor of the Apostle Peter and kisses his ring. "Good morning, Your Holiness."

Peter also kneels and kisses his ring.

"You know, Peter," says the pope as he takes a seat and indicates that the others should sit as well, "you have a very strong name, and you should be very proud of your father. Through faith he brought the Chalice of Gabriel and the message of God from the Moon to the rest of us on Earth and thus, facilitated the Great Judgment. And now, he has been chosen once again, along with you, his son! Father and son will now do God's will together!"

The pope looks from Peter to Matt and asks, "Tell me, what do you need from me? I am your humble servant."

"Thank you very much, Your Holiness," answers Matt. "We have been tasked with finding three relics that the archangels left on Earth. I already brought one of them to Rome—the Chalice of Gabriel. And Peter was fortunate to locate the second one, the staff of Raphael, in a small church in England. We believe that the third relic is the sword of Saint Michael, and we are fairly certain that he left that holy object with Pope Gregory the Great here at the Vatican. That's why we were in the Passetto di Borgo the other day.

"As you are aware, several structures are now rising out of the ground in Siberia. We were told by descendants of the nomads who live in that area that they were left there by three of the archangels—Gabriel, Raphael, and Michael. Those structures, or perhaps a better word for them would be weapons, seem to have been used to protect the Earth many years ago from some type of danger. And now, at this time, when an asteroid is on track to hit the Earth in just five days, the archangels have given us the ability to take advantage of their devices for our defense. The three relics are the keys that unlock their power.

"We believe that the sword, the only key we still need to find, was placed for safekeeping in the hand of a statue of Saint Michael. That statue was once located in the Hall of Perseus at Castel Sant'Angelo, but it is no longer there. We are hoping that because you have held the Chair of Saint Peter since the time of the Great Judgment, you may know where the statue is now."

"Well, Raphael, you have made much progress! But first, I must say that the structures of the angels are not weapons. They are the tools that the angels use to protect God's creation for His little creatures. As to where the statue is now, I am afraid I do not know. The living quarters in Castel Sant'Angelo have not been used since the time of Pope Francis, who went home to Heaven after Jesus returned and pronounced His Judgment on mankind. At the beginning of the thousand years of peace, many of the Church's relics were distributed around the world. I know that I gave permission for that statue to be sent somewhere, but I cannot remember where, and it may take too long to locate those old records. To save time, you should investigate the places where Saint Michael has appeared in the past. That is the best advice I can give you."

186

The Matteos are crestfallen at the pope's words but the pontiff reassures them by saying, "Do not fear, for I know that God would not send you on this quest for naught. You will prevail, my sons. Now, if there is nothing else that you need from me, I will leave you to continue your task."

Rising from his chair, the pope blesses the Matteos and embraces each of them before an attendant ushers them out of his office.

"We're back to square one," says Peter when they are outside of the pope's office. We still have no idea where the sword is."

"Well, we know where it isn't, and we do have a clue. The statue may be somewhere Saint Michael has already appeared. So, back to the Library we go. But this time, we'll be more focused in our search."

Within minutes, Peter and Matt rejoin Jennifer, Sergeant Gonzalez, and Francesco Scarpone. After summarizing their meeting with the pontiff, they direct their efforts toward researching all the apparitions of Saint Michael.

At about noon, Jennifer comes upon a book about the Sanctuary of Monte Sant'Angelo sul Gargano, commonly known to the English-speaking world as Saint Michael's Cave. "That's it!" she shouts. "Look, everyone, I found it!"

As the team gathers excitedly around her, she points to two photographs. "This photo was taken of the chapel at Saint Michael's Cave in 1970. And this one was taken of the same chapel last year. See? In the newer photo, the statue of Saint Michael is at the entrance of the chapel but it wasn't there before!"

"Wow! We got it!" exclaims Matt.

Excited by this discovery, the team members congratulate each other with hugs and high-fives.

"Ah, Signore Matteo, you may have located the statue, but you will not be able to get close to it soon," says Francesco. "The roads leading to the Sanctuary at Monte Sant'Angelo are closed now. Normally, it takes approximately four and one-half hours to drive there from Roma but with so much snow covering those mountain roads, it is not possible to drive there now, and a snowstorm has grounded all flights."

Matt sighs. "I guess we'll have to wait until the storm ends. But when it does, we'll need to get there as quickly as possible."

"Yes, of course. I will contact the Italian military to see what can be done."

When Francesco Scarpone leaves the Library to make arrangements for transportation to the shrine, Matt, Jenn, Peter, and the Sergeant walk to their rooms in anticipation of a successful conclusion to their journey. On the way, the group decides that as soon as the weather permits, Peter and his father will be the ones to make the trip to the Gargano Peninsula.

The Malignant, who is ever watchful for opportunities to strike at his enemies, is aware of these new developments in the Matteos' mission. He cannot see exactly what is going on, however, thanks to Saint Michael, who destroyed his Flame of Discernment.

In a rough and raspy voice, the Evil One raises his claw-like hand and shouts, *"You are who You are, and I am who I am. What can You do to me that You have not already done? Look at me, I am a horror! But I will be victorious in the end. For I revel in horror, and horror will triumph! HAHAHAHAHAHAHA!"*

CHAPTER
FORTY-THREE

The countdown for the missile launch continues at T-minus thirty-five hours. Time is running extremely short.

With snow still falling in Rome, all air traffic in and around the Eternal City remains grounded. The Matteos and Sergeant Gonzalez, their faithful military escort, wait in the Matteos' living quarters for Francesco Scarpone to let them know if he was able to make travel arrangements to Monte Sant'Angelo.

When they finally hear a knock at the door, Matt rushes to open it and finds Signore Scarpone clutching a sheaf of papers in the hallway.

"I have some news for you," he says with a serious expression.

"Come in, Francesco. Please."

Entering the room, Signore Scarpone declines a seat and without delay, launches into a description of their current situation.

"All air traffic is grounded, almost certainly until morning. However, I have been able to secure an all-terrain, six-wheel-drive military transport vehicle, and also a military snow-removal vehicle. *Le Forze Armate italiane*, the Italian Armed Forces, will escort you up the mountain roads to *Il santuario di San Michele Arcangelo*. Under these weather conditions, the drive will most likely take at least six hours. If you leave now, you could arrive at the cave at about ten o'clock tonight. The telephone lines are down in the Gargano area, so I could not contact Father Manelli at the Sanctuary. But there is perpetual adoration of the Blessed Sacrament there, so the small chapel will be open. Signore Matteo, this is the only option if you want to leave now. If the storm is over by tomorrow and the roads and runways are cleared, air travel will resume then. So, you can either go with the military now, or wait for a flight tomorrow. I am so sorry."

"Please, there is nothing to be sorry about." Matt pats the signore's back in gratitude. "We appreciate everything you've done for us during these difficult times."

Matt stops to think for a minute, and then turns to the others.

"I don't think we should sit around and wait for the weather to improve because it may only get worse before it gets better. As we already discussed, Peter and I will make the trip to Saint Michael's Cave, and we'll go now, with the Italian military. Jenn, you and Gonzalez should remain here until we return." Turning back to Francesco, he adds, "It will only take us a minute to pack. We'll be right with you."

Francesco takes a seat to wait for the pair while Peter rushes to his room and Matt packs his things with help from Jennifer.

A short time later, Peter returns with his suitcase and a heavy coat and gloves. Father and son shake the sergeant's hand and give Jennifer a hug and a kiss. Then, they follow Francesco out the door.

Looking on as they leave, Jennifer blows a farewell kiss at the two most important men in her life. "I love you both!" she calls out.

Matt smiles back at his wife. "We love you, too!"

In blowing snow, Matt and Pete climb into what can best be described as a Hummer on steroids. The large, snow-removal truck leads the caravan of heavy vehicles eastward across the southern edge of the Apennine Mountain Range toward the Adriatic Coast. In spite of the intense storm, most of the roads are drivable except for a section deep in the mountains that needs to be cleared by the Italian military's giant "snow blower on wheels."

After they pass the city of Pescara, the road continues south along the Adriatic near the resort town of Termoli, and then turns east. From there, it goes uphill. It's a slow climb up Monte Gargano, with switchbacks and occasionally necessary road-clearing as they approach the town of Monte Sant'Angelo.

At nine o'clock that evening, they finally arrive at the Sanctuary, relieved that the trip didn't take as long as they had feared. When the military vehicles finally come to a halt, Matt and Pete find themselves in a large parking area reserved for tourist buses, about four blocks away from the cave. The driver advises the Matteos to walk the rest of the way because the large snow removal vehicle cannot negotiate the narrow street that leads to the Sanctuary.

Peter and Matt thank their driver and exit the vehicle, only to sink immediately into ten inches of snow. The wintry conditions don't faze them but they make slow progress navigating the last four blocks to the Sanctuary of Saint Michael the Archangel. In the distance, they can see their destination with the majestic bell tower that looms over the tiny village. When they arrive in front of the basilica the bells peal the hour, as if announcing their presence.

After they step inside the church, they pause briefly to shake off the snow that has accumulated on their coats and boots while they look around to get their bearings. When Peter spots a flight of steps that leads down into the cave area, he takes off running.

Shaking his head at his son's impulsiveness, Matt begins his own descent, but soon hears a cry from his son far below.

"Dad, it's NOT HERE!"

Now running down the steps himself, Matt stops at the final set of stairs and stares at the statue at which Peter is pointing and shaking his head in disappointment.

"God help us, Pete! That's Padre Pio!" moans Matt.

While they stand there in disbelief, a priest walks out of the nearby chapel and scolds them in a soft but firm voice. "Gentlemen. This is a Holy place and Our Lord is present here. Please be quiet and reverent."

"Sorry, Father," apologizes Matt in an equally soft voice. "I'm Doctor Raphael Matteo, and this is my son, Peter. We're here from the Vatican in search of the statue of Saint Michael that was located at the entrance to the cave. We just drove five hours to get here, but the statue is not here."

"Yes, I've been told about your search for Saint Michael's sword."

"Father, the statue that was here came from Castel Sant'Angelo in Rome. The sword that statue holds is the actual sword that Saint Michael gave to Pope Saint Gregory the Great!"

"*Che peccato*! I did not know," says the priest with a groan. "I am so sorry that it is not here, but I do know where it is."

"Oh, that's great!" says Peter, a little too loudly. "Did you move it to another area of the Sanctuary?"

Before answering, the priest guides the Matteos to an area away from the chapel. "No, it is not here right now. You see, I am from Milan, but the pastor at San Giovanni Rotondo, where Saint Padre Pio is buried, is from Padua. Every year, we make a bet when our hockey teams play against each other, and this year, my Milano Vipers lost. Our agreement was that if I lost, I would send a statue of Saint Michael to San Giovanni Rotondo for one week and he would send a statue of Saint Pio of Pietrelcina here to take its place. Saint Michael left for San Giovanni three days ago. You should speak to

Father Enrico Strazzabosco at the Shrine of Padre Pio."

"Dad, we passed San Giovanni an hour ago," whines Peter.

When the priest notices Matt and Peter exchanging glances, he adds, "Our telephones were not working during the storm, but they are back in service now. I will call Enrico. I will ask him to wait at the church for your arrival."

At T-minus twenty-nine hours and thirty minutes, NASA is making last-minute orbital adjustments to the ANUBIS satellite, and the Matteos are trudging back to the military vehicles for their trip to the Shrine of Padre Pio.

The roads are clearer now, so it's not long before the convoy stops in front of the old church in San Giovanni Rotondo.

There are three churches in this small town, one of the most popular tourist destinations in Italy after Saint Peter's Basilica, the Basilica of the Chalice, and the Basilica of the Ark. The original church where Saint Padre Pio prayed when he arrived at the town's Capuchin Friary is now used a chapel. The church of Santa Maria delle Grazie, Our Lady of Grace, was built later to accommodate the thousands of pilgrims who visited Padre Pio while he was alive. And after he died, an even larger church was built for the tens of thousands who regularly overwhelm this small mountain village, especially now that he has been canonized a saint.

Father Strazzabosco, caretaker of Our Lady of Grace Church, has been waiting for the Matteos. So when he hears the sound of the approaching military vehicles, he rushes out of the church to greet his visitors.

"Doctor Raphael Matteo and Mr. Peter Matteo—welcome! I am honored to meet such celebrities! First, Father Minelli called me, and then His Holiness, Pope Peter himself, called! Imagine that! Each of them told me of your quest. Come! Come inside and let me show you Saint Michael's sword. I believe your search has ended!"

CHAPTER
FORTY-FOUR

I n T-minus twenty-eight hours and fifty minutes, three missiles will be launched to save the human race. But while the countdown continues in Houston, many of the world's leaders are en route to London for a G-20 Summit meeting to discuss the possibility of an ice age. At least, that is what the press release states. What the political elites will actually be discussing is how to make sure they and their policies will survive if the asteroid hits.

If the missiles fail in their mission to break up or destroy the leftover piece of Prometheus, officials of the federal government of the United States and their families will enter secure facilities located in the deep salt mines of the west, the Colorado Rockies, or the mountains of Pennsylvania and Virginia. Similar arrangements have been made for other leaders around the world to enter bunkers in the South American Andes, ice caves in northern Europe, or secret tunnels across Russia, China, Africa, and Australia.

Aside from protecting their families, the most pressing problem the elites face is not how to protect themselves but how to keep the knowledge of their actions for self-preservation from the public—the little people, the common folk—the ones who will most assuredly perish. If the asteroid hits, scientists estimate that it will create a fifty-mile-wide crater that will throw enough debris into the atmosphere to block the Sun for years and ultimately kill a large percentage of life on Earth.

"Come, gentlemen. There, near the tabernacle, is the statue of Saint Michael. And there is his sword." Matt and his son have followed Father

Strazzabosco into the small chapel adjacent to the Church of Our Lady of Grace in San Giovanni Rotondo.

Overjoyed, Peter runs up to the statue and smiles when it begins to glow in the statue's hand. Prying it from the archangel's tight grip, he holds it proudly while Father Strazzabosco looks on in wonder. Matt is standing nearby, but instead of showing an interest in the object he has been searching for all this time, he seems to be distracted. He is looking around the chapel with an odd expression on his face. "What is that smell?" he finally asks with a sharp intake of breath. "It's awful! It smells like rotten eggs!"

When the foul stench reaches Peter, he looks toward the back of the chapel and is riveted by the sight of a dark cloud with two red, piercing eyes glowering inside it. The dark cloud grows and pulsates, and transforms itself into a beast—the beast of Gehenna, the Malignant.

Horrified, Peter shouts out a warning to his dad and the priest, who turn and stare at the ghastly creature that is beginning to glide up the aisle.

Instinctively knowing what is happening, Father Strazzabosco takes out his cross and runs forward to confront the beast. Raising his crucifix high above his head, he yells in defiance, "Leave my church immediately! I command you to leave this house of God!"

With one quick swipe of his arm, the Malignant flings Father Strazzabosco into the air and across a row of pews. Landing against the far wall, the young priest falls into a crumpled heap on the floor, mortally wounded.

Fearing the Evil One's power, Matt and his son retreat to the shelter of the altar. But when the sword in Peter's hand glows intensely and inexplicably increases in size, Peter rushes forward, leaving his father cowering at the altar. With heavenly conviction, he walks confidently down the aisle to confront the Malignant face-to-face.

"Hand me that sword, mortal! Or you will not leave this place alive," snarls the Evil One.

The foul-smelling breath of the beast encircles Peter with the odor of seven thousand years of rotting flesh. The sickening scent causes his eyes to water and forces him to work hard at preventing himself from vomiting. But when the beast reaches out to grab the sword from his hand, his reaction is automatic. He raises the weapon high above his head and lops off the beast's hand in one swift strike.

Screams of fury erupt from the Evil One as his claw-like hand falls to the floor and black blood shoots out of his stump. The rancid blood sprays onto the adjoining pews and burns through the wood like acid.

With his severed hand wriggling and twitching on the floor, the Malignant's anger increases to a fevered pitch and the stench inside the church grows more and more pungent. When the hand bursts into flame, the beast jerks backward and howls deafeningly. The unholy sound penetrates the Matteos' souls, but it doesn't last long.

Unexpectedly, the beast stops screeching and breaks out in an evil grin. *"You fools!"* he cackles. *"You think you can stop* me*?! I am the prince of hell!"*

While the Matteos look on, the beast raises his handless arm and smiles evilly as a new claw-like structure emerges from the raw and bleeding stump.

Flexing his new hand, the Malignant keeps his eyes fixed on Saint Michael's sword and lunges toward Peter with an outstretched arm. But Peter zigzags out of reach and raises the sword again, ready to strike if the beast gets too close.

Just as he is about to slash at the untiring demon, the monster stops and stares past him with widening eyes. An intense light has burst forth from the Tabernacle, and a white mist is forming around the container holding the Holy Eucharist. Rooted into place, the Malignant scowls at it with an expression of fear and loathing.

Around and around swirls the mist, until it eventual forms itself into an indistinct face and a pair of clear blue eyes.

"I AM," thunders a voice from the mist, *"and you have defied Me for the last time. I warned you not to put Me to the test. You were once banished by My Son. Now, I will finish this."*

Behind the Malignant, a swirling cloud of wind forms like the inside of a tornado, and the thunderous voice proclaims, *"BEGONE, SATAN!"*

From the Tabernacle, God the Father takes a deep breath, and blows. The tremendous force of wind that God creates knocks the Malignant off his feet and sends him tumbling down the aisle. In an attempt to withstand the incredible force, Satan grabs onto passing pews but he is no match for the Breath of God. Now sliding sideways, he loses his grip and is sucked into a portal-like opening in the spiraling tornado.

"NOOOooooooooo……" screams the Evil One in panic and alarm.

Drawn deeper and deeper into the spiraling wind, Lucifer, Satan, the Devil, the Evil One, the Malignant, slowly disappears as if he were being flushed down a toilet. When he is no longer visible, the portal closes, and God the Father vanishes as if He were never there.

When silence and calm returns to the church, Matt asks, "Are you okay, Son?"

At first, Peter doesn't answer. He is captivated by the sword in his hand which is slowly returning to its original size and color. "Dad," he finally declares, "I had some doubts before, but I don't doubt *anything* now!"

With fatherly pride, Matt smiles at his son, but then remembers something. "Hey!" he shouts. "Where's Father Strazzabosco?"

Recalling where they saw the beast throw him, they rush to that part of the church and find the priest lying on the ground with another, older priest kneeling over him. The older priest is bearded and dressed like a Capuchin monk, and he is wearing fingerless gloves on both hands. One of his hands is on Father Strazzabosco's head, and with the other, he is making the Sign of the Cross over the younger priest's body.

Enthralled, Matt whispers to his son. "That's Padre Pio! It's Saint Padre Pio of Pietrelcina!"

Rising slowly, the saint turns toward the Matteos and makes the Sign of the Cross over each of them. Then, he vanishes from sight.

When Padre Pio is no longer visible, Matt and Peter notice that Father Strazzabosco is struggling to sit up. Hastening to his side, they lift him by his arms into a standing position.

"Father, you're okay?" they ask, baffled by his obvious good health. "We thought you were dead! That thing threw you so hard...!"

"Yes, I'm fine. My head is a little sore, but I think I will live. What happened?"

Not knowing quite what to say, Matt and his son glance at each other, momentarily stumped for words. Although the pair have experience many miraculous events in recent weeks, they are still surprised when they occur. Speaking for both of them, Matt responds, "Father, it was absolutely amazing! We have so much to tell you! Where can we go to explain it all?"

Moving his limbs around stiffly, the priest replies, "Come with me to the rectory. We can talk there, and you can sleep in the guest house overnight. It is late, and the roads are treacherous in the snow. You can leave for Rome in the morning."

Jennifer is getting ready for to retire for the night when she hears a knock at the door.

"Mrs. Matteo, it is Domenico Bertulli."

Shrugging into her robe, Jennifer pads over to the door and opens it slightly.

"Yes?" she asks.

"Good evening, Signora! I have wonderful news! Your husband, he call me from San Giovanni Rotondo! They have the sword of San Michele! They must remain there tonight because of the bad weather, but they will leave for Roma at sunrise."

"Oh, my goodness! Thank you for that fantastic news, Signore Bertulli! But San Giovanni? I thought they went to Monte Sant'Angelo."

"*Sì*, he say he has a grand story to tell you. He wish you good night and he will see you soon."

"Thank you very much, Signore!"

Bowing slightly, Domenico responds, "*Buona notte, Signora Matteo. Buona notte.*"

Although the Malignant is now out of the equation, Prometheus is still the x-factor. Ever present, it is continuing to twist and roll toward Earth like a runaway train heading for the end of the line.

CHAPTER FORTY-FIVE

The countdown of ANUBIS continues at T-minus twenty-one hours.

In less than one day, the three Cold War-era nuclear missiles will be launched to intercept Prometheus. If their mission fails, Prometheus will strike the Earth three days after that, so Matt, Jenn, and Peter have only those three days to bring all the keys to Siberia. However, even if both of those missions are successful, the Earth is still heading toward a full-blown ice age.

Matt and Peter left San Giovanni Rotondo at dawn and now are well on their way back to Rome. They are expected to arrive within the hour. Jennifer and Sergeant Gonzalez are passing the time by meeting for breakfast at their customary table in the Vatican's ornate dining room. After breakfast, Domenico Bertulli and a Swiss Guardsman stop them on the way back to their rooms.

"Signora Matteo, your husband call me again. He is outside the city and will arrive in fifteen minutes. He want you and *il sergente* to meet him in the Basilica of the Chalice. Now that you have all three keys, Major Ralston and your Consulate booked you on a flight to Siberia."

"That's perfect. Do you have details yet?"

"*Sì.* The first leg of your journey will take you to *Mosca*…how you say? Moscow? on a flight that will be four hours. There will be a plane change in Russia that will bring you to the archeological dig six hours later, if there are no delays from the weather. No military flights are available now, so you will be on one of only two commercial flights that fly from Roma to *Mosca* every day. The first flight leaves in an hour, which may be too soon, but the next flight leaves at 6:30 tonight. I will let you know as soon as I get more details about which flight you will be taking. Also, Pope Peter, he wants to meet with all of you before you leave Roma. May God be with you and your family!"

"Thank you very much, Domenico. You have been extremely helpful throughout this entire ordeal. In fact, I don't think we could have come this far without you! Please let Pope Peter know that we will meet with him whenever he wishes."

Leaning in, Jennifer gives Signore Bertulli a small kiss on the cheek. Then she and Sergeant Gonzalez follow the Swiss Guardsman to the basilica.

Because of the heavy snowstorm that followed the closure of the Basilica of the Chalice to the public, there aren't as many people as usual in the garden surrounding the church. Even so, there are still a few hundred pilgrims huddled near the propane heaters provided by the Vatican. As Jenn and Sergeant Gonzalez follow their escort to a side door of the basilica, they offer their unspoken admiration and thanksgiving for the dedication of those resolute believers.

When they enter the now-quiet house of prayer, the scene inside takes their breath away. Two thirteen-foot-tall archangels in full battle armor are standing majestically beside Gabriel's chalice and Saint Raphael's staff, and the relics themselves are sparkling like diamonds. The symbols that correspond with each angel's silo at Tunguska are dancing on their golden breastplates, and the three stars of the Orion Constellation are represented by twinkling brilliance on the belts around their waists.

Enchanted by the spectacle, Jennifer and Sergeant Gonzalez tiptoe to a front pew, but after they are seated they notice that the staff and the chalice are shining even brighter than when they first arrived. Unknown to either of them, Saint Michael's sword is also increasing in brilliance as the vehicle carrying it nears Saint Peter's Square.

Maneuvering carefully through the snowplowed streets of Rome, the two military vehicles transporting Matt and Peter finally pull up in front of Saint Peter's. Escorted by the Swiss Guard and members of the Italian military, the Matteos enter the Vatican gardens through a side entrance and pass through the assembled pilgrims. The pilgrims watch with intense curiosity as Peter carries Saint Michael's sword into the church.

When the sword arrives inside the building, a third being in full armor, more majestic than the others, appears at the altar. It is Saint Michael the Archangel.

200

Holding tightly to the sword, Peter walks toward the front of the church while the three archangels line up beside each other and beckon Matt and Jennifer to approach them.

Without a word being said, the Archangel Gabriel escorts Jennifer to the chalice and hands the holy object to her. The Archangel Raphael hands the staff to Matt and then directs Peter to stand between his parents with the sword.

The result of the archangels' maneuvering is that each member of the Matteo family now holds one of the keys to the salvation of the Earth.

Their responsibilities now complete, the archangels ascend toward a mist that has formed near the church's ceiling. Just before they disappear into the cloud, Saint Michael looks down upon the astounded trio and declares, *"Remember, we obey the Commandments of God."*

When the archangels are no longer visible, the sword, the staff, and the chalice lose their brilliance and return to their original states. In the silence that ensues, Peter turns to his dad and whispers, "What he just said is similar to the words on the silos in Siberia—*From the Commandments of God!*"

"Yes, I know," responds the senior Matteo in a similar whisper. Then, with a glance at his wife, he declares in a stronger voice, "We need to get moving. These keys have to reach the silos as soon as possible. The missiles will launch early tomorrow morning. But if they fail, there will only be three days after that to do what needs to be done, and we're going to lose almost twelve hours in travel time alone."

"Nothing yet, Matt. We missed the morning flight out of Rome, and the next flight doesn't leave until 6:30 tonight."

"That's not soon enough, Major! We'll be waiting around and doing nothing for almost an entire day!"

"Dad, listen," says Peter. "I can't believe I'm saying this, but let's not get too upset yet. There are still almost three days left to get to Siberia."

"Yeah, but remember Murphy's Law. If anything can possibly go wrong, it will."

With a tap on Matt's shoulder, Sergeant Gonzalez interjects, "You know, Mr. Matteo, Murphy was basically an optimist!"

CHAPTER FORTY-SIX

At T-minus fifteen hours, President Bush at a meeting with her chief of staff.

"Madame President, the underground bunker in Colorado has been renovated for you, your family, and your staff members. The vice president and the cabinet members will be moved to the shelter in the salt mines so neither of you will be in the same place at the same time. The senators and congressmen will also be separated from each other."

"Levar, I'm not going to the bunker. I'm the leader of this nation, and I will remain here in Washington. The shelter below the White House is where I will stay."

"But Madame President, I strongly advise…"

"No, stop right now. I AM STAYING HERE. The Secret Service has been notified and arrangements have been made. This conversation is closed. The Matteos have found the three keys, and they are on their way to Siberia. I'm sure…well, I'm as sure as I can be…that they will succeed. There is also a plan in place to revive the Gulf Stream. They will use two of the HAARP transmitters—the one in Alaska and the one in Colombia. When the asteroid is deflected or destroyed, the HAARP transmitters will bounce their radio waves off the ionosphere and into the oil spill area. According to the experts, the radio waves will heat up the water and start it flowing around the coast of Florida again. They believe that one of the main reasons the Gulf Stream has not started up again is that the change in climate has cooled the water down too much."

"Yes, ma'am."

With a shuffling of papers, the president continues.

"Levar, please tell the staff that they have the right to choose whatever they want to do. They can go to the mountains or stay here in Washington. I'm constantly monitoring the progress of each of the missions that can potentially save us. I'm in direct communication with NASA in Houston, and I'm receiving continual updates from Major Ralston about the Matteos. Unless you have anything else that is urgent, this meeting is now over."

Gathering up his paperwork, the chief of staff excuses himself and leaves the Oval Office.

Special arrangements have been made for the Matteos and Sergeant Gonzalez to fly on the commercial Alitalia flight that leaves for Moscow at 6:30 p.m., even though it is later than they wanted to leave. The Vatican sent them an aluminum case with foam cushioning to transport the sword and the chalice, but Peter will need to carry the staff because it's too large to fit in a case. The precious objects will remain with the travelers at all times; they will not be stowed with the luggage.

The group has been given reserved seats in the first-class section and they will be the only occupants in that area of the plane. Upon arriving in Moscow, they will be escorted to a private military jet, since there are no direct commercial flights to Krasnoyarsk, the closest major city to the Siberian excavation site. A tilt-rotor aircraft will then transport them from Krasnoyarsk to the dig. If the weather cooperates, their total travel time is expected to be ten hours. That will give them two hours of wiggle room before ANUBIS' missiles are launched.

Major Ralston is also on his way to Russia. After a private discussion with President Bush, the leader of the free world decided that he should join the Matteos in Krasnoyarsk and accompany them to the angels' silos. The major is now enjoying the luxury of a private jet, as there were no commercial flights available at the last minute.

The temperature in Siberia is currently -40°C (-40°F), but thankfully, there is no snow predicted for at least another week. Doctor Kirk has been spending most of his days at the excavation site because the temperature surrounding the silos is a steady 30°C (86°F). In fact, the rest of the crew is also spending most of their time there just to keep warm.

At T-minus nine hours until launch, the clock is ticking down fast. After the missiles are fired, it will take another three days for them to rendezvous with Prometheus. If their mission is unsuccessful, the asteroid will hit the Earth six hours later.

CHAPTER
FORTY-SEVEN

The majority of the more influential members of the world's political, financial, and business classes have known about the potential for a worst-case scenario for a long time but the rest of society is just coming to grips with it. With every discussion now centering on the real possibility of a confrontation between Earth and what the press is calling "Prometheus, the Planet Killer," fear and panic is taking hold around the world. However, the elites are ignoring all of that. Instead of using their considerable resources for the good of their communities, they are intent on saving only themselves and their families.

Although there are many places where faith and prayer are being renewed, greed and avarice are once again tightening their grip on mankind. Many of those who regained their faith after the Judgment and the one thousand years of peace granted by God seem to have lost it again. They are forgetting everything that God has given to them, and are once again complaining to Him. They say, "Yes, you gave all of that to us then, but what have you given to us recently?"

Will human beings ever learn?

At nine o'clock in the morning, less than four hours remain until the launch of ANUBIS. Matt, Peter, Jennifer, Sergeant Gonzalez, and Major Ralston are all sitting together in the commercial version of the military's Osprey tilt-rotor aircraft. When the pilot announces their arrival at the dig site, they look out of their windows with curiosity at the three silos that are still rising out of the tundra.

In preparation for landing, the Osprey converts from airplane mode to helicopter mode, and slowly descends near the archeological site's command center. As soon as it touches down, the group deplanes and proceeds toward the building with the keys. At their approach, the large "angel tools," the name Pope Peter has given to the silos, begin to hum and vibrate.

"Peter!" exclaims Doctor Kirk. "It's so good to see you again!"

"Hello, Doctor! I'm glad to be back. Let me introduce you to my father, Doctor Raphael Matteo, and my mother, Jennifer Matteo. I'd also like you to meet Major Ralston and Sergeant Gonzalez. Both of them are from NASA."

"Welcome to all of you! Come now, let's unlock our silos. Oh, you may want to remove your heavy coats now. It's quite warm out there."

Matt opens the aluminum case holding the chalice and the sword and hands the holy cup to his wife. Then he picks up the sword and joins Peter, who is holding the staff. When they are all ready, they follow Doctor Kirk outside.

As the structures come into view, the sound of singing fills the air, and a white mist forms around each of the structures. In the twinkling of an eye, the Archangels Raphael, Michael, and Gabriel emerge from the mist, each of them standing above the silo bearing his name.

As if it had been rehearsed ahead of time, the Matteos walk directly up to the silos that correspond to the key that each of them is holding. Peter stops in front of Raphael's silo with the staff, Jennifer brings the chalice to Gabriel's silo, and Matt stands before Michael's silo with the sword. When they are all in place, the keys in their hands begin to glow.

"All right!" declares Matt after a quick glance at his wife and son. "Let's do this together! At the count of three, insert your keys. Ready? One, two, THREE!"

In unison, the Matteos insert their holy relics into the matching areas on each silo, producing an instantaneous reaction that causes all of them to take a few steps backward. A plasma-like energy field has materialized around the silos and seems to be pulling each of them upwards. At the same time, the humming sound stops, and an eerie quiet settles into the area.

Fascinated, the onlookers watch as the Archangels Gabriel and Raphael disappear, leaving the Archangel Michael, dressed splendidly for battle, standing even taller above the site.

"Dad," whispers Peter, "we inserted the keys. What do we do now?"

Matt studies the silos and notices that they are now higher out of the ground than they were in the last photographs he saw, and more of their etchings are exposed. He bends down to take a closer look, but the Archangel Michael chooses that moment to speak.

"Remember," he says with dignity, *"we are the guardians of God. We are directed by Our Lord, and act only upon His Command."*

When he finishes speaking, he rises up into the sky and disappears.

"What does that mean?" asks Peter. "Have we failed?"

Matt doesn't respond because he is on his hands and knees examining the newly-exposed etchings.

No longer held in check by the presence of the heavenly visitors, everyone at the site is now free to walk over to Matt to see what he is looking at. He is studying a new design that is repeated on all three structures. It appears to depict rays of light shining onto similar-looking silos.

While the bystanders marvel at the new design and speculate on its meaning, Peter notices that there is only one area on the angels' tools that still seems to be active: the brightly glowing letters of the Greek words, Από τις εντολές του Θεού.

"Dad, Saint Michael just told us that the archangels don't act unless they are commanded by God."

"Yes?"

"Well, the Greek statement on each panel means, *From the Commandments of God,* and it's still glowing on each silo. What are we supposed to do now? We only have about three days left."

"I don't know, Pete."

While the Matteos wonder what to do next, Major Ralston and Sergeant Gonzalez walk around each structure, awestruck by what the objects may mean for the world. The silos are dormant at the moment, but their Greek inscriptions are glowing brightly.

"Major Ralston, can we get back to the Vatican as soon as possible?" asks Matt. "We must be missing something. Maybe there's still something in Rome that we need to find. That Greek inscription could be a clue."

"Hmm... According to my watch, ANUBIS will launch within the hour," says the Major, thinking aloud. "We're in in the middle of Siberia. Traveling back to Rome will take at least one and a half days. That would give you only one and a half days after that to solve the mystery, and that would be working non-stop; no sleep. If you're sure you want to go back, we need to return to the Operations Center now so I can get started on the arrangements."

"All right, let's go."

Back at the control center, Major Ralston talks on his satellite phone while the team and Doctor Kirk discuss the amazing events that just occurred. About twenty minutes later, the Major approaches them with news.

"The Russian military will hold transportation for you at Krasnoyarsk. When you arrive in Moscow, you will be put on a non-stop charter flight to Rome. Weather permitting, you should be back at the Vatican in fifteen hours. The sergeant and I will remain here at the excavation while the rest of you go back to Rome. If anything happens here while you're gone, I'll contact you immediately."

After some hasty goodbyes, the Matteos once again don their heavy coats and make the trek outside to the waiting Osprey.

CHAPTER
FORTY-EIGHT

O n the second leg of their trip back to the Vatican, the travelers are on their way to a military base just outside of Moscow. When they arrive at the base, a military convoy will escort them to the city's main international airport where they will board a private jet to Rome.

All of them—save one—are getting some much-needed sleep on the plane. Try as he might to get some rest, Peter keeps waking up. His mind is very unsettled; he keeps thinking about the Greek inscription on the silos. Every time he stirs, he reads over the Temple Mount scrolls on his laptop, hoping to gain some insight into its riddle.

The countdown finally reaches its conclusion at three a.m. Central Standard Time on October 10.

"7, 6, 5, 4, 3, 2, 1. Ignition…"

"We have confirmation. All three missiles have launched. Burn time for the rockets will be twenty minutes. All of them are on course."

If everything goes according to plan, Prometheus will be destroyed at 2:30 a.m. EST on October 13.

If not, at about ten o'clock a.m. EST on the thirteenth, Prometheus will impact the Earth.

In the White House, President Bush is also awake. She has been monitoring activities at NASA's mission control center on closed-circuit TV while she puts the finishing touches on a speech that she will deliver that morning.

According to information her staff released to the press, the topic of her speech is the G-20 Summit. However, that is not what she intends to discuss. Instead, President Bush will talk to the nation about ANUBIS, Prometheus, and the icy conditions that are currently gripping the planet and creating a new ice age.

"This is Charles Stark from ABC News' Washington Bureau. Reports coming to us from Rome indicate that Gabriel's Chalice has been removed from its display case in the Basilica of the Chalice. The Vatican recently closed that basilica to visitors, however, many tourists are still gathering in the garden surrounding the church, as well as in Saint Peter's Square and the area around the Basilica of the Ark.

"Unconfirmed reports from Saint Peter's Square state that Roman citizens and tourists are having visions of angels. They say they are hearing unusual sounds and categorize them as 'choirs of celestial voices.' In addition, many tourists describe a large golden rod that they say was carried out of the Basilica of the Chalice.

"Our office in Rome contacted the Vatican about these reports but there have been no comments from Vatican officials. The Vatican's spokesperson would only say that they closed the Basilica of the Chalice and moved the holy chalice to a secure location out of fear that the relentlessly heavy snowfalls could compromise the integrity of the roof. We questioned the stability of the roofs of Saint Peter's Basilica and the Basilica of the Ark, but the spokesperson assured us that the roofs of all Vatican City buildings are inspected daily. However, if deemed necessary, they will also close others for the public's safety.

"Meanwhile, there is new information coming out of Siberia. As we stated in prior reports, there is an ongoing international archeological dig headed by the Smithsonian Institution at the site of the mysterious 1908 Tunguska blast. Scientists are examining three metallic-like structures that are reported to have been buried in the Siberian tundra for over a century. Recently, the Russian military has increased their presence in the area and all sightseeing activity has been halted. We have contacted the Smithsonian Institution and the Russian government for details, but neither of them has commented at this time.

"Please stay tuned to this station for continual updates. This is Charles Stark, ABC News-Washington."

The world is in chaos.

Extreme, wintry conditions have established a death grip on the northern half of the planet. Northern seaports are closed because of ice-choked waterways and northern refineries are shutting down around the planet, causing oil prices to rise on a daily basis. Harbors in New York, Savannah, Seattle, San Francisco, and Baltimore are all closed, with similar closings developing across Europe, Russia, China, Japan, and the Unified Nation of Korea.

Smaller lakes, tributaries, rivers, and streams are completely frozen over, and ice is now beginning to form in the larger bodies of water. Each of the five Great Lakes is a mass of ice, and Niagara Falls is frozen solid, which hasn't happened since the early 20th Century. Towns, cities, and nations that rely on surface reservoirs for their drinking water are now in crisis mode. Many of them are being forced to melt snow and ice because their reservoirs are frozen solid.

The severe economic conditions have created a worldwide recession, and many companies are laying off workers. Others are scrambling to relocate to the Southern Hemisphere where it is still relatively warm. The extreme cold has not yet affected South America, South Africa, the island chain of Indonesia, New Zealand, or Australia.

Protests and riots are now commonplace across the U.S., Europe, Russia, and China because of twenty percent worldwide unemployment and insufficient food. Martial law has been declared in many American cities—New York, Chicago, Baltimore, Washington D.C., Seattle, San Francisco, and Pittsburgh—as well as in Paris, Oslo, Berlin, Moscow, Beijing, Lisbon, and many other cities around the world.

Adding to the chaos, doomsday rumors are now rampant. Amateur astronomers are continuing to blog about Prometheus while government officials are dismissing those reports as false. However, those same officials are privately preparing to bring their families to underground bunkers at a moment's notice.

The only positive note in all of this is that many around the world are beginning to return to their faith. Millions are flocking to their local places of worship to participate in continuous prayer vigils and other religious services.

It's funny how faith increases in times of crisis.

The ANUBIS missiles are finally on their way! The team at NASA is ecstatic at their success in pulling off such a complicated program in a very short period of time. But the news is not all good. Only two of the missiles are on course. The three weapons—nicknamed Michael, Gabriel, and Raphael—

were supposed to burn for twenty minutes in order to reach optimum velocity, however Gabriel, missile number two, flamed out in ten minutes. Instead of providing the world with an additional chance of destroying Prometheus, that missile will wander uselessly throughout the vastness of space for an unknown period of time.

The military's plan to destroy Prometheus was doubtful from the start, but the failure of Gabriel has cast it in an even more dubious light. The two remaining missiles must be precisely on target, for at two days and eighteen hours until the hoped-for destruction, there is no more room for failure.

In Saint Peter's Square, the faithful continue to remain vigilant. Even though the temperature has been hovering around 0°C (32°F), no one has left the area, and more are streaming in every day. The pilgrims are praying continuously while huddled around large propane heaters to keep warm, and volunteers are sustaining them with hot soup, fish, and bread.

In the Vatican Library, Francesco Scarpone and Domenico Bertulli are now working alongside the Matteos. They are all desperate to find anything related to the archangels and their "commands from God," as it states in the Greek text. Hours fly by, but no matter how hard the group searches, they are no closer to solving the Greek riddle.

Well past midnight, everyone is hungry and tired. During a rare pause for a food and restroom break, Matt tells his wife, "Jenn, I think it would be better if you went to our room and got some sleep. Signore Bertulli is going home to rest, so Pete, Francesco, and I will keep the fires burning. I know you want to help, but we can handle it for a while. Besides," he says with a smile, "you keep nodding off, and you almost hit your head on the table several times."

"I'm sorry, you're right," grins Jenn. "I *am* exhausted, but you must be as tired as I am. We're not as young as we used to be. Let the two youngsters keep the fires burning. Come with me to our room, Matt. Come to bed."

Matt closes his eyes and lowers his head briefly. When he looks up, Jennifer and Peter are watching him closely.

"You're right," he sighs. "Peter, you and Francesco are on your own. I'm exhausted, and I'm going to try to get a few hours' sleep. Wake us immediately if you find anything at all."

Jennifer gives Peter a hug and presses the intercom for the Swiss Guardsman. As they walk out the door, she looks back at her son to give him a wave goodnight, but he is engrossed in his work.

Four o'clock the next afternoon, Francesco Scarpone is sound asleep in a chair in the Library while Peter is valiantly trying to keep himself from nodding off. He and Francesco have worked through the night and well into the next day, but Matt and Jenn still haven't returned. Peter has tried to keep going, but he is finally done. He leans over the table, puts his head into his arms, and gives in to sleep.

Across the pond, President Bush's press conference has just begun. It is a news conference that other leaders around the world will soon repeat.

CHAPTER FORTY-NINE

Standing at the podium with President Bush are Press Secretary Nora Langley, Doctor Stefan Bell from the Sagan Observatory, and Doctor Carol Sinberg from NASA.

"Good morning," begins Mrs. Bush. "If you reviewed the statement we released about this press conference, you're expecting me to talk about the G-20 summit. However, that will not be my topic today. As you know, we are currently approaching what some scientists are calling an ice age. Unusually cold winter weather has gripped the northern half of our planet and is causing extreme difficulty for everyone. Gas shortages, food shortages, water shortages, and job layoffs have pushed the world's economy into a deep recession. But all of this is the result of a self-inflicted wound.

"The oil spill in the Gulf of Mexico has halted the flow of the Gulf Stream, the current that brings the warm waters of the Gulf of Mexico around the coast of Florida and into the northern Atlantic Ocean. That warm water helps to regulate the temperature of the planet. Without it, our world is rapidly cooling. Although the spill has been successfully cleaned up, the Gulf Stream has not resumed its flow. Within forty-eight hours, we are prepared to initiate a strategy to heat the waters of the Gulf of Mexico, which we pray will start the Gulf Stream flowing again. Detailed information about that plan will be forthcoming, but now, I want to address the rumors that are circulating on various social media and alternative news websites."

The president pauses to collect herself before she has to deliver more bad news.

"Contrary to what has been reported by officials from our government and other governments around the world, an asteroid is indeed heading toward the Earth. The heads of all the major world powers jointly decided to wait until there was a plan in place to deal with it before we announced the situation to our nations."

President Bush is forced to wait until the buzz of reporters' questions and comments dies down low enough for her to continue.

"The asteroid is the size of Manhattan Island. It is a rather large chunk of one piece of the Prometheus asteroid that broke off from the main body as a result of our mining operations, and this piece is now racing toward our planet. Within approximately two days, it will be close enough to be visible with the naked eye. Our best scientists have assured us that it does not pose a direct threat to our world at this time. However, it will pass within only 10,000 miles of us, and any change in its path could bring it directly into our atmosphere. That is why we took the Shuttle Atlantis out of retirement and asked her brave crew to perform a dangerous mission on our behalf.

"When the world united after the judgment of mankind, we were promised one thousand years of peace, and all governments destroyed their weapons and nuclear materials under the Euro-American treaty of 2030. However, we have recently learned that not all of the weapons were destroyed, and we are now putting those remaining weapons into service— not to destroy humanity, but to save it. We discovered that a 20th century satellite code-named ANUBIS has been circling our planet all these years with a payload of three nuclear missiles.

"Yesterday, we sent five astronauts into space on the shuttle Atlantis. Their mission is to reactivate the satellite and direct its missiles to intercept the piece of Prometheus that is threatening our planet. The three missiles have been launched successfully, and two of them are on schedule to rendezvous with the asteroid tomorrow morning. The third missile was defective and has been sent out into deep space.

"I am confident that our plan to deflect or destroy the asteroid will succeed. I firmly believe that God will not abandon us after His Son deemed us worthy of His Judgment and His one thousand years of peace.

"I will now answer a few of your questions. Press Secretary Nora Langley will respond to remaining questions after I leave the podium."

The president looks over the sea of raised hands.

"Ah, okay, Joe Abernathy from A-CNN. You'll be the first."

"Thank you, Madame President. There have been reports from Europe and Japan that government leaders there are moving into protected underground facilities. If this is true, doesn't that mean that the asteroid is

218

expected to hit the Earth?"

"Joe, there are emergency plans and procedures in place for every government, including our own, that are to be implemented during all presumed or actual crises. I cannot comment on the actions of other governments or their officials, but I am not going anywhere. My family and I will remain here, in the White House."

Pointing out into the crowd, she says, "Next question. Sarah from Fox News."

"Madame President, the price of gas is now over nine dollars a gallon in some areas and there are riots all over the country due to shortages of food and water. What is the federal government doing about this?"

"Sarah, I have given permission for National Guard units to be activated nationwide so that our governors can utilize the Guard's manpower as they see fit. I have also released our oil reserves to ease the price of gas, and I have directed the United States Coast Guard to use its icebreaker ships to unclog seaports near our refining facilities so we can start producing more gasoline, and to allow food and water to arrive from southern areas."

President Bush scans the room and announces, "I'm looking for Greg from AP. Oh, there you are, Greg. Go ahead, please."

"Thank you, Madame President. My sources at the Tunguska archeological dig in Siberia tell me that there has been an increase in military flights in and out of the area, with connections to Rome. There is also increased activity in Saint Peter's Square and the garden around the Basilica of the Chalice of Saint Gabriel. Can you comment on these reports, and do they have anything to do with Prometheus?"

"Greg, I have no comment at this time. I suggest that you attend Pope Peter's next press conference. Thank you, everyone. Nora will now field more of your questions. God bless us all."

A question is shouted out from the audience as President Bush leaves the podium.

"Madame President! President Bush! If the missiles fail and the asteroid hits, are we all going to die?"

CHAPTER FIFTY

At nine p.m., Peter's parents have returned to the library vault and Peter and Francesco have awakened from their naps. All of them are now searching through multitudes of scrolls and documents about Old Testament events. With a little less than twenty hours until the missiles collide with the asteroid, the team is becoming increasingly anxious.

"Dad, after God gave Moses the tablets of the Ten Commandments, the Israelites built the Ark of the Covenant at God's command, and placed the tablets inside it. They carried the Ark with them into battle and essentially used it as a weapon to defeat their enemies. We know that the Ark was found during the Great Judgment at the site of King Solomon's Temple, in the area where the Holy of Holies was located. We also know that they found written descriptions of how Solomon was able to unlock the Ark's power with a sacred ring that was given to him by Saint Michael. We all know that, right?"

"Yes, Pete. All of that has been very well documented in recent years. What's your point?"

"Look at these drawings of the Ark being used in battle. The illustrations are similar to the symbols on the silos at Tunguska. The Ark, or should I say what is in it, may be what the phrase, *From the Commandments of God,* pertains to. The silos may need to be activated by the Ark of the Covenant. Well, actually, by the tablets of the Ten Commandments."

"Hmm, that actually sounds reasonable."

"Yeah, maybe, but something is still confusing me. According to these other documents from an old Coptic church in Ethiopia, Menelik I, son of the Queen of Sheba and King Solomon, brought the Ark of the Covenant from

Israel to Ethiopia. Many Ethiopians believe that when Menelik arrived in their country, he placed the Ark in a chapel in the city of Aksum. So at the time they found the Ark at the Temple Mount in Jerusalem, it puzzled me that it wasn't in Ethiopia, and that there was no mention of a ring belonging to King Solomon."

"Signore," interrupts Francesco Scarpone, "the Ark, it was not really found in Jerusalem. Well, *sì*, it was, but it wasn't."

At that unexpected comment, everyone turns and stares at Francesco and Matt urges him to clarify his statement. "Please explain, sir. We don't need another riddle at this point."

"*Sì, sì*. When they found Solomon's Temple, Pope Peter wanted to be there when they entered the Holy of Holies. I was with him, and when we entered that area of the temple we saw an altar where the Ark must have been placed so long ago, but it was not there. We were *molto triste*, very sad, but suddenly, the room was illuminated by a light so bright that we could not look at it. Before us appeared Saint Michael with six other angels, and they were carrying the Ark. They said it was God's will that when the temple was found, the Ark would be returned to its original location from its resting place in Ethiopia. God wants the temple to be rebuilt so that the Ark can remain there permanently. That day, Saint Michael gave Pope Peter a ring that controls the Ark's power. You know that Solomon's Temple is being reconstructed now and should be completed in three years. But you may not know that the Basilica of the Ark was built to hold the Ark until the temple could be rededicated to God."

"That's the last piece of the puzzle!" cries Matt. "I can't believe you didn't tell us this sooner! We need to get that sacred ring from Pope Peter, and we need to bring the Ark of the Covenant to Tunguska! Let's get moving! There isn't much time before the missiles hit the asteroid!"

Banging on the intercom button, they shout at the Swiss Guardsman to open the vault door, and then rush to Pope Peter's quarters. But it's now almost ten p.m. and Pope Peter is getting ready to retire for the evening. Directed to wait in an adjacent room, they pace the floor while the pope makes himself ready to meet with them.

"Good evening, everyone. I was told that you need to see me, and that it is quite urgent."

Matt kneels to kiss the pope's ring. "Yes, Your Holiness. My son has deciphered what the angels have been saying! They've been telling us that they will act only with the 'Commandments of God.' So Peter figured out that we need the Ark of the Covenant with the stone tablets of the Ten

Commandments, and the ring of King Solomon."

"Please explain."

"Your Holiness, the silos will only become active if the Ark is opened in front of them. We know that you received the ring of King Solomon from Saint Michael and that it controls the power of the Ark. Both the Ark and the ring need to be brought to Siberia. Have you looked inside the Ark? We need to expose what is inside it to the silos. We can take the holy items to Siberia ourselves, or perhaps you would like to travel there with us to open the Ark yourself."

"Doctor Matteo, there is nothing in the Ark but the two tablets that Moses brought down from the mountaintop. I would dearly love to go to Siberia, but I am too old to make that trip. And I do not know if the ring will share its power with any of you since none of you have been chosen to be guardians of the Ark. If you know your Biblical history, when unworthy persons were exposed to the Ark, they experienced a horrible fate. God's power is in the Ark and God's power is in the tablets."

"Your Holiness, if my father were not worthy of this task, he would not have been told to go to the Moon and the Sinai, and he would not have been miraculously cured. He would not have been chosen to do those things if he were not also worthy of the honor of guarding the Ark. Time is running out. If the missiles don't stop the asteroid, we will have only a short period of time to get the Ark to Russia to activate the structures the archangels left for our use. Any delay in getting there will cause our mission to fail. Your Holiness, we need the Ark, and we need the ring. Please."

Pope Peter stares thoughtfully at the Matteos. Then he smiles and excuses himself from the room. Within minutes he returns carrying a small, jeweled box.

Addressing Matt, he says, "Doctor, this ring was given to me by Saint Michael when the Ark of the Covenant was brought to Jerusalem by the archangels. He told me that it would bring forth the Commandments of God, which is something I have not understood until this very moment. It is obvious to me now that he was referring to these specific events. Please guard this ring, for it will control the power of the Ark."

After accepting the box, Matt opens it to reveal a large, gold ring emblazoned with a Star of David surrounded by the names of all the archangels. It glows as he admires it, so he removes it from the box and places it on his right hand.

Initially, the ring is too large for Matt's finger, but as those present watch in wonder, it gradually shrinks in size until it fits him perfectly. But a few minutes after putting it on, he makes an announcement.

"Um, I feel strange. There's a warm feeling traveling up my arm and all over my…" Matt stops speaking when the warmth consumes him. His legs become limp and he begins to fall but Peter grabs him and lowers him into a resting position on the floor. Matt feels as if he's lying on a cloud. He is in a state of peace so intense that he does not want it to end.

Conscious but not able to will his body to move, he remains on the floor until his mind tells him that he is not on a cloud, but on a cold, marble floor. Within a minute of that understanding, he is able to move again and slowly raises himself into a sitting position.

Somewhat embarrassed, he looks down at the ring and tries to remove it. But try as he might, it won't budge. He continues to struggle and tug at it until Pope Peter reaches out and grasps his hands.

"Raphael, stop. You will not be able to remove the ring until its job is done. You are worthy; you have been chosen. Go, and let God's will be done."

Matt looks at Pope Peter, and at his wife and son. "That was another wonderful gift from God! It was amazing! I don't understand why I've been chosen again but if God wants this done, we have to get moving, *now*. If the missiles fail, we'll have less than six hours to stop the asteroid, and we don't even know how we're going to get there yet! Peter, call Ralston in Siberia. Let him know that we solved the riddle!"

Eager to assist in any way he can, Pope Peter calls his secretary into the room and asks him to help the Matteos find a way to get to Siberia as quickly as possible. He also issues instructions to his ever-present Swiss Guard to retrieve the large container that was used to transport the Ark from Jerusalem to Rome.

With snow crippling half of Italy and Europe, winter is continuing to cement its grip on the Earth. Rome has been shut down, and all air travel has been grounded.

The Matteos are so close, and yet so far.

CHAPTER FIFTY-ONE

"Ralston here. Go ahead, Peter."

"Major, we solved the riddle, and it involves the Ark of the Covenant! We need to bring the Ark to the silos, but there is a problem. All air traffic in Rome is grounded. Officials at the Vatican are trying to make arrangements for us to leave, but is there anything you can do?"

"Let me call the embassy in Rome."

"Okay, let me know if you can do anything."

"Ten-four. I'll call you back as soon as I can."

Major Ralston hangs up with Peter and immediately contacts his liaison at the U.S. Embassy.

One hour later, the Matteos are still in the room outside of Pope Peter's office, waiting nervously for someone to let them know how they will be getting to Tunguska. They have spent their time praying for assistance, so when Francesco Scarpone enters the room, they know he will have good news.

"My friends, we have made arrangements for you to take the train to *Aeroporto Internazionale di Napoli,* the airport of Naples. There is no storm south of here, so you should arrive in *Napoli* within three hours. Major Ralston says your flight to Russia will need to take a southern route because of bad weather, so he has made arrangements for you to fly from Napoli to Ankara, Turkey. From there, the Turkish government has cleared you to fly to New Delhi on a military transport plane. From New Delhi, you will take a commercial flight to Krasnoyarsk. Your total travel time is estimated to be eighteen hours."

With a knowing smile, Matt shakes Francesco's hand. "Once again, thank you for everything you've done, Francesco." Turning to his fellow travelers, he adds, "So, if it's going to take us eighteen hours just to get to Krasnoyarsk, we'll have only four hours to get the Ark to Tunguska."

Always the doubting Thomas, Peter exclaims, "What happens if there are more weather delays?"

"Say a prayer that we have good weather," says his mother.

Turning back to Francesco, Matt asks, "When do we leave?"

"The *Carabinieri* have set up an escort for you and the Ark to *Stazione Termini*, the main railway station in Roma. It is about 13 kilometers, or 8 miles, from here. The train for Napoli leaves in one hour. *Buona fortuna! Che Dio benedica a tutti voi!* Good luck! And may God bless you on your journey!"

Peter calls Major Ralston again as the family makes their way to the vehicles that are waiting for them in Saint Peter's Square.

"Major, we're on our way to catch a train to Naples."

"Good! An Air Force transport plane is waiting for you there. The Turkish government will take over in Ankara, and the Indian government will handle the final leg to Siberia. There's a weather front heading to Krasnoyarsk, but we'll worry about that later. Arrangements have been made for both ground and air transportation, so you'll get to Tunguska one way or another. A worst-case scenario would add an additional two hours to your travel time, but that will still give you about an hour or so to set up. Godspeed to you all."

Peter briefly wonders whether he should reveal anything to his parents about the news of potential weather delay but he quickly decides against it and pulls up his collar against the blowing snow.

While the family climbs into the waiting SUV, five other vehicles are arranged in defensive positions around the truck that is carrying the Ark of the Covenant. When everything is ready, the convoy squeals out of Saint Peter's Square toward Termini Station.

Cold weather and food shortages are continuing to take their toll on the world's populace. Across the United States, the National Guard has been deployed to quell the continuing riots and general unrest. Similar emergency actions have been taken across the European Union, with military personnel and armored vehicles assigned to many cities. Even in the Far East, riots are occurring in Beijing, Tokyo, and Seoul.

Across the globe, those who are able are rushing south to warmer areas, and the continuous stream of new arrivals is placing a tremendous strain on the infrastructures of warmer cities. In the United States, droves of winter-weary families are heading south to Texas and southern Florida, clogging their roadways and filling their hotels and motels to the brink.

But churches and other houses of worship are delighted that they have to keep their doors open twenty-four hours a day. They are also experiencing a steady influx of people but they are grateful for the crowds who are praying for divine intervention.

With Prometheus lumbering ever closer, amateur astronomers worldwide are using social media to contradict their governments' official positions. They are defying orders to stop spreading their so-called lies about the looming disaster-in-the-making. Contrary to what citizens around the globe have been told, these observers are certain that Prometheus *will* hit the Earth but the people in power are doing everything they can to clamp down on the truth. All around the globe, websites, blogs, YouTube videos, Facebook, email and Twitter accounts are being shut down. Some world leaders are even placing citizens in jail for spreading what they describe as "absolute falsehoods."

When they are about fifteen minutes outside of Naples, a train conductor approaches the Matteos with disturbing news.

"The engineer has informed me that all transit workers at Napoli Centrale, the main train station in Napoli, are on a sympathy strike with the garbage collectors. Army personnel have been sent to assist you, but you will not be allowed to leave the train once it reaches the station."

Matt glances at his watch. There are only fifteen and a half hours until the missiles rendezvous with Prometheus, and if they fail, only twenty-one and a half hours until the asteroid impacts the Earth. Lowering his head, he takes hold of Jennifer's hand and the two of them pray together fervently.

CHAPTER FIFTY-TWO

The train station is in chaos. The Matteos have been forced to wait while the striking workers block all attempts by the train's personnel to unload their cargo or let their passengers disembark. Suddenly, the train car they're in begins to rock violently.

"What's going on?"

"I think they're trying to overturn the train!"

Just as suddenly as it started, the violent shaking stops. Calm engulfs the train, and a deep voice calls out, "You can go on your way now."

Alone in their passenger car, the Matteo family and Sergeant Gonzalez quickly leave the train. Once they are on the station platform, they sigh in relief at the Italian military personnel who are unloading their precious cargo from the baggage car.

"Hey, look!" calls Peter, who is pointing toward the crowd. The others turn to see an astonishing sight—the crowd of strikers has parted like the Red Sea, and an illuminated path is winding through them toward the exit. Shouting to the others, Matt motions for them to follow as he leads the way.

With the crate holding the Ark right behind them, God's agents follow the path toward a freight elevator that will bring them up to street level. Hanging back while the others enter the elevator, Peter steals a glance over his shoulder and sees a comforting sight: the Archangel Michael, with sword extended, is standing above the train in all his glory while the sea of people all around him is on their knees.

When they exit the elevator onto the upper level of Napoli Centrale, they are delighted to see that the illuminated path is once again lighting their way. The presence of the Ark compels the throngs of train travelers in the lobby to kneel as the holy object passes them by, and gives comfort to the missionaries. The path leads them to a convoy of vehicles that has been waiting to take them to the airport that serves the city of Naples.

"Thank God we have divine guidance," says Peter as he looks at his watch, "but time is still running out. The missile should hit the asteroid in fourteen hours, so we only have twenty hours to complete a 900-mile trip to Turkey, a 2,000-mile trip to India, and another 2,000-mile trip to Siberia. And even after all that, we still have to get to the dig."

"Peter, you sound like the Israelites who were lost in the desert for forty years! Faith, Peter, faith."

The convoy speeds off for the airport. Thankfully, there is no snow in Naples, but it is only 0°C (32°F).

In Washington, D.C., it is six o'clock on the evening of October 12. In thirteen hours, the two still-functioning missiles are due to hit the asteroid Prometheus. If they fail like the first one, the asteroid is projected to hit the Earth at approximately 1:15 on the afternoon of the thirteenth of October.

A majority of U.S. Congress and Senate members and their families have already left D.C. for the protected bunkers and deep underground shelters. But President Bush is still sitting in the Oval Office. Apart from her chief of staff and a few loyal assistants, all other federal workers have left the White House.

The National Guard is maintaining a heavy presence in the city. They are patrolling all the intersections between the White House and the Capitol, even though they are aware that the city's buildings are now mostly empty. Rioting in the area has stopped, but it is because of the threat from the sky and the heavily-falling snow, not the military.

There are now ten inches of snow on the ground in D.C., and snow drifts exceed two feet in height. The blizzard that is pummeling the area extends through Baltimore and Philadelphia and is forecast to cripple New York City within twenty-four hours.

That is, if Prometheus doesn't do it first.

Since there is no one left in the White House to prescreen calls, President Bush is now answering her own phone.

"Hello? This is the president."

"Uh…Madame President?"

"Yes, Major Ralston, it's me."

"Okay…Well, ma'am, the Matteos are on an Air Force plane heading to Ankara. They should land there within two hours, and the Turkish military is waiting to fly them and the Ark to New Delhi, a four-hour trip. Another four hours will get them to Krasnoyarsk, and then it's one more hour to Tunguska. Taking into account the transfer times between flights and assuming no bad weather, they should be here at the dig within eleven hours. Ma'am, time is running out. Any hiccups in the schedule…well…"

"Yes, I know, Major. Keep me posted on all developments, and call me at any time. I'm not leaving Washington." After a slight pause, the president adds, "Major, in case I don't get the chance, I want to thank you and the people at NASA for your vigilance and dedication through all of this. And please extend my thanks to the Matteos when you see them."

"Thank you, I will, Madame President. I know we will prevail."

At the end of the conversation, Major Ralston turns off his satellite phone and looks over at Doctor Kirk. "I *hope* we will prevail."

The expression on Doctor Kirk's face is not encouraging.

"What is it, Doctor?"

"I received an updated weather report a few minutes ago. A major storm is heading this way and it should hit us about the same time the Matteos reach Krasnoyarsk. Flights out of Krasnoyarsk will probably be grounded until the storm passes and the runways are cleared."

"Then it's a good thing I arranged for two Sno-Cats to be waiting at the airport as backup! If necessary, they will arrive by land instead of air."

"That was very wise, Major, but Krasnoyarsk is 644 kilometers, or 400 miles, away. Unless those Sno-Cats can travel at 160 kilometers per hour, which is equivalent to your 100 miles per hour, we are doomed."

Lucifer, the pride-filled angel, now sits on a cold rock on a barren world deep in the outer reaches of the universe. It is dark there, and silent. There are no sounds, no wailing or grinding of teeth. There are no minions there, either—no followers. Lucifer is alone, banished from his former existence. Deprived of any connection with the weak and no longer energized by the power of sin, he grows more and more feeble and pathetic.

But even though Lucifer's throne sits empty in Gehenna, the wailing continues and the putrid smell of rotting souls maintains its depressing presence in the forlorn hallways of hell.

One evil soul in hell is about to make the most the empty throne. Aware of Satan's absence, the soul of Victoria Bokor walks steadily toward Lucifer's throne room. When she arrives at the heavy doors, she confidently pushes them open, and with single-minded purpose, marches to the front of the darkened room, not stopping until she climbs the steps in front of the throne. At the top, she glances around, smiles smugly, and lowers herself onto the throne of hell.

A few minutes after she is seated, she begins to transform. Her former human-like form becomes more like that of a dragon, with black, scaly skin and large, tattered wings. When the transformation is complete, she bellows loudly in approval— an alternative version of the prince of hell.

Gehenna may have a new tormentor for now, but one day, a battle will most assuredly ensue for ultimate control of the realm of darkness.

CHAPTER FIFTY-THREE

At 7:38 p.m. EST, about 18.5 hours until total destruction if the ANUBIS mission fails, good news finally seems to be on the side of the Matteos. Their flights are on time and there are no weather delays.

When their Air Force military plane lands in Ankara, it is immediately diverted to a remote end of the airstrip, adjacent to the Turkish military aircraft that is standing by to fly them to New Delhi.

As they wait on the tarmac to board the next plane, a cold wind blows across the airfield. Jennifer shudders and puts an arm around her husband. "That wind went straight through my soul. Are we going to make it, Matt?"

Matt tries to relieve his wife's anxiety by giving her a kiss on the cheek. "Everything will be okay, Hon. Everything will be okay."

In just a few more minutes, the Ark is stowed securely and the travelers are buckled in and ready to take off on the second leg of their trip. While the pilots wait for permission to depart, Peter once again checks his watch.

"Dad, we now have less than eighteen hours to get to the dig. I figure that with a good tail wind, we'll get to Krasnoyarsk in about eight hours, and then it will take ten more hours to get to Tunguska. If the weather holds, we'll be okay, but what happens if it doesn't?"

"Son! Be vigilant in your faith! Remember, we will prevail!"

Turning away from Peter, Matt leans over to whisper into Jennifer's ear. "It's gonna be close."

As they bid farewell to Turkey, Jennifer squeezes her husband's hand in unspoken support.

Joe Toteda has repositioned the large telescope on the patio outside of the Moon's visitor's center. When the Garden of Eden was still open to the public, visitors were able to use that telescope to get a closer look at the planets and the other heavenly bodies. Now, Joe is using it to keep track of Prometheus, hoping to get a firsthand view of the missiles' impact.

The missiles named Michael and Raphael are now passing the Moon on their journey toward the asteroid. In five hours, the leftover chunk of Prometheus will be about 300,000 miles away from the Earth, but only 120,000 miles away from the Moon. For the people of the Moon, they will only be tiny specks in a sea of stars, but they may be able to follow their progress as they attempt to stop the leviathan.

On an abandoned oil rig in the cold North Atlantic Ocean, a pirate TV station is preparing to override worldwide programming in a bid to broadcast a critical message around the world. The rogue program begins with a sign that says *"Government should be afraid of the People. People should not be afraid of the Government."*

The sign is replaced by an announcer whose face is disguised by a Guy Fawkes mask, a well-known symbol of protest. The mask's over-sized smile, red cheeks, thin mustache, and pointed beard came to represent anti-government dissension after it was featured in the movie *V for Vendetta* in the early 2000s.

"People of the world, be forewarned. Your governments are lying to you. We are now at the End of Days. The Prometheus asteroid will hit the Earth. It will not miss. The feeble attempt to destroy the asteroid in flight will fail. Prepare yourselves, just as your leaders are doing for themselves and their families. They are going into bunkers and caves while the rest of us will perish, unprotected and…"

Unaware that Special Forces units from the European Union are quietly boarding the oil rig, the commentator continues his rant from the makeshift studio.

"…and again I say to you: do not be fooled by the power-hungry tyrants who are…"

Startled by a sudden commotion outside the door, the broadcaster does not stop his tirade. He attempts to finish his comments while Special Forces commandos knock down the door and barge into the studio.

"They are here now! I must…"

Worldwide, TV screens now show nothing but static. It is T-minus eleven hours.

CHAPTER FIFTY-FOUR

Surprisingly, the temperature in New Delhi is bearable compared to the double-digit, subzero temperatures that await God's messengers on the Siberian tundra. The height of the Himalayas has so far prevented the extreme northern weather from moving further south but colder weather won't be an issue if the two remaining nuclear missiles aren't able to destroy Prometheus or change its trajectory. As the asteroid tumbles around in space on its silent approach toward Earth, the planet is still in danger.

The Turkish aircraft lands in New Delhi, India at eleven p.m. Eastern Standard Time on October 12. With faces pressed to the windows, the travelers watch as their aircraft is guided close to the commercial jet that has been ordered by the Indian government to wait for them.

Once they're off the Turkish airliner, Jennifer walks directly to the Indian plane to get settled for the next trip. But Peter and his dad are a little too anxious to be confined in their seats yet again. They take advantage of the break in flights to walk around outside and to keep an eye on the crate containing the Ark of the Covenant as it's transferred from one aircraft to the other.

"Peter, we're one-third of the way there now. I believe…no, I *know*… that we will succeed in our mission."

"I pray that you're right, Dad. I hope all of our time and effort is worth it."

Matt puts an arm around his son as they walk toward the Indian plane's airstairs. "Give Ralston a call before we board. Let him know where we are and tell him that we should be in Krasnoyarsk in about eight hours."

The weather in Siberia doesn't look good. Snow is now falling, and it is forecast to continue for several hours. Preparations are being made to try to keep the Krasnoyarsk airport open for the critical arrival from New Delhi, but only time will tell if that will be possible.

At 4:30 a.m., Major Ralston is awakened at the archeological site by an incoming call.

"Major? It's Peter Matteo."

Struggling to rouse himself, the Major responds sluggishly, "Yes, Pete. Where are you?"

"We're just boarding the plane to leave India. How's the weather in Russia?"

Stifling a yawn, Ralston replies, "Colder than a witch's…heart. And it's snowing in Krasnoyarsk, but I don't think it's snowing here yet."

"Will we be able to land?"

"The Russian military has been ordered to keep a runway open so you can land, but if you aren't able to fly out of there, I arranged for ground transportation to get you here."

"Okay, great. Any new activity at the silos?"

"No, everything is quiet. But they're still generating heat so the area surrounding the dig is comfortable—about seventy degrees."

"Okay. I'm sorry I woke you. I know the time difference is five hours. See you soon…I hope."

"I'm praying for success, Peter—for you and your parents."

When the call ends, Major Ralston mumbles, "And also for the rest of mankind."

Peter relay's the major's comments to Matt and then father and son enter the airplane. With the Ark safely stowed one more time, the cargo doors are slammed shut, and the plane taxis for takeoff.

The flight to Russia will take them over the mighty Himalayan Mountains. All of their flights have been uneventful so far, but that may not last long. As soon as they cross over the high mountains, the wrath of winter will hit them smack in the face.

In the city of Krasnoyarsk, the snow is relentless. Russian military personnel are scurrying around the airport, doing everything they can to keep the runway clear of ice and snow. They are also installing high-intensity lights along the airstrip to ensure that it is sufficiently illuminated for a safe landing.

CHAPTER FIFTY-FIVE

The Indian 797 aircraft is now twenty minutes out of Krasnoyarsk. Until this part of the trip it has been flying high above the raging snowstorm but now it is beginning to descend directly into the maelstrom. The previously calm and level flight is swiftly becoming a roller coaster ride.

"Krasnoyarsk Control, this is flight 10399 on approach. What is your status?"

"Flight 10399, the runway is clear. Extra lights and emergency vehicles have been deployed."

"Ten-four, Krasnoyarsk. Visibility here is zero."

"Flight 10399, follow our beacon and begin autoland sequence."

Boeing 797s are equipped with an autoland system that works without pilot intervention. The software places the aircraft's computer in control of landing the plane in adverse weather conditions.

"Ten-four. Autoland is active."

As the Boeing 797 descends slowly through the clouds, its passengers are holding on for dear life and its precious cargo in the luggage bay is being tossed relentlessly against it restraining straps. When the aircraft drops to less than 3,000 feet, it breaks out of the clouds and enters the blizzard's whiteout conditions.

When Peter can't see anything out of his window, he mumbles under his breath, "Uh, oh…how are the pilots going to land this thing if they can't see five feet out of their window?"

On their final approach to Krasnoyarsk, the Matteos hold each other's hands and pray as the computer guides the plane. At 1,000 feet, the runway lights become visible and the plane continues its way down. When it finally reaches the ground, it slams onto the runway, bounces up, and slams down again.

The runway has only an inch or so of snow on it, but it is covered in almost invisible "black ice." When the 797 hits the ice, it slides sideways, forcing the pilot to reverse the engines in an attempt to stop the uncontrolled motion. But when he tries to assist the engines by engaging the brakes, his efforts cause the large aircraft to skid into the deep snow alongside the runway.

The snow does nothing to stop the plane, however. When the landing gear hits the white fluff, the wheels buckle under the plane's belly and essentially transform it into a huge toboggan. Sideways motion unchecked, the plane continues to slide on a direct path toward the airport's terminal building. With the large building looming in front of them, the passengers who aren't crouching in their seats in fear are watching out of their windows in horror. Passengers and crew brace for impact, while people in the terminal scatter in the face of the oncoming jet.

Heads bowed, the passengers prepare for the worst. Incredibly, though, the sliding motion soon stops, leaving nothing but quiet sobs in the large cabin. With its wingtips only fifteen feet from the building, the plane sways back and forth, then steadies itself and settles deep into the snow. In the quiet, Matt glances out of his window and rejoices to see the Archangel Gabriel kneeling between the plane and the Krasnoyarsk airport terminal building.

While the plane's evacuation slides automatically inflate and unfurl outside of the aircraft, the pilot and crew members rush into the cabin to check on their passengers. Relieved that no one is hurt, they join the others who are looking out of the windows at Gabriel, who is now standing next to the plane. With everyone watching, Gabriel takes hold of the fuselage and lifts it clear of the snow. The pilot is puzzled by Gabriel's action until he understands the angel's intention. Rushing into the cockpit, he releases the lock on the cargo doors to allow the ground crew to unload the Ark of the Covenant from the area of the plane that the angel has freed from the snow.

Due to the importance of their mission, the Matteos are allowed to slide down the evacuation chutes first. They wait alongside the plane until they are satisfied that the Ark has been safely unloaded, then they proceed into the relatively empty terminal, thankful and relieved that yet another crisis has been averted.

But inevitably, Peter's impatience once again gets the better of him.

"Dad, we need to get going! We have only eight hours before

Prometheus could hit the Earth, and it looks like flying to Tunguska is out of the question!"

"Doctor Matteo?"

Hearing an unfamiliar voice, Matt turns around to face a colonel from the Russian Army.

"I'm Doctor Matteo," responds Matt.

"Sir, we have two Sno-Cats waiting outside for you and your family. Under these conditions, if you leave now, it will take about eight and a half hours to get to Tunguska."

"Oh, Dad, we won't make it! If the missiles fail we won't have enough time!"

"Son, there's no time for discussion. Let's go. Show us the way, Colonel."

The family and their precious cargo proceed quickly to the Sno-Cats—large, turbocharged, all-terrain vehicles powered by natural gas and equipped with tank treads. The Sno-Cats are Major Ralston's ground transportation backup plan.

The group climbs into the lead vehicle while the Ark is loaded into the second one and tied down securely.

When the driver closes the door, Jennifer leans over and whispers into Matt's ear. "Now I'm really getting worried."

"Keep the faith, Hon," says Matt with conviction. "But it's gonna be close."

The top speed of a Sno-Cat is sixty miles per hour and under normal conditions, each vehicle has a range of three hundred miles. But that is not far enough to get them to the remote Tunguska dig without refueling. In another act of prescience, Major Ralston asked the Russian government to modify these two behemoths so they could carry enough fuel for the entire trip. Agreeing to his request, the government ordered two auxiliary fuel tanks to be welded onto each of their roofs.

Light snow is now falling in Krasnoyarsk, but in this area of the world conditions can worsen at any time and they cannot afford a setback. Matt fastens his seatbelt and closes his eyes in silent prayer. *Lord, if You really want to save Your planet, we need Your help now, more than ever. We may not make it without You.*

As the passengers begin their journey toward Tunguska, they are unaware that yet another problem has been narrowly averted. A major snowstorm that was affecting the dig site has passed over it, and is now heading away from the area. But even with that assistance, time is still running out.

CHAPTER FIFTY-SIX

A natural early bird, Major Ralston has been awake for several hours when he receives his first call of the day at a little after eight o'clock on the morning of October 13.

"We're leaving Krasnoyarsk now," says Peter. "All flights are grounded, so we're traveling by Sno-Cat, thanks to your foresight."

"Peter, you know you still have over four hundred miles to cover in only eight hours. If the weather and traveling conditions are good, you'll be able to make it here in time. But if the weather turns bad…"

"Yeah, I know. I'll keep you posted on our progress. But if conditions are right, would it be possible for us to be picked up by plane along the way?"

"Maybe; the storm has already blown through here. Keep your phone turned on. I'll keep track of you through your GPS coordinates, and if it seems possible, I'll try to arrange an emergency pickup. The Russians have some Ospreys at the airport in Krasnoyarsk."

With a thirteen-hour time difference between Tunguska and the Oval Office, it is still the evening of October 12 in Washington, D.C., and the missiles are due to impact Prometheus in two hours. President Bush is pacing the media room and following progress reports on a large, split-screen monitor. One side of the monitor is broadcasting the actions at NASA Mission Control in Houston, and the other is monitoring Stefan Bell's activities at the Sagan Observatory.

Focusing on Doctor Bell, the president watches as he guides the building's large telescope to the area of the sky where the explosion is expected to occur. When the time comes, images from the telescope will be transmitted directly to the president's monitor. The leaders of many other countries across the globe are also monitoring the missiles' progress through the nearest observatories.

Outside the city of Krasnoyarsk, the weather has deteriorated rapidly and the Sno-Cats and their precious cargo are making slow progress. What was previously light snow is now a blizzard with near-whiteout conditions.

In this area of the world, paved asphalt roads are few and far between. That's why the group is traveling on a road of hard-packed gravel. The rough road is not affecting the travelers or their cargo, though, because of the two feet of newly-fallen snow that is cushioning their ride. Their real problem, like a giant gorilla in the room, is time. The minutes are ticking away like an endless drip from a faulty faucet.

As the Sno-Cats continue to traverse the Russian countryside, the blizzard finally begins to lessen. When they are two hundred ninety kilometers, or one hundred eighty miles, northwest of Krasnoyarsk, they enter the city of Lesosibirsk and it is no longer snowing.

Because it seems that the weather is improving, the travelers are hopeful that they can make up some of their lost time, even though they know the roads are still treacherous because of the extreme cold and heavy snow cover. The air temperature where they are now traveling is a manageable -20°C (-4°F), but as they continue northward, they know that the temperature will drop much further and conditions may even worsen.

The group tries their best to fight off a growing sense of discouragement by chatting about mundane matters. This distraction works well until their attention is unexpectedly diverted by an abrupt change in their vehicle's momentum and speed.

Grabbing onto whatever they can inside the vehicle's interior, they brace themselves as their Sno-Cat suddenly turns off the gravel road and veers down a rough bank. Initial attacks of panic turn into wonder and surprise when they realize that the two vehicles are now traveling down a frozen river and that this new route is actually providing them with an unusual, but smoother, ride north.

Amid sighs of relief, Matt and Jenn marvel at the skill and ingenuity of the Russian drivers and settle back for the remainder of the trip. But Peter remains glued to his wristwatch.

"The missiles are due to hit Prometheus in twenty minutes!" he groans. "I asked Major Ralston to give us updates, but I haven't heard from him in a while. Maybe he hasn't called because things are going well and we won't need to activate the silos after all."

"I hope you're right, son," mumbles Matt. "But my gut is telling me otherwise."

At NASA headquarters in Houston, Senior Engineer Brooke Jensen is monitoring the progress of the two remaining missiles. She is keeping a close watch over their telemetry signals, which are being broadcast to Earth on a four-second delay. She also has a direct-link hookup with Stefan Bell at the Sagan Observatory, who will broadcast views of the event through the monitors connected to his telescope.

"All right," says Doctor Bell. "Raphael should impact first, and then within seconds, Michael will hit. 10, 9, 8, 7, 6, 5, 4, 3, 2, 1."

The four-second delay in communication signals is agonizing and seems to last for an eternity. Brooke and the entire team in Houston, along with Stefan Bell, President Bush, and other world leaders and scientists in observatories around the world, wait and hope.

Raphael misses Prometheus. The missile passes the asteroid and continues out into space on an endless journey. However, Michael makes a direct hit. Telemetry from Michael ceases when a brilliant flash of light from the nuclear warhead's impact flashes from the surface of the wayward asteroid.

When the blast's image fills the large screen at Mission Control, jubilant roars of victory pass through NASA headquarters and similar facilities across the globe.

"We did it! We hit Prometheus!" trajectory technicians shout in jubilation.

Lost in thought, Brooke ignores the excitement around her as she studies the images sent from the observatory and waits for further data in order to confirm the asteroid's destruction. Minutes tick by while the computer-controlled telescope continues to track its target. Then, as debris from the blast clears the screen, the worst possible scenario unfolds.

Eyes widened in distress, Brooke jumps out of her chair and shouts, "We failed! Prometheus is still intact! Check trajectory! Tell me if it was deflected toward us, and get Bell on the phone, *now*!"

"Madame President, this is Stefan Bell. We hit Prometheus, but we did not stop it or destroy it. It has not altered course. The super computer at NOAA is plotting its current course and projects that it will enter our atmosphere in six hours and twenty minutes somewhere over mainland China. If it does not burn up when it hits the atmosphere, it will most likely continue on a southwest track and land in the Atlantic Ocean near the eastern coast of the United States. That would produce a tsunami that would destroy everything along the North American coast from the Chesapeake Bay to Key Largo. The tsunami would also travel eastward across the ocean and affect coastal communities in Europe and Africa. There may also be extensive damage in the Southern Hemisphere, and the debris that will be thrust high into the atmosphere will plunge this world into darkness. God help us all!"

Numb and in shock, President Bush hangs up the phone, and for a few precious minutes, sits alone in her office. She knows that leaders across the world are receiving the same dire news but that is not comforting. With a deep sigh, she summons the loyal staff members who chose to remain with her at the White House.

On the way to the town of Lesosibirsk, Peter has finally received the call he was waiting for. He listens attentively to the speaker, but does not respond to the awful facts he is hearing. When he ends the call, he lowers his head into his hands and in a quiet voice, relays the grim news to his parents.

"Mom, Dad, the missiles failed. It's all on us now. There are only six hours left, and we're not even near Lesosibirsk yet." Voice quaking, he asks, "What are we going to do?"

Jennifer's hand flies to her mouth in panic, but Matt remains calm. "Peter, continue to let Major Ralston know where we are. If the weather improves, he can still dispatch those Ospreys to pick us up."

With a tap on the driver's shoulder, Matt describes the urgent situation to him but the driver replies, "We are at full throttle now. We will do our best."

Still traveling on the frozen river, the Sno-Cats pass upstream of Lesosibirsk a short time later, but they still have almost 483 kilometers, or three hundred miles, to go.

The asteroid is now projected to hit the Earth at about one thirty a.m. the next day, October 13. With less than five hours for the world as we know it to remain in existence, President Bush resolves to speak to the nation.

At a little after eight p.m. EST preparations for the speech are completed and the president is scheduled to go on the air in about fifteen minutes.

Except for King George of England and Pope Peter in Rome, other world leaders are choosing to remain silent on the situation.

CHAPTER FIFTY-SEVEN

"**M**y fellow Americans, I come to you this evening with a heavy heart. I am about to give you some information that will frighten you greatly. However, it's important to remember that as Americans, we have always faced any obstacle with strength and fortitude, courage and resilience. That is why I know we will overcome all difficulties that may arise during the coming months.

"Fellow citizens, there is no way to sugarcoat this news. As a result of mankind's greed and interference in God's universe, a large asteroid is on a path to hit the Earth within five hours. The deep-mining operation on the asteroid Prometheus generated a quake that caused the asteroid to split apart, and a large piece of it was sent directly into our path.

"The best minds in the country came together and devised a plan to either destroy the asteroid or deflect it away from our planet, but it failed. All is not lost, however. As we speak, a group of American patriots is on a mission bestowed upon them by God Himself to prevent the asteroid from colliding with Earth. I am not at liberty to divulge the details of that mission, but I am requesting your prayers for its success.

"At this time, I am prepared to give you important instructions that you need to follow immediately after this broadcast. Do not panic. If you follow all instructions given by me and your federal and local disaster agencies, we will get through this crisis.

"If the asteroid does not burn up as it travels through our atmosphere, it is projected to enter the Atlantic Ocean off the eastern coast of the United States. All residents of low-lying areas on the East Coast, from the

Chesapeake Bay in Maryland to Key Largo in Florida, need to begin immediate evacuations to inland locations in advance of a tsunami that will likely result from that impact. The Department of Homeland Security and local disaster preparedness agencies are gearing up to deal with any and all of the aftereffects of this event.

"My fellow Americans, I firmly believe that God would not have given us one thousand years of peace only to abandon us in our hour of need. Let us all pray unceasingly for our fellow Americans, and for the people of the entire world. God bless us all."

Similar words from King George are simultaneously filling the airways of the United Kingdom, and states of emergency are being ordered for the coastlines of the United States, Europe, and Africa.

In deference to the leaders of the United States and the United Kingdom, Pope Peter waits until their speeches are concluded before he goes on the air himself.

"Dear people of the world, as children of God, I encourage you this morning to return to faith in your Heavenly Father and in His only Son, Our Lord Jesus Christ.

"God has given all of us, His children, the gift of free will, but we reward His generosity by rejecting Him through our woeful lack of faith in His Heavenly guidance and power. For that reason He will not intervene in events that we ourselves have created. It is therefore up to mankind to undo what mankind has done. God is all-merciful, however, and He has left to us His guardians and the tools that are necessary to make amends. But first, we must discover the way to use those tools. I urge you to pray for the three individuals who have been chosen by God to summon the power of the archangels, the guardians who have been tasked by Him to protect His children. Please join together in praying that God's chosen three will understand how to direct the guardians to employ their tools in our defense before our time runs out.

"My dear people, prayer is essential, for with prayer, anything can be accomplished. Please join in solidarity with me and other spiritual leaders around the world to pray for the security of our planet. Let us all take a moment to reflect deeply on the actions of humankind that have caused these difficulties."

Pope Peter bows his head and closes his eyes. Several minutes later, he says, *"Let us pray. In the Name of the Father, and of the Son, and of the Holy Spirit. Amen. I believe in God, the Father Almighty, Creator of Heaven and Earth…"*

Following the speeches of the three world leaders, news of the impending events swiftly encircles the globe, and a multitude of prayers are lifted up. Millions of people come together to pray in their homes, in their houses of worship, on their way to higher ground, and deep inside their bunkers.

With millions of people heading inland to escape the ocean's wrath, roads in the soon-to-be affected areas are quickly becoming jammed and traffic is coming to a standstill. For those who can't or won't leave, as well as for those who are not in immediate danger, churches and other spiritual centers worldwide have opened their doors to anyone seeking shelter and prayer.

Strangely, there is minimal panic around the world. Instead, an eerie calm settles over everyone, and a general sense of faith and duty prevails, binding everyone together with a compelling need to provide assistance to one another during the crisis. There is no chaos, and people everywhere are unselfishly helping their fellow men.

This behavior is shocking but extremely gratifying to the millions who chose wisely at the time of the Judgment. It seems that mankind is finally realizing that human beings are not the ones in control of their world. They may be finally acknowledging that God and His Son are the ones in charge, and that man's interference in the planet and in the universe that God created, will no longer be tolerated.

But not everyone has heard about the world leaders' broadcasts. Major Ralston, Sergeant Gonzalez, and the crew at the dig site are off the grid at their remote location in Russia. The Matteos and their two drivers are also out of telecommunication range as they continue to travel toward the three silos.

The Sno-Cats are traveling as fast as they can but time is slipping by. As the seconds count down, Peter is becoming increasingly agitated. Unable to contain himself, he calls out to his father in panic.

"Dad! We won't make it! We have only two more hours to get to the dig, and by my calculation, we're still one hundred fifty miles away! We lost! We failed!"

No sooner has Peter finished his bleak announcement when a powerful voice fills the Sno-Cat from every direction at the same time.

"Peter, My son. Remember what I told My prophet Habakkuk, who was waiting for a response from Me to his complaints. The revelation I provided to him revealed My response. Although its fulfillment was far off, it occurred

247

in the end. My revelations do not lie, and My prophet finally realized this. He ultimately said, 'If it make any delay, wait for it; for it will surely come.' Like Habakkuk, you have little faith."

When the voice stops speaking, a profound silence fills the Sno-Cat until the shrill sound of Peter's ringing cell phone startles everyone. In an attempt to grab the phone quickly, Peter drops it clumsily to the floor, so Matt picks it up and answers it.

"Hello?"

"Hello, Peter? It's Major Ralston."

"Major, it's Matt."

"Oh! Where are you? Time is getting short!"

"Yes, we know. We're on the Yenisei River, about one hundred fifty miles out."

"You're on a river? How did you...? Never mind. The asteroid is getting dangerously close, Matt. I'm going to send an Osprey to pick you up—Ark and all. The weather has mysteriously cleared up so tell your drivers to activate their locator beacons. The Osprey will track their transmissions to find you."

"Will do, Major. See you soon."

"I hope so, Matt."

On the Moon, James, Christine, and Joe watch in horror as Prometheus streaks silently past them. Now 120,000 miles from the Earth, it will soon be visible to the Earth's inhabitants.

While the residents of the Moon fervently pray that the Earth will be spared, the Golden Tree of God in the Garden of Eden provides some measure of comfort for them as it continues to shimmer and sparkle brightly.

CHAPTER FIFTY-EIGHT

J ust before midnight, President Geraldine Bush stands in the Oval Office before a painting of her grandfather, President George W. Bush. Reaching out, she touches the frame lightly and whispers, "Well, Grandpa, I think my crisis is a little greater than yours ever was. Please pray for me. Please pray for us all."

As she concludes her prayer, Chief of Staff Levar Daniels barges into the room.

"Madame President?"

"Levar? I thought I was the only one awake. Why aren't you in the bunker?"

"We just received an update from the Sagan Observatory. They determined that Prometheus was damaged pretty significantly by the missile strike. The blast left a deep crater on the asteroid and caused fissures to scatter across its surface."

"What does that mean, Levar? Are we out of the woods?"

"Not really. The scientists at NOAA re-ran simulations of the asteroid's projected path. Most of the scenarios show that because it was weakened by the missile strike, our atmosphere will probably burn it up more than we thought so it may be somewhat smaller when it hits. But instead of entering the Atlantic Ocean, it will hit land anywhere from west of the Bermuda Triangle to the Gulf of Mexico. Central Florida may be hit the hardest."

"So, you mean that all the people in Southern Florida who are evacuating northward toward Orlando would have been better off if they had stayed where they were?"

"I'm afraid so. The computer is targeting ground zero as the I-4 corridor in Orlando."

"Levar, that will occur about an hour from now!"

"Yes, and you can see Prometheus in the sky right now. It's coming at us from the east."

"Holy cow! Levar, you need to go to the bunker now! Go on, get out of here! Go, be with your family!"

President Bush gives Levar a hug, and pushes him out of the door. Then, she steps outside the Oval Office to search the night sky. It is only twenty degrees outside and she is not wearing an overcoat, but the cold is not her concern.

"Do you hear an airplane approaching?" asks Jennifer.

The crew of the Osprey searches the frozen river near the travelers and locates a clear spot 100 meters, about 328 feet, upriver from them in a large, flat area. When the Sno-Cats arrive there, they pull up as close as they can so the crews can transfer the Ark of the Covenant to the Osprey as quickly as possible.

When they board the aircraft, Peter takes another look at his wristwatch. "Mom, Dad, we only have forty-five minutes to get to the dig and do whatever it is we need to do once we get there. Boy, God is really putting my faith to the test!"

The Osprey takes off and heads north. It is now 1:30 p.m. on October 13, a bright, sunny day on the tundra, even though the temperature is -30°C, or -22°F.

The asteroid will impact the Earth in about fifty minutes, giving the Matteos only ten minutes to get the Ark into place. They know that they need to stop Prometheus far enough out in space to avoid fallout on Earth, so the thirty-minute flight to the dig seems like hours.

When the plane finally circles the excavation site in preparation for landing, the Matteos watch the three structures begin to shine.

President Bush has moved back inside the White House and is sitting alone in the chapel at the far end of the West Wing. She left instructions with the Secret Service members who have remained with her that she should only be disturbed if the Matteos are successful.

The asteroid's trajectory will cause it to enter the Earth's atmosphere somewhere over India and then proceed westward. Levar was led to believe that it would be visible from Washington, however, due to the Earth's curvature, its dramatic entrance will only be visible in the Southern Hemisphere.

The two major observatories that will monitor the event for the scientific community are Mount Stromlo in Australia and the Palermo Astronomical Observatory in Sicily. The moment Prometheus makes its debut the world will see it broadcast live by video crews around the world who are ready to film it as it streaks through the skies.

Within twelve minutes, Prometheus will enter the Earth's atmosphere.

At the dig, the crate containing the Ark is unloaded from the Osprey and gently placed on the tundra. The Ark's dimensions are approximately 131 cm long, 79 cm wide, and 79 cm high (52"×31"×31") and it is covered completely in gold. Two large angels face each other on the top, and more angels and seraphim are carved into the sides. Four golden loops are affixed to each corner where long wooden poles were inserted to carry the Ark during Biblical times. The original poles were not found with the Ark, so Major Ralston has provided two long metal pipes as replacements.

After the Ark is removed from the crate, the major inserts the pipes into the loops so that he, Peter, Matt, and Sergeant Gonzalez can carry the Ark toward the silos of the angels. Grunting and straining, Peter and Matt have trouble lifting their end while the sergeant and the major, who are more physically fit, seem to have no problem with the holy object's weight.

When they reach the silos, they position the Ark so that it is facing the three structures and nearest to the one dedicated to Saint Michael. The silos beam brightly as they remove the pipes from the golden loops.

Wearing the ring that Saint Michael gave to Pope Peter, Matt takes the lead and steps up to the Ark. Since he is the chosen one, everyone else waits while he gingerly lifts the chest's lid.

The lid of the Ark of the Covenant is connected to the rest of the chest by a thick strap of leather along the rear that acts like a hinge. Two golden chains are also attached to the lid, with one end fastened to the chest's rear panel, and the other connected to the lid's underside. Matt discovers that this design enables the top to be fully tilted back without falling off.

As he pushes the lid back, his jaw drops at the sight of the two stone tablets of the Ten Commandments. While he contemplates this, he notices that a mist has begun to form inside the chest. It appears suddenly, and soon, brightly-colored lights swirl within it as it rises to the top of the Ark, flows over its sides, and drops gently to the tundra.

Moving away from this strange vapor, Matt scurries around the chest and joins the others, who are standing nearby. The mist continues to pour out of the Ark but nothing further occurs.

"Dad, nothing is happening!" cries Pete. "What do we do now?"

"I don't know!" his father shouts worriedly. "The last time we were here we inserted the keys into the keyways, and now we even brought the Ark. I don't know what else to do!"

"Matt, it must be the ring," hollers Jennifer. "Honey, try the ring!"

"Try it how? Point it at something, like the Green Lantern?"

"Solomon used the ring to seal his documents, right? It's embossed with raised images. Look around the Ark to see if there's a place the ring will fit into."

Matt walks up to the rear of the Ark and searches its surface. Among the images of angels, he is surprised to find an indentation in the shape of the Star of David that matches the image on the ring. Reaching out, he places the ring into the spot, but nothing happens.

He is just about to say something when a loud, piercing shriek comes out of the Ark, and blinding lights burst outward toward each of the three silos. The keyways holding Gabriel's chalice, Michael's sword, and Raphael's staff, glow in the bright light, and from within the light appear the three archangels—each of them standing next to the structure named for him.

In the next moment, a plasma-like burst of energy envelopes the silos and rushes skyward with a roar. Everyone present shields their eyes and ears, and around the globe, people everywhere turn to watch the bright column of energy as it streaks skyward.

Unseen by humans, Prometheus is enveloped within this field of energy five hundred miles from the Earth. The power of the Ark causes the asteroid to shudder and explode into thousands upon thousands of small fragments that plunge into the Earth's atmosphere. These meteors range in size from 100 to 1,500 feet in diameter, and they are headed toward the western coast of the United States.

At the Tunguska dig and all around the world, cheers erupt at the spectacular meteor show that is now streaking across the sky. The television crews that are broadcasting live images of the remains of Prometheus quickly post videos on the Internet so they can be viewed by as many people as possible.

"Madame President!" A Secret Service agent interrupts President Bush in the White House chapel. "Prometheus has been destroyed! Please come to the media room! You'll want to see this for yourself!"

President Bush jumps up from her seat and hurries to view a live broadcast from TV crews in India. As soon as she enters the room, an agent hands her a telephone and indicates that the call is from the Chairman of the Joint Chiefs of Staff.

"Are you seeing this?" asks Mrs. Bush excitedly.

"Yes, ma'am. I have bad news, though. It's true that Prometheus was destroyed, but now there are thousands, or rather tens of thousands of smaller space rocks that are heading toward the eastern coast of the United States. Computer tracking indicates that they will strike the surface of the Earth beginning in the ocean near the Bermuda Triangle and then proceed westward into the Gulf of Mexico. Many of them will fall harmlessly into the water, but some of them will most assuredly hit land across the state of Florida, from Melbourne on the east coast to Naples on the west coast."

Seemingly rooted into place, the onlookers at the dig are still standing behind the Ark when the Archangel Michael approaches it and gently lowers its lid. Then, he walks over to Matt and says, *"From the Holy Spirit, from the Almighty Father, and to His Son. So shall it be with you."*

The Archangel Michael holds out his hand toward Matt and waits. At first, Matt looks questioningly at the archangel, but then he removes Solomon's ring and places it into the guardian's hand. Michael nods his head and moves to stand in front of Peter, who automatically holds out his right hand and allows the ring to be placed on his finger.

"You have been chosen to command the Ark," intones Saint Michael. *"As your father was chosen, so shall it be with you, to your son and to his son, until the end of time."*

From around his neck, Michael removes a gold medallion on a gold chain. The medallion is round and about two and a half inches in diameter. On one side is an image of the Star of David and on the other is an image of the Constellation Orion encircled by four bands with the names of the seven archangels in English, Aramaic, Hebrew, and Greek. Michael places the medallion around Peter's neck and then unsheathes his sword and raises it skyward.

Summoned by their angelic leader, the Archangels Gabriel and Raphael station themselves beside Michael. Then, all of them bow their heads to the new Commander of the Ark. An intense flash of light follows and reveals the four remaining archangels—Uriel, Remiel, Sariel, and Raguel descending from the heavens to surround the Ark.

With the Ark of the Covenant thus protected by their fellow archangels, Michael, Raphael, and Gabriel walk to the silos and remove the sword, the staff, and the chalice from their keyways. When they return to the Ark, all seven archangels, along with the Ark, disappear in another flash of light.

Stunned, everyone present enters into a state of shock. They remain that way until they begin to realize that they are very cold, and that it has started to snow. As a group, they scamper into the warmth of the command center, where they gather around Peter. Each of them takes turns examining the medallion but none of them fully comprehend what has just occurred.

While the others try to make sense of what they have seen, Doctor Kirk grabs his coat and walks out of the building to take another look at the structures he has been studying for such a long time. A short time later, he rushes back inside and shouts, "THE SILOS! COME! THEY ARE SINKING!"

The group rushes out of the building and enters the now-freezing dig site just in time to see the three silos sink completely back beneath the surface of the earth. When they are no longer visible, the area's EMF detectors scream out in unison, warning everyone that the silos are once again projecting electromagnetic fields to advise humans that they are now intruding into protected space. At the piercing sound, the team runs back into the command center to don the protective gear that they wore when they first arrived there.

When everyone is once again protected, Jennifer, Matt, Major Ralston, and Sergeant Gonzalez surround Peter, who is still examining the medallion. Looking up at his dad, Peter says, "I'm the one who has been chosen to control the Ark and I'm supposed to pass the responsibility onto my son, but I'm not married and I have no son. I'm not even dating anyone."

"Well, I guess you'll have a son one day."

"There was a girl you were pretty serious about in college," says Jennifer. "Maybe she's the one."

"Courtney O'Brien? I haven't seen her in years, Mom. She wanted to go into politics. We tried to keep in touch, but I don't even know where she is anymore."

With one hand on Peter's shoulder, Matt says, "If she's the one, she'll get in touch with you."

Clearing his throat to get the group's attention, Doctor Kirk addresses them while Major Ralston places a call on his satellite phone.

"It seems that our job here has been completed. The silos have disappeared back into the ground and the ground is quickly freezing over in that area. I'm going to suggest that the Russian military cordon this location off from the public. We'll close down the dig and make preparations to leave as soon as possible."

"Stop!" shouts Major Ralston as he shuts off his phone and rushes back to the group. "We're not safe yet! That energy beam we saw at the silos hit Prometheus and broke it up into thousands of smaller pieces! And it's still on a trajectory to hit the Earth!"

Amid gasps and cries of disbelief, the major continues to impart the dire news he has just received.

"When the asteroid exploded, pieces of it became so hot, they're almost molten. NASA estimates that they're probably close to 700°F, and they don't believe they'll cool off much, if at all, before they hit us. We don't know the size of the larger rocks, but they estimate the smaller ones to be between 100 to 500 feet in diameter. All of them should reduce in size by almost seventy percent as they travel through the atmosphere and some of them will burn up completely. Those that don't will be heading toward the southeastern coast of the United States. In about twenty minutes, they will start landing in the ocean west of Melbourne, Florida. There is no threat of a tsunami now, but there will still be extensive damage across the Florida Peninsula. The meteorites will create fireballs when they hit the ground, and that will cause havoc. We need to pray that most of them hit water instead of land."

"Holy cow!" shouts Peter. "Major, get back on your phone. We need to get back home!"

It is almost two o'clock in the morning, Eastern Standard Time, and the coastline of South Florida is almost deserted. Only a few people remain—those who were not deterred by the warning of a tsunami.

On the shoreline of the city of Melbourne, a group of people has gathered on the beach to watch the red-hot meteorites from Prometheus streak across the sky.

They are watching fire rain down from the heavens.

CHAPTER FIFTY-NINE

S till awake at 2:15 a.m., President Bush is anxious and upset as she watches continuous coverage of fireballs falling from the sky in Central Florida like a rainstorm from hell. People living under the five-mile swath of meteorites that are streaking across the peninsula are being awakened by explosions, and are finding their homes and cars engulfed in flames.

The governor of Florida has reassigned the National Guard from riot control to fire control to assist local fire departments in their efforts to battle the thousands of blazes that are popping up all over the central corridor. Fortunately, many of the meteorites are landing in the Gulf of Mexico after passing harmlessly over the state in a spectacular celestial display. But those that are hitting land are causing a great deal of destruction.

Hours ago, President Bush declared a federal state of emergency for Florida and authorized Homeland Security, FEMA, and military personnel from bases around the state to assist local officials with the crisis. While our president is coping with the catastrophes that are unfolding in a section of our country, many world leaders whose nations are not affected are just beginning to emerge from the bunkers where they took refuge.

As the president's subordinates return from the bunker under the White House, they are being put to work answering their boss' phone, which is ringing nonstop. The more important calls are being put directly through to the president, but the majority are being answered by White House personnel. When Stefan Bell from the Sagan Observatory calls, he is immediately connected to the president.

"Yes, Mr. Bell? Do you new information for me?"

"I have good news, ma'am. The meteor shower over Florida should subside within a few minutes. Most of the smaller meteorites have fallen into the Gulf of Mexico, and a few of the larger ones that we're still tracking will not make landfall. We don't believe the meteor shower will reach Texas or Mexico. It should end over the Gulf."

"That's good news, Doctor Bell!"

"Yes, it is. But there is one more thing. We don't know how the falling meteorites will affect marine life in the Gulf, because when all those hot rocks fall into the water they will undoubtedly raise the water's temperature."

"Well, that may actually work in our favor! We do need to raise the temperature of the water to get the Gulf Stream moving again, but I'm sure NOAA will have something to say about that. Thank you for the information, Stefan. I need to take more calls now, so I have to hang up. I see that the governor of Florida is on hold."

Pope Peter is praying a Rosary with the faithful inside the Basilica of the Ark of the Covenant. The large church is filled to capacity, and millions of others are praying with them as they watch the live broadcast by Vatican TV.

The pope is about to pray the concluding prayers when he suddenly stops and looks over at the altar. An area of brightness has materialized in front of it and the unmistakable sounds of an angelic choir are being heard throughout the church. Stunned by the beautiful music and the bright lights, the congregation has fallen silent, and the TV cameras are capturing it all.

The intense lights near the altar shine brightly for a few moments and then materialize into a vision of four angels supporting the Ark of the Covenant. The angels, later identified as Uriel, Remiel, Sariel, and Raguel, set the Sacred Ark down in a place of honor near the altar and take up protective positions in front of it. Three bursts of light follow and descend into the church to become the Archangels Gabriel, Raphael, and Michael.

Transfixed by the sight of seven powerful angels standing at the front of the revered basilica, the congregation and the global television audience wait with bated breath for what will happen next. But it seems as if the angels themselves are also waiting for something.

Minutes tick by, but when nothing further occurs, Pope Peter rises hesitantly from his seat. He takes a few cautious steps toward the angels but stops in his tracks when a deep and thunderous voice fills the entire church.

"*I AM WHAT I AM*," the powerful voice announces.

In an instant, the Son of God materializes among the archangels.

The awesome sight of Jesus, the Lord of Heaven and Earth, standing in front of the church in all His Glory, causes Pope Peter and the entire congregation to drop to the floor in adoration.

"*My children,*" Our Lord says, "*My Father has chosen from among you a new Commander of the Ark. The power of the guardians has been shared with him to protect you, My precious creatures. However, you must be ever watchful. Do not interfere with My Father's universe. All of the heavens are His creation. Avoid the failures of your past; keep safe this beautiful garden that you have been given to live in and share of its bounty. You are an inquisitive lot, and you will continue to venture forth to explore My Father's vast creations, but this warning I give to you all. Do not venture to the constellation of the archangels. Do not go to Orion.*"

With a look of love, the Lord Jesus reaches out and places His hand on Pope Peter's head. Then, He disappears from sight.

At Our Lord's touch, the pontiff falls to the floor and rests peacefully in the spirit. The archangels Michael, Raphael, and Gabriel surround him instantly and place the chalice, the staff, and the sword beside him. Then, raising their eyes toward heaven, they announce in unison, "*Our task is now complete,*" and also disappear from view.

The archangels are on their way home. They are returning to Orion.

"*This is Olivia Parra with WESH TV Orlando. It is now 2:30 a.m., and I am reporting to you from the roof of the SunTrust building a few miles from downtown Orlando. As we pan our cameras south, you can see the firestorm wall that begins at the junction of I-4 and the Florida Turnpike. Hundreds, if not thousands, of fires are erupting on the ground as the firestorm proceeds in a southwesterly direction. At this time, we have no reports of injuries or deaths resulting from the meteorite strikes, but as you can hear, it sounds like a war zone out here. Meteorites are exploding in the air and on the ground. Reports from Tampa and Sarasota reveal that this five-mile wide swath of terror is turning toward the west and is exiting our state south of Sarasota. From there, it is heading out over the Gulf of Mexico.*

"*Information received from across the state indicates that the larger meteorites are traveling further west. Here in the Orlando area, the balls of flame are estimated to range in size from softballs to basketballs. Unconfirmed reports from Fort Meyers say that some of the fireballs in that area are four feet in diameter and larger.*

"*This is Olivia Parra, WESH TV Orlando.*"

After signing off the air, Olivia gazes out over the rooftops at the burning landscape of Central Florida. She loses her struggle to hold back tears and is soon sobbing freely. Wiping her eyes with the back of her hand, she turns to her cameraman, who is also watching the rain of fire.

"What must those people be going through out there?" she cries.

A few miles south of Olivia's location, fire departments from the cities of Kissimmee and Haines City are racing to three of the area's famous theme parks—Universal Studios, SeaWorld, and Walt Disney World.

At Disney World, Captain Bob "Skeeter" Davis from the Kissimmee Fire Department directs Squadron Three down the theme park's Main Street. The well-known street is now unrecognizable, as it has been turned into a flaming inferno by the meteorites that are streaking down from the sky like the British cannon balls at Fort McHenry during the War of 1812. The fireballs are descending every fifteen to twenty seconds and are filling the air with whooshing and screaming sounds.

"Captain! We just lost Pumper Two, and three men are down!" shouts a lieutenant.

Captain Davis grabs his radio to command his team. "Get everyone into the tunnels under the park! Go down the stairway near City Hall! We're going to have to let it all burn!"

Members of the Kissimmee Fire Department race to the protection of Disney World's underground city while dodging screaming balls of flame. Before Captain Davis enters the tunnels himself, he takes one last look at Cinderella's Castle, which is taking direct hits.

Most of the firefighters are able to make their way safely into the tunnels, but some of them are not as fortunate. The ones who are still on the surface are scurrying around, trying to find shelter wherever they can while the ones below wait out the bombardment with nervous concern for their comrades.

The meteorites pummel the State of Florida relentlessly for fifteen minutes until they finally clear land and move out over the water. As thousands upon thousands of meteorites enter the Gulf of Mexico, the surface of the water appears to boil like a steaming cauldron. Thankfully, the larger pieces of Prometheus strike the water twenty miles away from land.

"Madame President, Governor Menendez is on line three."

"John, my prayers are with you and all of your fellow Floridians. What is the situation down there, and what can we do to help?"

"Thank you for your concern, Madame President. The initial numbers are sixty-three dead and two hundred injured, with property damage in the billions. Thank God for the four inches of snow on the ground; it's helping to deter the spread of even more fires. Most of the meteorites have stopped falling now; however, there are still a few wayward strikes along the coast. The main firestorm is now over the Gulf."

"I'm glad to hear that it's left Florida, John, and I'm so sorry about the loss of life and the extensive damage in your state. From what I've observed from the videos coming out of Orlando, we're extremely lucky that many more lives were not lost. I'll extend that emergency declaration for you, and we'll get keep FEMA and Homeland Security forces deployed as long as they're needed."

"Thank you again, Madame President. I'm sorry to have to cut this call short, but there's a chopper waiting to take me to Orlando to view the situation there, and then I'm heading west to Sarasota. I'll call again later."

The president hangs up the phone and buzzes her secretary.

"Yes, Madame President?"

"Thank goodness you're there, Marjorie. I wasn't sure if you had returned from the bunker yet."

"Yes, I'm here, ma'am. What can I do for you?"

"Get me in touch with Bell at the Observatory. I need to find out when all of this is going to end."

The Matteos, Sergeant Gonzalez, and Major Ralston, are traveling back to Krasnoyarsk; they can't wait until they're back home in the U.S. On the way to the city's now-familiar airport, Major Ralston gets a call on his satellite phone. He talks for only a few minutes and ends the call quickly.

"That was NASA Mission Control in Houston. Florida was hit pretty hard. Fires are raging from Orlando to Sarasota from hundreds of meteorite strikes, but the snow on the ground is keeping them from spreading. The meteorites have now moved away from land and are striking the Gulf of Mexico."

"That's awful!" worries Jennifer, who voices the sentiment that is felt by all of them. "I just want to go home!"

"Home will probably have to wait a while longer, Jennifer. President Bush wants to meet with all of you. I should warn you that your family has become quite famous around the world; by now, everyone has probably heard about you. After the president meets with you at the White House, Pope Peter has requested another meeting in Rome, and…Oh, I almost forgot! The archangels made another appearance! And they brought the Ark of the Covenant back to its basilica!"

Smiling widely at that news, Matt responds, "Well! Now we know where the angels went after they left us at the dig! But Major, I don't want any of the attention that's undoubtedly going to be heaped upon us when we get home. However," he amends thoughtfully, "we probably won't have much choice in the matter."

Noticing that Peter has been very quiet, Matt looks at his son, who is fingering the ring on his finger and staring at the medallion around his neck.

"Is anything wrong?" he asks, as he reaches over and gives Peter a little shake.

"Oh, sorry, Dad, I was just thinking. Saint Michael said, 'My son and his son, and so on until the end of time.' Dad, I'm not worthy of any of this."

Jennifer puts her arms around her son and holds him like only a mother can. "God is not going to give you anything you can't handle. I'm sure you'll find a wife when the time is right, and then you'll have the son that God has promised you. Remember what I told you: the right person will come along, and she'll be the one who's destined to be with you. You'll do fine. You always do."

CHAPTER SIXTY

O n the morning of October 15, President Bush is preparing to meet with the Matteo family in the Oval Office when General Parkins arrives unexpectedly.

"Madame President, I need to speak with you."

"Of course. But please make it as brief as possible."

"Thank you. We devised a plan to warm up the Gulf by using the two HAARP transmitters. In about twenty minutes, we're holding a meeting in the Situation Room with Doctor Emil Gurov from NOAA and Lieutenant Colonel Strum from HAARP Command."

"Excellent! I'm glad to hear that we're moving forward on that problem. I should be able to join you after I greet the Matteos. Thank you, General."

A staff member standing outside the door waits for the General to leave the room and then pokes her head in. "Madame President, the Matteos are here."

"Very good. Notify the photographer, and then send them in."

A few minutes later, Peter walks into the room, with Matt and Jennifer following behind, hand in hand.

"Peter Matteo! Welcome to the White House!" greets Mrs. Bush. "Hello, Doctor Matteo, Mrs. Matteo. It's a pleasure to meet all of you!"

"Hello, Madame President," replies Matt. "Thank you for inviting us here. It's quite an honor!"

The official White House photographer begins snapping photos while the president talks with her guests.

"Raphael, the honor is all mine. The people of the United States... actually, the people of the world...owe you their very lives! You and your family have become very famous. Many of the world's leaders want to meet with you."

"Yes, we've heard that. As a matter of fact, right after we leave here this morning, we're taking a flight to Rome to meet with the pope. Then, it's on to Europe and the Far East."

The photographer snaps several posed photos of the president greeting her guests, and then, when she leaves them to walk over to her desk, he takes more casual photos of the Matteo family. While the family is being kept busy, President Bush removes three boxes from the top left-hand drawer of her desk and then returns to the group with a broad smile.

"Now, let's get down to the real reason I asked you here today. I am pleased to bestow upon each of you the Presidential Medal of Freedom, for your valor in the face of insurmountable odds, and for the successful completion of your God-given mission to save the world."

Approaching each person in turn, the president removes the prestigious medals from the boxes being held by a staff member, and places one of them around each of their necks.

The Presidential Medal of Freedom is the highest civilian award in the nation. It is worn around the neck suspended by a blue ribbon with a white stripe running down its outer edges. The medal is a circle formed by five golden eagles touching each other wing tip to wing tip, with a white enameled star over a red pentagon in the center. In the center of the white star is a circle of thirteen golden stars over a blue background.

Leaning over his son, Matt whispers in his ear. "Another medal for you to wear, eh?"

Peter smiles as the photographer snaps away.

"Again, I thank each of you on behalf of a very grateful nation, and I wish all of you the best in the coming days. I know you're going to be very busy!"

The president shakes each person's hand and says, "Thank you for coming in today. I hope we'll meet again some day. My chief of staff will escort you out, and one of the other staff members will give you a personalized tour of the White House. I hope you enjoy visiting the people's house."

Smiling widely, the Matteos thank the president and follow Levar Daniels out of the Oval Office.

As soon as the room has been cleared, Mrs. Bush walks through a door on the opposite side of the office and heads directly to the Situation

Room where she greets General Parkins, the head of the Joint Chiefs of Staff; Doctor Gurov, and Lieutenant Colonel Ben Sturm.

"Okay, gentlemen. Tell me what you have."

General Parkins clears his throat to respond, but Doctor Gurov speaks first. "Excuse me, General, but I have information that may have a direct impact on this meeting."

Receiving a nod from the General, he turns to address the president.

"We have new data on the situation in the Gulf of Mexico. After the meteor shower, people living in the area tell us that the overall temperature of the water has increased more than ten degrees and is continuing to rise. They also say that a current has formed on the water's surface in the area of the Florida Straits. We have no official confirmation of any of this yet because the Southern Atlantic sensors were destroyed by debris from Prometheus. So we ordered a research vessel based in Key West to travel through the Straits and up the eastern coastline to monitor the currents. We should have more information later today."

"Doctor, what are you saying?"

"Ma'am, if it is true that a current is flowing through the Florida Straits and entering the Atlantic Ocean, well, that will tell us that the Gulf Stream has become active again. We think the fallout from Prometheus provided the energy that was needed to jumpstart the current and get the warm water flowing back into the Atlantic. Give me twenty-four hours, and I'll let you know if we still need to implement HAARP. We may not have to use those transmitters to heat up the water after all. Besides, weren't we just chastised for interfering with God's creation?"

Silence fills the room while each of them recalls what God has said over the past few days.

"Yes, we'll meet again exactly twenty-four hours from now," directs the president. "Lieutenant Colonel and General Parkins, I know you have the technology that could help us in this hour of need, but I don't want to deploy that technology if we don't absolutely need to. Thank you, Gentlemen."

After the military men have left the room, President Bush pulls Doctor Gurov aside for a private conversation. "Emil, I pray that you are correct. I'm afraid that the use of the HAARP technology would do more harm than good, and in my opinion, I don't think it will work. And I especially don't want to risk the ire of our Heavenly Father again."

The Matteos are in the air again, on their way back to Italy to meet with Pope Peter. But this time, they are enjoying some rare, first class treatment.

Unexpectedly, they are ushered to the first row of the Alitalia 797, where the seats turn into miniature bedrooms with full mattresses and individual entertainment centers.

"You know, Jenn, I could get used to traveling like this!" chuckles Matt as he admires his accommodations.

"From your lips to God's ears, Hon!" replies his wife with a grin.

Peter adds, "This sure beats the rear deck of an Osprey!"

CHAPTER SIXTY-ONE

I t is 3:50 a.m. on October 16 when the Matteos finally reach their hotel in Rome. Their meeting with Pope Peter is at ten o'clock later that day so Matt and Jenn decide to catch a few extra hours of sleep. Peter had enough sleep on the plane so instead of relaxing like his parents, he sets up his laptop in his room and begins to review the next project his boss at the Smithsonian has assigned to him.

During the meteor shower, a small, 3.1-magnitude earthquake shook the island of Bermuda. At the time of the quake, a salvage ship was recovering an old Spanish galleon one mile off the coast, in the area known as the Bermuda Triangle. After the earthquake, the tips of three golden pyramids inexplicably appeared on the ocean floor not far from the galleon, in a pattern aligned with the stars of Orion's Belt. When told of the discovery, the Smithsonian Institution heralded it as the possible site of the lost city of Atlantis.

The salvage crew sensed a terrific opportunity to increase their bounty so they promptly abandoned their work on the Spanish galleon and moved their ship close to the new discovery. When they were in place, they contacted the Smithsonian and volunteered their services. Since they were already in the area, the Smithsonian readily agreed to accept their help.

As soon as they received approval, they began the tedious task of excavating the pyramids with their large underwater cannon. But after blowing away almost ten feet of sand, they still had not reached the base of any of the structures.

Their underwater sonar equipment indicated that the bases were located deep beneath the sand, beyond the range of their sonar's detection.

Using simple geometry, the crew estimated that the height of the pyramids were a minimum of 290 feet, and they calculated that it would take at least ten years to remove enough of the ocean floor over the ten-acre site to completely uncover the structures.

With a keen understanding of the enormity of the task and the limits of his vessel, the captain of the salvage ship forwarded their findings to the Smithsonian and wisely decided to abandon the task to others. He suspended their activity at the pyramids and returned to the site of the Spanish galleon, recognizing that a larger and better-funded expedition would be needed if there was to be any hope of fully uncovering the submerged structures.

Engrossed in reviewing the data that Stanley Jameson sent about these discoveries, Peter doesn't realize how much time has passed until the phone in his room rings.

"Hello?" he says curiously.

"Peter? It's Mom. It's almost eight o'clock. Are you going to join us for breakfast?"

"Oh, wow. I didn't realize the time. I'll be down in fifteen minutes. Make a plate for me, okay?"

Rushing through a shower and a shave, Peter changes into fresh clothes and joins his parents for a buffet breakfast in the dining area of the Michelangelo Hotel.

The NOAA research vessel *Blue Lagoon* remains on course, steadily following a strong underwater current through the Gulf of Mexico. Sonar readings of the flow have thus far guided the ship through the Florida Straits and toward the islands of the Bahamas off Florida's southern coast.

The crew is anxiously watching the readings to see if they indicate a northern turn, which would provide proof that the Gulf Stream has returned. When the readings show the turn, the crew members shout for joy, and Captain Segurra immediately places a call to Doctor Gurov at NOAA headquarters.

In Rome, Pope Peter is running late for his meeting with the Matteos. It's almost 10:30 when he is finally able to join them in the meeting room near his office.

"God bless you all this morning! Thank you for accepting my invitation. How was your flight?"

Before responding, each of the Matteos greets the pontiff by taking his hand and kissing his ring. But after Peter kisses the pontiff's ring, the pope does something that surprises everyone. He grasps Peter's hand, and kisses the Ring of Solomon. Noting his guests' wide-eyed looks, the pontiff nonetheless continues as if nothing unusual has occurred.

"You are all very quiet today," he says. "Is everyone well?"

Recovering from the pope's surprise gesture, Peter replies, "Yes, we are all well, Holy Father. My parents and I had a wonderful flight. We were honored to be placed in first class, and it was a wonderful experience! I wouldn't mind traveling like that all the time!"

The pontiff smiles. "Yes, I know what you mean. But you must be wondering why I invited you all back to the Vatican."

When the family nods their heads in agreement, Pope Peter reveals his reason.

"Doctor Matteo, you, your beautiful wife, Jennifer, and your powerful son, Peter, have completed a critical mission in the service of God and man. You were chosen, and you decided to serve. Each of you deserves a special place of recognition here at the Holy See. To that end, I have commissioned an artist to paint a portrait of you and your family. The portrait will be placed on permanent display in the narthex of the newly-named Basilica of the Archangels, the former Basilica of the Chalice. I have changed the name of that beautiful house of prayer because we are placing your three artifacts on display there—the chalice, the sword, and the staff. From the many photographs that have been taken of each of you, the artist will create a painting that the world will be proud of. Please follow me to the church now, and I will show you where the painting will be displayed, and how the three holy artifacts will be presented for veneration."

The Holy Father and the new world heroes surprise the many pilgrims who are visiting the Vatican that day when they are seen walking through the garden behind Saint Peter's with their Swiss Guard escort. The group enters the church amid loud and enthusiastic applause.

The space designated for the family's portrait is just to the right of the basilica's entrance. The pope stops to point out the area and then continues into the basilica with the Swiss Guard guiding them through a crowd of tourists. At the altar, the pope draws the family's attention to an ornate case of bullet-proof glass that contains Gabriel's chalice, Raphael's staff, and the sword of Saint Michael.

Peter's presence near the holy objects once again causes a profound reaction in each of them. They all begin to glow, and a brilliant light appears alongside them at the altar.

Within that light, the Son of God once again materializes in all His glory. Gazing at the Matteo family lovingly, he says, *"I bring you good tidings from My Father. We are pleased that you have completed your task and We acknowledge that Peter has been charged as Commander—guardian of God's people. Peace be with you all."*

Behind the group, the more reverent in the crowd of awestruck tourists prostrate themselves on the ground in adoration, while scores of others point their cameras and cell phones at Our Lord in an effort to capture His image. Eventually, though, everyone is humbled by the divine experience, and a profound silence descends upon the crowd.

With His hand raised in blessing, Jesus smiles at His children and disappears into a cloud that has formed near the ceiling.

After Jesus departs, the artifacts stop glowing and everyone present turns to Pope Peter for guidance in understanding the event. But His Holiness' only comments are directed to Peter Matteo.

"My dear boy!" he exclaims, "Apparently, *you* are the reason for our joy at being honored by another visit from Our Lord! It appears that Our Heavenly Father wanted to greet you personally! This is truly a time of miracles!" Then, leaning close to Peter, he speaks in a quieter voice meant only for him. "Come now. Let us go back to my office. I want you to tell me everything that happened at Tunguska."

Amid more applause and shouts of greetings from the pilgrims inside and outside the church, the Matteos follow His Holiness back to his living quarters in the Vatican complex.

CHAPTER SIXTY-TWO

resident Bush is once again in the Situation Room, waiting to begin the follow-up to yesterday's meeting. The first to join her are General Parkins and Lieutenant Colonel Strum. Doctor Gurov arrives a few minutes later.

"Thank you all for coming," says the president. "Please present your status report."

Seizing the lead, General Parkins speaks first. "Good morning, Madame President, the HAARP facilities are ready."

Eyeing the general icily, President Bush asks, "They're ready? Can you guarantee that what happened before the Great Judgment earlier this century won't happen again? Surely you remember that the HAARP facilities blew up a South Korean patrol boat and nearly brought us into war."

Turning to the doctor, the president asks, "Doctor Gurov, I gave you twenty-four hours to provide me with good news about the Gulf Stream. What have you learned?"

"Ma'am, I do have good news for you, but that is an understatement. The Gulf Stream has reemerged! It's a little weaker than it was prior to the oil spill, but it appears to be increasing in intensity. At its current rate, we expect it to be back to normal within six months."

"That is *wonderful* news! But are you absolutely sure about that, Emil? I don't want to get our peoples' hopes up if it's not true."

"Yes, it's true, ma'am. We verified that the current has returned. There is a bit of news that's not as good, though. The cold climate will be with us for a while longer, until the Gulf Stream returns completely. Temperatures should gradually return to normal but we don't know how long that will take. I fear this winter will be…um…let's say…extreme."

President Bush pauses for a few seconds of relief, and silently contemplates the good fortune of the Earth's inhabitants. Even though hard times will last for a while, it looks like they dodged a major bullet. A moment later, she says, "It seems that our place in the universe has been preserved by the guardians of this planet, with help from Peter Matteo and his parents. I fervently hope that all of us will learn from this experience. We must finally realize that any tampering with the natural order of God's creation will bring dire consequences to mankind. We must never forget what has happened, and we must always remember that dreadful things can occur in the future if we repeat our mistakes, for we are not the masters of the universe. Pope Peter and I have discussed this at length, and we will be addressing a special session of the United Nations to reinforce that message."

Matt and Jennifer are happy to be back at home in Colorado Springs after the whirlwind activities of the past few months. Exhausted, they are planning a short vacation to Brazil to wind down and celebrate their unbelievable accomplishments. They also want to go somewhere warm even though as Coloradans, they are veterans of wintry weather. With current temperatures in South America in the high 70s, it will be cooler there than normal, but warm enough for them.

In D.C., Peter is also glad to be home. After so much time away, he busy in his apartment, trying to get it and himself ready to go back to work. He has done loads of laundry, has restocked his pantry, and is now dusting the living room. As he works, a news report interrupts the music he has been listening to on the radio.

"We have a breaking news event. Another earthquake on the southwest coast of Bermuda has caused an upheaval of the ocean floor. An area of land about fifty acres in size has risen out of the Atlantic, and a tsunami is reported to be heading toward the southeastern coast of the United States. Coastal cities have been warned of flooding, as the sea is expected to rise about six feet. But there is more to this story. Three pyramids have risen out of the new land mass in the Atlantic, along with several small buildings. Preliminary investigations of the structures suggest that the persistent rumors of a lost city of Atlantis may have been true. News crews will be sent to the scene and our sister TV station, WBFF in Baltimore, will have photos as soon as they are available."

Stunned by these developments, Peter rushes to the phone to call his boss, Stanley Jameson. But before he can pick it up to dial, it emits a loud ring. Bringing the phone to his ear, he hears, "Hello, Peter? I was hoping you would be home! This is Jameson. I need you here ASAP! Those pyramids in the Atlantic…It's *Atlantis*!"

"Yes! I just heard it on the news!"

"This is amazing! We must arrange some time for you to fill me in on everything that happened, but right now, I need you here. You're going to Atlantis!"

"Okay, I'll be there within the hour." Peter puts down his cleaning supplies and gets ready to go to work.

Before leaving the apartment, he calls his parents. "Hello, Mom? It's Pete."

"Peter! Have you been watching TV? Have you seen the pyramids?"

"No, I haven't seen them yet, but I'm on my way to the Smithsonian right now. They're sending me over there!"

"Oh, Peter, they look like the Pyramids of Giza, but they have golden tops, and there are many buildings near them. It looks like a small city!"

"Yes, I heard the description on the radio. They think its Atlantis, Mom!"

"Wow! Dad will be shocked to hear that! Listen, as long as I have you on the phone, I should tell you that we're planning a trip to Brazil. We want to relax for a while where it's a bit warmer than here."

"That's great! You guys deserve to take a break. Tell Dad about my new adventure, okay? Love you, Mom."

"Love you, too, Son. Good luck!"

Courtney O'Brien, Chief of Staff for Senator Ted Collins of North Carolina, is taking a day off today, intent on spending the day as a tourist at some of the Smithsonian museums. It's sunny in D.C. now, but the air is crisp and there is still snow on the ground. While she is in the National Museum of Natural History, a warm front crosses over the city, and it begins to rain.

Peter is also in the Natural History Museum. His meeting with Stanley Jameson has just ended and he is leaving the administrative area and walking purposefully toward the building's main exit. He wants to head directly home to pack for his trip to investigate the buildings that have recently protruded from the Atlantic Ocean.

In his haste to exit the building, Peter rushes hurriedly out of the door, not noticing that it's raining. But just behind him, Courtney sees the downpour and stops before she exits.

When he's outside in the rain, Peter's clothes rapidly become soaked, so he abandons his plan to walk home and searches for a passing taxi. In the museum doorway, Courtney wonders how she will be able to catch a cab without getting wet.

When a taxi stops at the curb, Courtney can't believe her luck and starts down the steps to hail it, not noticing that there is a man standing nearby in the rain. Peter, who has been hunkered down against the downpour, runs for the cab that he summoned, and when he reaches it, climbs in quickly and slams the door against the torrent.

While the cab is waiting to pull out into traffic, Peter glances out of the side window. When he sees a woman's wet figure standing at the curb, he shouts to the driver, "Hey, wait a minute! I'll share my ride with that lady. I don't want her to get stranded in the rain." With a nod from the driver, Peter opens the door and slides over on the seat to make room for his taxi-mate.

Grateful for the ride, Courtney quickly climbs into the cab and turns to thank her rescuer. But when she looks at the person sitting next her, she stares at him in open-mouthed astonishment. "Oh, my goodness!" she exclaims. "Peter?"

Surprised, Peter turns toward a familiar voice. "Courtney? Courtney O'Brien?"

As the cab speeds off, the two friends catch up on each other's lives while high overhead, Saint Michael smiles and turns back toward his home in the Orion constellation.

At NASA headquarters in Houston, scientists and flight technicians are still tracking the two nuclear missiles that missed Prometheus. The first one shut down prematurely and will eventually impact the Sun without any further consequences. But the second one is traveling out into space at 5,000 miles per hour and is expected to impact the planet Mars in about eleven months. Notified of the missile's trajectory, the NASA exploratory colony that has been recently established on the red planet has begun emergency preparations. At this point, NASA does not know exactly where the missile will land on the planet's surface, but the scientists are watching and waiting, hoping that the inhabitants of Mars will remain safe.

EPILOGUE

I t is now September of a new year, and Peter is still leading the archeological excavations at Atlantis. The mild summer is promising to lead to another cold winter, but meteorologists are hopeful that the Earth's climate will return to normal by springtime.

Courtney, Peter's fiancée, has quit her job with Senator Collins and has joined Peter at the site. The couple, who is planning their wedding for the following June, will honeymoon in Rome because Peter wants to see the completed portrait of his family that is now on display in the Basilica of the Archangels.

Although the newly-engaged couple has already shared much of their life stories with each other, there is one thing that Peter has not yet shared with his wife-to-be. Courtney knows that Peter is the new Commander of the Ark, but he has not told her that his offspring will inherit that same mission. He will wait until after the birth of a son to share that news with her.

In Colorado, the senior Matteos are happy and content. Matt is enjoying a quiet retirement but Jennifer keeps herself busy by volunteering at a local hospital. Neither of them was able to contain their joy when Peter and Courtney announced their engagement, and they are eagerly anticipating the prophesied grandson.

Meanwhile, on Mars, the exploratory colony of astronauts is thriving. The errant nuclear missile hit the planet about four hundred fifty miles north of their location with no direct effect on them. However, because of the missile's explosion, man's actions are once again resulting in changing God's creation. The crater created by the blast released the water that once flowed freely across the planet and as a result, water is now gushing over the red planet's surface and filling up a long-dried river bed that lies adjacent to the NASA colony.

The temperatures on Mars normally range from sixty-eight degrees during the day to minus one hundred forty-one degrees at night. However, the sudden influx of water over the normally dry surface will inevitably create a new topography on the planet, and make a drastic change in its climate. Many scientists predict that the changes will occur within a few years, but others say they will take many generations. As for how the impact of water on Mars will affect the planet and what type of life may spring forth from it, only time will tell.

But if life does arise from this incident, it will be a living thing that mankind has had a direct impact in creating—not God.

On the Earth, the new leader of hell is trying desperately to lure mankind into sin, while the Malignant continues to rebel against his creator in the desolate place of his banishment. Staring into the darkness of space, he continually cries, *"I will prevail in the end, and You cannot stop me!"*

The Lord looks down on Satan and listens to his ranting. Finally, He manifests Himself in front of the beast on the cold and lonely rock.

"Lucifer! You were told not to interfere with the human race, but you continued to defy Me. That is why you are here. But I see that even here, you remain defiant. Therefore, My guardians will take you to another place—the place of the archangels. There, you will remain under their watch until the passing of the thousand years that will signal the end of your exile."

At the Lord's command, seven archangels appear on the barren world and surround their fallen brother. Then, as quickly as they appeared, they depart—with Lucifer.

An instant later, at the very moment Lucifer is placed in the Orion Nebula in the constellation of Orion, an intense burst of light shines throughout the cosmos. The light from that event will take 1,300 years to reach the eyes of the people of Earth—over three hundred years after the one thousand years of peace end. What will that light foretell?

Humans are stubborn creatures. Despite God's specific warnings and despite everything that they have been put through, mankind continues to interfere in God's creation. The latest disturbances caused by human beings on the planet Mars are rippling across the cosmos and will eventually intersect with the lives of all of the people of God.

But that is another story, to be told at another time.

About the Author

Frank A. Ruffolo resides in South Florida, where he and his beautiful wife, Christine, raised two wonderful children.

After taking early retirement from a forty-year career in purchasing and purchasing management, he discovered a passion for writing and took up a second career as an author, independently releasing two novels—Gabriel's Chalice, a science fiction adventure, and The Trihedral of Chaos, an action adventure.

Now Frank is working with Linkville Press to release his first murder mystery, The Jack Stenhouse Mysteries.

Always writing, Frank is busy putting the finishing touches on four more novels while conducting research on a fifth.

Follow Frank on Facebook (Frank A Ruffolo or Frank A. Ruffolo author) and Twitter (@ruffoloauthor) to read about his future releases.

www.ingramcontent.com/pod-product-compliance
Lightning Source LLC
Chambersburg PA
CBHW050715180626
46814CB00002B/450